I0541018

Curandero

R. L. Mosz

Copyright © 2018 R. L. Mosz

All rights reserved.

ISBN: 978-0-692-96431-6

Cover art by Elizabeth Daniel

CONTENTS

Why so downcast, O my soul?

1—Un Sueño

"Sammie?" Maureen shielded her dramatically made-up eyes from the gust of wind as she gazed down at her pretty daughter on the rocks below.

"What?" Samantha looked up, preparing to release Dreamer from the leash so they could run down to the beach.

"You're . . . you're not going for a walk right now, are you?" For once her mother's confident voice sounded uncertain.

As if in response to the question, Samantha released Dreamer; and the agile brown dog leaped eagerly away for the shoreline. "I won't be gone long, Mom." She didn't want to argue. There had been an assault about a mile south along the oceanfront last week, but the crime was committed late at night, and it was currently morning. In any case, the perpetrator had turned out to be the victim's former boyfriend, not some stranger still on the loose.

"It's going to rain pretty soon. Look at the sky."

"I'll be back before then."

Her mother wouldn't let it rest, however. She continued to stare uneasily, succeeding in making Samantha feel guilty.

"I'll just go down to Esperanza Point and back. Fifteen minutes. Dreamer is restless and needs a run."

Maureen's expression appeared resistive. Samantha stamped her foot in annoyance. "It's not dangerous, Mom. That guy was just her ex-boyfriend, and he's in custody now."

"Uh-huh." She nodded. "Well, that's good." Something else was bothering her. The wind flapped the skirt of her garish muumuu, and she attempted to shield her styled gray hair from the weather.

"Mom?"

At last her mother relented, just as Samantha knew she would. "I dreamed a strange dream about the beach last night."

"Oh, Mom." Her mother was always having some extraordinary dream. She fancied herself a great prophetess or something. If Samantha didn't hurry, it really would be raining before she returned from the walk.

"Just don't bring back any stray birds if you find them. In the dream, you found something sick—I can't remember what—and it flew up into a tree. You tried to reach it, and you got hurt . . . terribly hurt." She glared indignantly at her daughter as if the tragic event had already occurred.

"Okay, no injured birds. Can I go now?"

"Wait, I'm not finished. After that, we had to call off the wedding."

"Oh, brother." Samantha rolled her eyes.

"You didn't marry Richard. It was a premonition dream, Samantha. You know what I mean. It frightened me."

"Mom, you know Richard and I would never call off the wedding in a million years. And I can't quit walking on the beach, can I? We live right above the ocean! I'll see you later. And stop worrying."

With a wave, Samantha picked her way through the stones and down to the sand below. Dreamer paused for a moment to allow her to catch up and then darted ahead again. It was a beautiful autumn morning, bright and clear; but thunderheads did indeed loom on the horizon. Samantha slipped off her sandals and pressed her feet into the glistening sand as she continued her walk.

"Dreamer, wait up," she warned. The seashore seemed benign enough, but she kept a watchful eye out just the same. Although she was reluctant to admit it, her mother possessed a perceptive ability which caused you to pay attention in the end. She passed several harmless-looking joggers, a young boy and his dog, and finally an older couple walking hand-in-hand.

"Hello!" The elderly man smiled.

"Good morning." Samantha nodded in return.

She began to relax and her thoughts turned, as they usually did, to Richard. Last week, they had enjoyed picnicking on the dunes and, afterward, sailing across the cove in his new boat. Samantha couldn't imagine her world without her confident, successful fiancé. If only the wedding weren't so far away; she was impatient to finally be able see him every day. She wished he didn't have to work such long hours. However, that was one of the things she admired most about him: his dedication to everything, including her.

Peering into the distance, Samantha shielded her eyes from the sun. Dreamer was playing with another dog just up ahead. After slipping her sandals on again, she hurried to catch up.

"Dreamer, knock it off!" Her dog was chewing on the strange dog's ruff. She tried to pull Dreamer back while glancing around impatiently for the owner.

"Rebel . . ." A soft, articulate voice spoke behind her, and the dog pulled itself free from Dreamer and trotted toward the sound.

Turning around in relief, Samantha was momentarily stunned. A cloud passed over the sun, and the morning darkened as thunderheads rolled across the sky. A man glanced up at her as he snapped a leash on the dog, his countenance somber. Her first impression was that he must be an addict or a homeless drifter living on the beach, wasted by some substance unknown. But as her eyes drifted to the sleek, healthy dog by his side, she realized something in her supposition was wrong. He wore a classy watch around his wrist, and his clothes were clean and new. The man's physique appeared emaciated, however, and his complexion sallow. There were frightening dark circles under his eyes.

"Hello." As he attempted a smile, his lips pulled back from perfect white teeth. He looked like a skeleton. "I'm Stefan." He nodded to her. "I was hoping to talk to you today and ask a favor of you."

Samantha hesitated before accepting his hand to shake and he noticed. His hand felt cold and dry. She had trouble meeting his eyes. What did this strange man want? Repressing a desire to grab her dog and run, she still wished she could get away.

"I've seen you walking your dog every day."

She cringed. The dream! But what possible threat could such a fragile man pose to her? He looked as though he were about to fall over. Sure enough, he collapsed on top of a rock while still looking up at her. She remained suspicious and kept her distance, refusing to feel too concerned. He tried to smile at her again but then looked painfully away.

"Are you all right?" Samantha couldn't help asking. Something was terribly wrong with him. She recalled her mother's illness three years earlier. That had never been as bad as this man's condition appeared to be.

He didn't attempt to smile again. "No, I'm not. I'm sick and I don't have much longer to live. I was wondering if you'd take my dog for me when the time comes." Rebel sat quietly by his side as if

4

he somehow understood.

She found herself flabbergasted by the request. He was ill! She instantly regretted remaining so aloof moments earlier. People must stare at him all the time, she surmised, probably thinking the same thoughts as she. When she didn't answer straight away, he glanced up at her again and continued.

"He's a really good dog . . . he's very well trained and only three years old. I'd hate to surrender him to some shelter, even though he is just a mutt. I suppose he's nothing special except to me. I've noticed how often you walk your own dog. I'm sorry to have to ask."

"It's okay," Samantha hastened to reply. "I'd be glad to take him for you. I live just up on the ridge."

She released Dreamer and settled herself next to Stefan. Rebel remained close to his owner. Samantha brushed dark curls back from her face, and he noticed how beautiful she was. Stefan breathed a sigh of relief and reached out to pet his dog. She would be sure to take good care of him.

"Are you seeing a doctor?" It was a silly question that she regretted the minute she uttered it. Of course he was seeing a doctor! She wondered why he wasn't in the hospital, though; he appeared so ill.

To her chagrin, he shook his head. "No, I'm not. I'm just . . . freewheeling it . . . on my own." He smiled weakly in the face of her concern. "I've been to the best of them. But it's past that point now, if you know what I mean."

"Oh." She felt at a loss for words. He was so young and just giving up. "Stefan," she began, unsure of how to proceed, but not willing to let the opportunity pass. "I know this very unusual doctor."

"No, thank you." He shook his head.

"Dr. Calderón is not just an ordinary physician. He advised my mother when she was sick with cancer, and she is actually doing very well now. He has a good success rate with hopeless cases." She wished she hadn't said that! Still, he had asked her to take his dog.

Stefan's pallid face appeared unmoved, and perhaps a shadow of annoyance passed over it. He ran his fingers through his sparse dark hair as if considering. Studying him more closely, she tried to imagine him well. It occurred to her that he must have been handsome and that the two of them were about the same age. She wanted to ask what his illness might be, but the question felt too intrusive.

"Stefan, please. You've got to give it a chance." Her boldness surprised her, but she was always trying to save something, to preserve life. It was just that it had never been *human* life before. "Think of Rebel."

"I am thinking of my dog. That's why I've asked you to take him. You don't understand—I've been through enough. The cure is worse than the disease. And it's not even a cure; it's experimentation . . . research." His gaze was intense. "Believe me, they've tried. There's just nothing more anyone can do."

"Not according to Dr. Calderón. I tell you—he's different!" Samantha insisted, anxious to get through. "He might be able to help you. . . ." Her voice trailed off. "It's difficult to explain. You have to meet him." An idea occurred to her. "Listen, my mother is having a garden party Saturday afternoon, and Dr. Calderón always stops by. Would you like to come and meet him yourself? I'll introduce the two of you, and you can just see what you think. I'd be happy to take your dog, but I wish that as a favor in return you'd do this for me. I don't expect any promises, only that you'll meet him and see what you think."

Closing his eyes a moment, Stefan sighed. He felt boxed in. There was something sweet and irrepressible about this woman; if he were his former self, he'd have turned on the charm in an attempt to win her over. But a giant anvil had fallen from the sky, destroying all that he was and leaving him quaking weakly in the aftermath for a few brief, remaining moments.

There was a clap of thunder overhead and drops of rain began to pelt down on them. "In here!" Samantha directed, pointing to an overhang in the cliff under which a cave opened. Grabbing the dogs, they hastened inside and resettled themselves in the grotto where they were safe from the downpour.

Stefan attempted to adjust his bony frame against the sand, and a silence grew between them. Samantha wondered what her mother was doing—probably worrying because she wasn't home yet. But the pounding rain on the raging surf was somehow reassuring, and they sat next to each other, witnessing the dramatic scene.

Samantha finally spoke, breaking the magic of the little spell. "Are you from Acantilado del Mar, Stefan?" To her knowledge, she had never seen him before.

"No, from the city. I was editor in chief there for *Paradise Magazine*."

She was dumbfounded. Editor in chief for *Paradise Magazine*! It was an enormously successful publication—one that she herself loved and held a subscription to—and he looked so young! For a moment, she wondered whether or not he might be lying to her, but one glance at his beleaguered profile told her otherwise.

"Really? I love that magazine. I have a subscription." She noticed a faint smile. "My girlfriends and I are trying to start our own publication about wildlife and the coastline . . . things like that."

"Really?" He turned to study her. "That's very ambitious of you." He shifted his position and actually chuckled. "How's it coming?"

She shrugged. "Well, there are a lot of problems with capital and other things. Right now, it's more like a newsletter than a real magazine. But it's gotten pretty elaborate. And we have over fifty paying subscribers."

He appeared interested. However, this young man of obvious talent, all alone in the world except for a black dog, was fading fast. He shook his head, appearing resigned. "Well, I wish you luck. It's a tough business, and the competition is merciless. Know your readers and target them. That's all I can say."

Samantha found herself beginning to feel sorry for this relative stranger and wanted very much to be his friend. She wondered about his family and other possible support. He must have known a lot of people connected to the publishing world. But she knew all too well about human nature. Her own mother had never been as ill as this man, yet had lost many friendships during that difficult time. People feared their own eventual decline and avoided facing others whose lives were hanging in the balance.

"I wish you'd come by on Saturday, Stefan, and meet Dr. Calderón. He was such a big help to my mother. He's too unorthodox for a lot of the other doctors, but many people have benefited from his therapies."

"Really?" He found his curiosity faintly aroused. "All right, Samantha." He sighed. "If you are generous enough to take a stranger's dog, I'll come and meet your doctor."

"Oh, that's great! C'mon, the rain has stopped. Let's walk back together, and I'll show you where I live."

They strode up the beach until they reached a wooden stairwell leading to the top of the bluff. "It's right up here," Samantha informed him, ascending the steps. He appeared to be breathing unevenly and clasped a palm to his hollow chest. She turned to face him, her expression grave. "Can you make it?"

"Let me rest for a minute." Attempting to catch his breath, he turned away and looked out over the ocean to hide the agony in his expression. There was a new pain traveling down his right side. He turned back to Samantha. "I'm okay now."

At the top, they paused again and then wound their way down a narrow path along the cliff, the two dogs trailing at their sides. "I live right over there," she informed him while motioning toward a lovely home. "And that's Dr. Calderón's house." She pointed again, this time to the left. "Is anything the matter?" she asked, noting his perplexed expression.

He shook his head. A dreamlike state passed over him as his gaze took in the towering Torrey pines intermingled with cascades of foliage, wild garden paths, and flowers surrounding the home—it was all strangely familiar. But he had never passed this way since his arrival in the small coastal town.

"That house . . ."

"It's beautiful, isn't it?" Samantha remarked. "I love the gardens. My parents and some of the neighbors complain, you know, about the weeds mixed in with the flowerbeds. Especially the dandelions. The seeds blow into their yards and land in the gardens."

"I've seen this house before." He attempted to analyze the situation. They had always been featuring houses in the magazine. Perhaps that was it. But it was not the sort of place that would have interested *Paradise Magazine*. It was too off the beaten path for one thing, and it wasn't luxurious enough. When you examined the place, it was almost modest in comparison with the other homes in the area. He squinted at the house again. The trees around him swayed in a gentle motion, somehow calming his shattered soul.

"Stefan?"

"I'm all right," he replied, turning back to his newfound friend. "What time is the party?"

Samantha snapped the leash back on Dreamer's collar. "Three o'clock." She could hear her mother calling in the distance. "That's my mother," she explained. "You'd think I was still a teenager."

"I'd better be going." He pulled Rebel toward him. Another silence followed as the wind stirred a patch of his dark hair across his face. She turned away, trying not to stare. His hair must have been curly and dark, she pondered, much like her own.

"Thank you for agreeing to take Rebel." He started down the path once more, this time in the other direction. She waved, watching him depart. Soon he disappeared from sight behind the ridge.

"There you are!" Maureen strode purposely toward her, annoyance and concern emanating in waves as her large form closed the gap between them. "Where have you been? Didn't I tell you it was going to rain? Well, at least you're not soaked." She stroked her daughter's shirt, reassuring herself it was dry. "How was the walk?"

"Fine." She stared at the crest in the distance.

"What's the matter?"

Samantha sighed. "Nothing. I . . . I met this man. I invited him to your garden party on Saturday."

"What?" Her mother appeared properly shocked. "Richard's

coming," she reminded her daughter, as if Samantha didn't already know. "What man? You didn't meet him on the beach, did you? Samantha . . ."

"He's really sick. He asked me if I'd take his dog when he dies. Is Dr. Calderón planning to attend? I told him to come so he could meet him."

"Yes, he's coming." Her mother glared a little. "Did you say he's sick?" She grew uneasy, thinking of her dream. "How sick? And how old is he?"

"I don't know. He looks old but he's young. And he's terribly sick. He has a lot of trouble breathing."

Maureen nodded, lapsing into her own thoughts. Samantha knew she was reflecting on her own illness. Her mother sighed. "Well, it's for the best then. It was a nice thing you did, inviting him." Her mother's expression remained grave, however, as she considered the matter. Her gaze floated out over the ocean and finally came to rest on the doctor's house. She smiled to herself and shook her head.

"Why doesn't he ever do something about those dandelions? They keep blowing over here all the time. I ought to send him my gardener's bill. It'd serve him right!"

Samantha glanced over at their neighbor's house. "Dr. Calderón says they have medicinal properties and that they are very useful plants."

"Right." Her mother's air was sardonic.

"He also says they're beautiful—his favorite flower!"

Maureen burst out laughing. "Right . . . his favorite flower. Wouldn't you know?" She shook her head again. "Well, I guess it can't be helped. It's all for the best then."

Samantha was silent as they turned for home, unsure of

whether her mother was referring to Stefan or the dandelions—
probably both.

2—*La Fiesta*

As Stefan approached the house on Saturday afternoon, he checked his watch for the time even though he knew it already. It was four o'clock. Never intending to be late, he'd inadvertently fallen into a deep sleep earlier in the afternoon, something he now only experienced on rare occasions.

Cars were parked up and down the street, indicating quite a crowd; and Samantha's home appeared more lavish than before with the sloping gardens perched above the roaring sea. He wished he could turn around and go back to his motel. Straightening up and attempting to appear well, he knocked on the front door instead. Voices and laughter drifted out the open windows.

"Stefan, hello!" With an enthralling smile, Samantha showed him in, her captivating eyes concerned. "I'm so glad you decided to come. I was afraid you'd changed your mind."

"Sorry I'm late." He tried to run his fingers through his hair, a former gesture of his whenever he felt ill at ease, but then realized how few curls remained. Embarrassed, he laughed to cover up his discomfiture. It sounded hollow and empty.

"Well, never mind. I'm just so glad you could make it." Smiling self-consciously herself, she led him into the living room. The atmosphere was still uncomfortable between them, unaccustomed as they were to the other's presence. "Try not to be horrified by my mother," she continued. "She's a bit of a dragon lady, but people usually like her in the end—I promise."

Stefan cringed. He disliked meeting mothers even under the best of circumstances. The present one made it almost unbearable.

"Well, hellooo!" a large woman cried out right on cue, purposely heading in their direction. Her gray hair was swirled up in a mass on top of her head, and she wore a sweeping skirt, fringed vest, and dangling earrings. Her expression intense, she appeared to be in her late fifties. "You must be Stefan. Welcome! I'm Maureen, Sam's mother."

"Hello, nice to meet you." Stefan extended his hand, and she clasped it in an iron grip of determination. The house was crowded with conversing, snacking people; but the dragon lady focused all of her attention on the new arrival.

"Sam told me she picked you up on the beach. Well, better you than some sick, mangy bird!"

"Mother!"

"I was kidding!" She laughed uproariously at her own joke, and Stefan could smell alcohol on her breath. His space invaded, he attempted to step back and collided into a lady seated behind him in a chair.

"I beg your pardon," he apologized, attempting to recollect his composure. As he straightened up, he experienced a searing pain in his chest which caused him to nearly faint. When he could breathe again, he turned back to Samantha.

"Stefan," she began, attempting to assist in some way.

"Stefan," Maureen barged in obliviously, "I don't know if Sammie told you or not, but I'm a cancer survivor. So you've come to

14

meet the infamous Dr. Miguel Calderón? Well, good luck. I tell you; even after all this time, I'm still not sure what I think of the man. Sammie, get him something to drink—he looks like he needs it. After he meets the doctor, I know he'll need it!"

Leading Stefan away by the arm, Samantha procured a glass of punch from a table and offered it to him. Maureen stared after them, a look of foreboding etched into her face, despite her buoyant demeanor. Stefan caught the look and wished again that he had never come. Long since past the point of being able to socialize, he sipped his punch in silence, trying not to breathe too deeply. It was becoming more difficult to recover after losing his breath so unexpectedly.

"Stefan, I'm sorry. She can be really obnoxious. It's embarrassing to introduce people to her sometimes, especially when she's had a few drinks."

"It's all right," he attempted to reassure her.

Over by the breakfast bar, a clutch of men his age lounged around, hotly debating the upcoming Super Bowl. Samantha gestured toward them. "Stefan, come over here. There's someone I'd like you to meet." She guided him across the crowded room. "Stefan, this is Richard, my fiancé. Richard, this is Stefan." Samantha stepped back and allowed them to shake hands in greeting.

"Hi, Stefan, nice to meet you." Richard smiled, but his robust countenance gave way to shock at the unexpected sight of disease and mortality staring him in the face. The men grew uncomfortable.

"Hi," Stefan replied, feeling as ill as he looked and leaning on the counter for support.

"Join in!" Richard, with his shiny blond hair and rosy cheeks, though somewhat hefty, was the picture of health itself. He yanked out a stool for Stefan in a friendly manner. Samantha touched his arm again. "I'll go see if I can find Dr. Calderón." With that, she vanished.

Stefan grinned at the group again. He was so emaciated at this point that he felt like a grimacing skeleton when he forced, with increasing difficulty, these smiles to come. The effort it required was draining away the last vestiges of strength remaining to him.

He pretended to listen to the idle chitchat and vain prattle; but his eyes drifted across the room to where several elderly people sat huddled together, their walkers and canes in a corner against the wall. There was where he really belonged, for he was no longer one of the young. He was prematurely old and infirm, awaiting death to snatch him away.

Richard and the others glanced over at him from time to time as if trying to think of something to say to make him feel more welcome and like part of the gathering. They appeared at a loss, however, and eventually looked away.

Samantha reappeared. "He's out in the garden," she confided kindly, pointing the way.

Rising up, he felt ready to collapse on the spot. The thought of meeting yet another doctor was the last thing he felt the will to do in his condition; his inward vow upon leaving the hospital was never to be tortured by another. But it was too late to protest—he'd promised; and besides, it would require more energy to back out now than to simply bend to the will of another.

He stepped out on the patio and cast his eyes across the shrub-bery. A tall, lean man tarried among the roses, sipping a glass of wine while examining the blossoms. Stefan walked over and stood at a polite distance.

The doctor looked up straightaway. "You must be Stefan." He extended his hand.

Stefan shook it. "Yes, I am. Nice to meet you," he lied.

"Why don't you sit down?" He gestured toward a bench and Stefan seated himself thankfully. He was growing winded again and felt like he needed to lie down.

Dr. Calderón continued his inspection of the rose blooms, quite at ease. "Such beautiful blossoms," he remarked offhandedly. "Quite exquisite. She pours so much poison on them though . . . into the ground, onto the leaves." He frowned, shaking his head. His jet black hair was parted in the middle and brushed against his shoulders. While the man was still oddly boyish looking, Stefan realized upon closer scrutiny that Dr. Calderón was probably in his early forties. "One has to wonder, is it really worth it?" He turned to Stefan with an engaging smile while gazing into his eyes. "Have you ever noticed the wild roses growing along the bluffs?"

Stefan remained silent, shaking his head.

"They're very beautiful too. A little weather beaten but with a charm uniquely their own. And no one takes care of them—they fend for themselves." He sniffed the air. "I can smell it, the poison. It must wash down to the sea. . . ." He broke off, observing Stefan for a moment. "Tell me, Stefan, what are you doing down on the beach?"

Stefan snapped back to reality, bracing himself for a sermon. Samantha must have given the doctor an earful. A reprimand was surely coming.

"Well, actually, I was taking a break . . . from treatment," he added. It was a falsehood, but he didn't want to offend the man. "I . . . I just felt like I needed a breather from it all."

Dr. Calderón nodded in understanding as he regarded Stefan. Stefan looked away, out over the ocean. The doctor stepped closer and seated himself on the bench next to him, placing his drink on a nearby table.

"Taking a break?" His gentle voice grew questioning. "What do you mean by that? Do you plan to continue with your treatment, then?"

Stefan shook his head. "No."

Dr. Calderón clasped his hands together and bowed his head. They sat immobile for what seemed like a long time, each waiting for the other to break the silence. Finally, Dr. Calderón spoke. "You must let me help you, Stefan. You'll need pain relief for one thing."

"No, I don't want anything."

"You will need it soon; trust me." The waves lashed against the rocks below as gulls circled overhead. "I will need you to request your medical records for me."

"You'd just be wasting your time."

The doctor hesitated again, studying his hands in his lap. "You'll need some relief from the pain," he repeated. "It will help you rest at least. You can't heal if you can't sleep."

"I don't want help anymore." Incongruous as it seemed, he laughed—an apologetic, self-effacing chuckle. "No one can save me at this point, so what's the use?"

"No one can save you, Stefan; but perhaps you can still save yourself."

Stefan stared at the horizon where ominous dark clouds were

gathering. He felt strangely challenged by this man. There was something compelling in his demeanor, as if he held a secret he wanted to reveal but only when the time was right. As his gaze met Dr. Calderón's again, Stefan felt pierced by the sincerity in the physician's dark eyes. Physicians rarely looked people in the eye; they preferred their charts and machines. It justified his rendezvous doing nothing down on the sand, but suddenly his world was thrown into even more turmoil. The wall he had felt so right in throwing up was developing a hairline crack. He wasn't going to allow it—he wouldn't fall back into the trap again.

Stefan stood up, wringing his hands. "I'm not feeling well. I should leave."

"Why don't you come see me in the morning, Stefan? That is my house right over there." He pointed next door. "Come at eight o'clock for breakfast." His voice sounded neither imposing nor entreating.

Stefan was struck once again by how youthful the man appeared. For some inexplicable reason, he found himself faintly afraid. The problem was that he felt so debilitated. In his weakened condition, he found it preferable to simply cave in and agree with the demands of everyone.

"Okay, I'll come." He continued to rub his hands together to allay his uneasiness. "I don't have any appetite though. Eating makes me sick. But I'll come if you want me to."

"Good. And feel free to bring your dog."

Samantha must have told him about Rebel. "All right." He turned to walk away, but that compelling voice called out behind him.

"Be sure to send for those records."

Stefan stopped in his tracks. He was slipping back into the ruse again. Couldn't a man on the brink of his death find a little peace down on the oceanside? Why did he have to pick Samantha, who just happened to live next door to another doctor? He should have chosen another. Resentment welled up in him, followed by guilt. His assets were close to depleted, and his insurance nearly capped off. There was no money left to pay for the help that would be of no use and that he didn't want. He would have to liquidate his remaining stocks and give the proceeds to the rich doctor. Perhaps Dr. Calderón could use the money to hire a gardener to get rid of the dandelions. After all, Stefan had no one else to leave it to—no grieving wife and no child. There was nothing left to him except an undying urge to smoke another cigarette. If only he could have a cigarette!

"You've given up the cigarettes?"

How could he have known he was thinking about a cigarette? "Yes, I've given them up," Stefan replied. There was a trace of anger in his voice.

Dr. Calderón nodded. "I'll see you tomorrow." It started to rain.

Stefan trudged inside, glancing around for Samantha, who he was now thinking of as his bad luck charm. The mother streaked toward him instead.

"Stefan! There you are! Come and have something to eat." She clasped his arm and stared intently.

"No, thank you. I . . . I don't feel well. I was just going to say goodbye to Samantha." He felt so exhausted he could barely hold his head up.

"Are you sure? Well, all right. Wait here—I'll run and fetch her. Can we offer you a ride, perhaps?"

"No, I'll be fine." His motel room was close by.

"Sammie!" Her voice boomed all over the house, and Samantha appeared, glancing about in irritation.

"Mom, do you have to scream, for—"

"Well, Stefan has to leave. He's not feeling well. He wanted to say goodbye to you."

"Thanks, Mom." She turned to Stefan, the annoyance in her brown eyes changing to concern. "Are you sure you can't stay longer? You just arrived."

"No, I'm feeling really beat."

"Well, let me walk you out." Clasping Stefan's hand, she waved to Richard across the room, and he smiled in acknowledgement; but Stefan detected frustration in the expression. It was not as if the man were jealous, Stefan thought grimly; it was merely Samantha's preoccupation with a pitiful charity case that appeared to be annoying him. She led him outside to the front entryway surrounded by dripping greenery.

"Thanks for inviting me." He struggled to appear grateful.

"Do you need help getting back? Where are you staying?"

"No, I'll be fine. I'm just down at the Budget Motel."

"Are . . . are you going to see Dr. Calderón again?" Her pretty face looked so hopeful.

Stefan nodded. "Yes, tomorrow morning."

"Really? That's wonderful, Stefan."

"Well, thanks for everything, Samantha," he managed, starting down the walkway. He wanted to get away from everyone to be alone with his pain and crushing fatigue. When he reached his car, he collapsed behind the steering wheel in relief. Stefan noted Samantha still watching him, so with a final wave, he turned the key in the ignition and pulled away.

The rain pelted against the windshield, and the visibility was poor. It was tragic how his perceptions of life had altered so radically. What if his car skidded on the slick pavement and slammed into a telephone pole? What if he deliberately pushed the pedal to the floor and aimed straight for the telephone pole? It would be a mercy. With his luck, he wouldn't die though, just wind up in even more agony.

Something passed in front of him, and he abruptly stepped on the brake to avoid hitting it. Opening the car door seconds later, he squinted into the driving rain to ascertain what it might be. He was certain it was something—perhaps an animal. A white cat darted out from under his car and turned momentarily in his direction. It must have missed the wheels, crouching at just the right instant to avoid impending death.

He knelt down and inspected the animal carefully. It appeared all right; in fact, seeing him stoop in the road, the cat hurried toward him and rubbed up against his knee. Stefan stroked the smooth, rain-splattered fur in relief. He felt better. It would have been a terrible thing to kill an animal.

"That's a good kitty," he comforted, tickling the cat's chin above the blue collar. There was an ID tag attached, and he turned it over to read the name: Milagro.

The cat darted away and leaped up on a ledge under the awning of a house where it attempted to clean the beads of water from its fur. Stefan remained kneeling in the street, the rain cascading down on him. The cat jumped off the sill and disappeared from sight, and he slipped back into his car and continued on his way.

3—*Una Esperanza y una Oración*

The following morning, Stefan awoke early. Rebel was already waiting by the side of the bed, leash in mouth and eyes intense.

"Okay, boy. I'm awake."

He eased himself out of bed, handling each familiar pain with kid gloves. Upon catching a glimpse of his appearance in the mirror, he experienced a deep shock. It was a skeletal face with the skin now barely stretched over it, his sunken eyes ringed with gruesome dark circles—especially prominent upon awakening. Stefan's hair had grown back in patches, some generous, others sparse. He closed his eyes a moment, collecting himself. How was it possible for his appearance to become so appalling in such a short expanse of time? At twenty-seven, he looked beyond old. Elderly people seemed simply timeworn. He appeared already dead.

It required a superhuman effort to boil water for instant coffee, and he halfheartedly tore open a breakfast pastry. Only able to consume half of it, he tossed the remainder to Rebel. The dog sniffed the object and then nudged it under the counter. Stefan sighed, too tired to retrieve it. What did it matter? The broken pastry would outlive him; it would still be around when he was six feet under.

After downing the coffee, he snapped the leash on Rebel's collar and walked to the car. Sliding gingerly into the front seat, he allowed the dog to settle himself next to him and turned the key in the ignition. They drove the short distance to the beach in morose silence. The storm was over and a new day beginning. Rebel, ever loyal and obedient, had abandoned his old way of racing ahead and tearing back every few minutes to find his friend. Now he merely trotted a short distance in front of Stefan when freed from the leash, the dog somehow aware of his master's infirmity.

When they reached the deserted shoreline, Stefan needed to rest and sat on his favorite rock. He found comfort when sitting on this particular rock. For one thing, it didn't hurt his bony frame, and for another, he felt almost beyond time—like the rock itself. Gulls circled overhead, calling out to him. For a moment, he imagined that they were heralding some secret message, his cure perhaps; but as fate would have it, he would never understand seagull language. If only the doctors could.

Stefan checked his watch. There was plenty of time. He watched Rebel chase the sea birds up and down the beach for a while and contemplated the unwanted new doctor. It was a waste of time—all of it—and he dug his heels into the soft sand in resistance to the idea of ever entering another hospital. No matter what anyone said, he was not going down that road again.

Feeling comforted by his resolution, he called to Rebel; and they started down the beach again. The walk was growing more difficult even in the short time since his coming to stay up on the cliffs in the rundown motel. Arriving at the staircase that he and Samantha had ascended the first time they'd met, he paused to rest and then took it slowly, Rebel waiting by his side as he struggled up each step.

Upon reaching the top, he turned to look back out over the vast expanse of open sea. A stab of pain in his chest caught him by surprise, and he nearly lost his balance. Seizing the railing for support, his heart pounded in his chest. The fall would have surely killed him. After closing his eyes a moment, Stefan snapped his fingers for Rebel to come, and they turned for Dr. Calderón's house.

"Sit," he commanded Rebel, and the dog obliged. "Stay." He looked over at the house. The same feeling of timelessness passed over him. "Where have I seen this house?" he muttered aloud, beginning to grow even wearier with the effort it required to search his memory again. His was a sharp, restless mind perpetually on the move, accomplishment and hard work having been his driving forces. Now in constant pain and with nothing to occupy himself with all day long, he found himself descending into the condition of a dullard.

After a final glance back at Rebel, he started up the walkway that led to the front door. He scanned the gardens with a critical eye for weeds and experienced a surge of triumph upon spotting some. Sure enough, there were the dandelions—just bursting with seeds and ready to blow to the four winds. It was irresponsible; the neighbors were right. Pausing a moment to catch his breath, he summoned the courage to knock on the front door. It immediately opened, and a woman peered out at him, holding a little boy.

"You must be Stefan."

"Yes, that's right."

"I'm Alicia. Come in. Miguel's in the kitchen starting his breakfast." She pointed the way, her expression neither pitying nor filled with concern. He found that a refreshing change of pace. Children's voices could be heard down the hallway, and Alicia turned in their direction.

The interior of the house was a mirror image of the outside—beautiful in an almost thoughtless fashion. The rooms were decorated with books, shells from the shoreline, paintings, and three dimensional artistic creations—many of them obviously fashioned by children. Inside the bright kitchen, he discovered the doctor again, sipping a cup of tea.

"Good morning, Stefan. Won't you join me?" He glanced up, appearing somewhat disheveled as he reached for the morning paper.

He grimaced. "I don't have much of an appetite." Seating himself across the table from Dr. Calderón, Stefan found himself growing anxious, as he always did, in the presence of gods in white coats. But Dr. Calderón wasn't dressed in a white coat. He was wearing a ratty bathrobe over his pajamas.

"Yes, I know." He glanced behind him. "Alicia?"

A boy who appeared to be about twelve years old stood in the doorway, leaning against the door jamb. "She's busy."

"Stefan, this is my son Roberto. Roberto, can you fetch that juice your mother just prepared for Stefan?"

Roberto stared at Stefan momentarily before hurrying off and soon returned with a glass filled to the brim with a thick green liquid. He placed it in front of Stefan.

"Here you go, Stefan." Roberto leaned one elbow on the table and studied their guest. "You better drink this, man."

"Thank you, Roberto." His father cast a look signaling him to leave, and with a compliant smile, his son obliged.

Stefan hesitated. The deep green color was off-putting, to say the least, and the contents shimmered eerily as they caught the sunbeam from the window. Feeling on the spot, he tentatively sipped the drink. It was pleasant enough despite the color. "What is it?" he asked, trying it again. The mixture seemed to agree with him.

"Just a few greens from the garden. Papaya juice, too," Dr. Calderón added, taking a large forkful of scrambled egg. "What have you eaten this morning, Stefan?" He studied Stefan curiously.

"Uh . . . well, just a cup of instant coffee. And half a breakfast pastry." He smiled weakly.

"A breakfast pastry?" The doctor appeared dismayed. "Throw them away. And no more coffee either." He turned to the local section of the paper. "When you're feeling better, I'll take you into town and buy you a cup of coffee, all right?

Stefan sipped the juice and remained silent. The ocean breeze wafted through the open windows, and he noted the blue water in the distance through a break in the trees.

"Do you live around here, Stefan?

"I have a room at the motel on Cedar Avenue."

"Good, that's close by Dr. Sandler's café. Brian works in conjunction with me, and after an initial consultation with you, he will directly oversee all your nutritional requirements as well administering several adjunct therapies." He handed Stefan a card. "Here's the address. Beginning next week, you'll only be eating there. The personnel at the café will be expecting you. When you are stronger, you will be able to manage the dietary requirements on your own. Initially, you'll be put on an extended cleansing fast and consuming mainly juices. After that the food will be very pure

27

and easy to digest."

Stefan clasped his hands together in front of him, trying to appear unperturbed despite feeling uncertain. Why, the man talked as though all was going to be well, that he would indeed be getting better, as if there were no question about it! He glanced over at Dr. Calderón. The doctor was obviously one of those holistic nuts, not quite right in the head.

Alicia stepped into the room and placed a bowl of liquid-like gruel in front of Stefan. "*Come esto*, Stefan." She leaned over and whispered something in her husband's ear. Miguel nodded and she disappeared.

Nearly finished with his glass of juice, Stefan stared half-heartedly at the cereal.

"Eat." Dr. Calderón took a bite of scrambled egg.

After a long sigh, Stefan began the laborious task of eating breakfast. He'd never been a breakfast eater; he preferred coffee and a donut on the go. The gruel tasted bland and the green drink—faintly of dirt. Then he remembered that the greens were from the garden. "Yes, but will all this save me?" he murmured under his breath, taking another bite of the cereal.

Dr. Calderón continued reading the paper. "Do you want to be saved?"

"Doesn't everyone?" Stefan chided. He recalled the incident only moments earlier on the stairwell. But at this point, as monstrously ill as he was, it seemed impossible to want anything other than an end to his suffering; and the most logical resolution to that was the specter of death looming before him. Everyone seemed to realize this except, of course, the man who sat eating his breakfast across the table from him. He talked of "feeling better" and "when you are stronger" and so forth, as if it were a fact that he, Stefan, would get better. But then all doctors spoke like that, including the ones he'd abandoned. After making the pronouncement that you had six months to live, they began trying to cure you when they knew it was impossible. What they were really attempting to do was wrestle all the money possible from the insurance company before your time ran out.

"Do you know what the difference is between a man and an egg, Stefan?" Dr. Calderón paused, awaiting a reply.

"Nope." He took a swig of the juice. It wasn't so bad, once you became accustomed to the aftertaste.

"A man can be unscrambled, an egg can't." He set the paper aside.

Stefan chuckled a little. He felt unsure. "Well, some things can never be undone." He stared Dr. Calderón in the eyes.

"A man can survive a thoracotomy," Dr. Calderón responded, stunning his companion.

How did he know? But, then, he was a doctor. Physicians knew things like that, being around sickness and death day in and day out. He was silent, too deep in pain to speak.

"But there are some things a man cannot live without." Dr. Calderón sipped his tea.

Stefan was in the dark about to what the doctor was referring. "Well, they're not cutting into the other one."

Dr. Calderón appeared amused. "That's not what I meant."

"They had no right."

"They were trying to save your life."

"All right . . ." Stefan rubbed his patches of hair, trying to think. "I'll agree to further treatment. Just no more cutting, okay?" His expression was resolute.

Dr. Calderón gathered up his dishes and wiped his face with a napkin. "If they hadn't performed that surgery, you'd be dead right now. I will need your records. Have the information faxed to my office—here is my card. It's imperative that you and I begin our program immediately. We can set up an appointment for Monday afternoon around four o'clock. Is that agreeable?"

Stefan nodded, finishing his cereal. "Fine."

"Good. Now, I must be going. Alicia and the boys are waiting for me. Let me see you out." Out of kindness he graciously took the time to lead his ailing new patient to the door and waved goodbye.

Stefan waved in return and, wandering back down the path, discovered Rebel curled up waiting where he'd left him. "C'mon, Rebel, get your butt up. It's time to go back to our derelict motel." Rebel eased himself up, stretched lazily, and wagged his tail.

They started off together, and Stefan glanced over at Samantha's house. The beautiful home appeared deserted this morning. He felt a little better—perhaps due to the greens. He tried not to feel it, but it was rising up in him nevertheless—a bit of hope that hovered in his chest like a delicate bird. It was futile; he knew it. Still, he'd found a rock to lean on, much like his favorite one down on the beach. He felt odd, uneasy, and again, perhaps just the tiniest fluttering of hope.

Monday afternoon, Stefan managed to find a parking space downtown and located the café. Once inside, he stepped up to the counter and cleared his throat.

"I'm a new patient of Dr. Calderón's."

"You must be Stefan Campeau." A man with a bushy beard

wearing a tie-dye shirt extended his hand. "I'm Dr. Sandler's assistant. He will be providing us with a protocol for you, but for now, we will simply offer you life-giving food. You can take a seat right over there." He motioned toward an empty table.

Nodding in compliance, Stefan sank into a nearby chair. The place was packed with visibly ailing people. Sitting alone at his table, he grew critical while surveying the pathetic bunch. Most were old and hunched over their tables, staring vacantly into space. A few were young and wasted like he was—wearing either expressions of resignation or bewilderment, depending on their apparent states of mind. What did any of them matter at this point? They were all outsiders now, vagabonds—wandering minstrels playing an all-too-familiar tune.

Beyond the gleaming windows, the rest of the world passed before his eyes. Professionals in business suits rushed off to meetings while sipping coffee in Styrofoam cups. Parents sauntered by with their children, pushing strollers and chatting amicably to companions. Everyone looked busy and animated.

The assistant reappeared and, with a smile, placed a plate of food before him. He also provided a large glass of dark liquid.

"What is this?" Stefan asked, staring in dismay.

"Steamed organic vegetables and brown rice. And a glass of vegetable juice." With that he vanished.

Sipping the liquid, he winced upon encountering a blob of pulp. He suppressed an involuntary gag reflex and forced it down. It took him a moment to recover from the ghastly experience. Downing a bit of water, he attempted to breathe again. The taste of dirt remained with him. He felt grit in his teeth and gums. Extracting a piece with his finger, he expected to see gravel. Instead, he discovered green globs that broke apart when rolled between his fingers.

Stefan glanced back at the assistant where he was running a blender behind the counter and caught his eye. "Everything all right?" he asked a moment later, standing next to Stefan's table again.

"What is this?" Stefan held up his finger.

"Oh, I apologize." He laughed and shook his dreadlocks. "Didn't run it through long enough. No worries, though. That's just spirulina."

Consuming the food on the plate was arduous, but finishing the drink proved even more so. At last, he checked his watch and snatched the ticket. The prices were outrageous for such meager fare. Stefan slapped a ten dollar bill down on the table and exited. He would have little need for his diminishing resources soon enough—why not throw it around? He had always been too tight with his money.

After his excursion to the café, he drove to the medical complex five blocks away. It was too early for his appointment with the doctor, so he lounged around the courtyard, soaking in the sun. Yet another enormous hospital towered up before him, threatening to blot out the sunlight in another few hours; and he repressed a shudder. Heaven forbid he should ever be admitted as a patient there. He swore fervently under his breath to never allow it—he refused to die in a hospital staring up at a ceiling. His hope was to perish looking out over the ocean. Why didn't they build the hospital by the seaside, he wondered, with all the patients' rooms on the side with the view? Apparently, your last moments weren't worth much.

His chest hurt and he clasped his hand over it, not that it helped; but it comforted him somehow. He checked his watch again and eased himself up, walking slowly over to the building to locate the correct office.

"You're the new patient?" The late middle-aged receptionist smiled pleasantly. Stefan nodded with relief. He was tired of glamour girls studying him with badly-concealed expressions of shock and pity. But as he glanced around the waiting room, he grew uncomfortable, remembering his previous medical escapades in the city. After accepting the paperwork, Stefan began filling out the application for being sick. He was overqualified, as usual. The endless wait began as patient after patient drifted through the cattle guards. He twisted in his chair, leafed through magazines, and chewed on his fingernails. The incision on his back hurt every time he leaned back in these particular chairs.

He suppressed the desire to walk out, strong as it was. A sick child's name was called. The boy rose up with his mother, quite at ease. He glanced over at Stefan and grinned. The skin on the child's nose was chipped and sunburned, and his front teeth were missing. Stefan smiled and nodded in return. There were children like him. It was a chilling thought. The minutes dragged by. Finally, he was the sole remaining customer in the waiting area.

"Stefan?" It was the doctor himself, standing in the doorway of an adjoining room.

Stefan stood up, wincing in pain. He hurried over, glancing around. It was after five o'clock. The appointment was bound to be rushed. Dr. Calderón placed his arm around Stefan, much to his patient's surprise, and led him down a hall into his office. With that he dismissed his nurse, bid the receptionist farewell for the evening, and shut the door behind them.

"Have a seat, Stefan." He motioned to a couch and Stefan gratefully complied. Dr. Calderón settled himself in a stuffed chair across the room and crossed his legs.

Stefan cleared his throat and glanced around the interior of the office with misgiving. Where were the files, records, charts, and X-rays? The bad news was nowhere to be found, and Dr. Calderón was not even wearing a white coat. He wore a dark pullover shirt, slacks, and Earth shoes. There was a desk, but it was across the room and pushed up to the window for a view. He couldn't bear the suspense any longer.

"Did you get my medical records?" Stefan questioned, having trouble meeting the doctor's eyes.

"Yes, Stefan, I have them. I thought we might discuss treatment now . . . your options, my observations and suggestions. There are some things I want you to do, in fact, that I strongly encourage for treatment. But of course, you'll have the final say in that." He smiled handsomely.

Stefan, however, discovered himself frowning. "Uh . . . all right." He shifted his position on the sofa, attempting to grasp the situation and wrestle some power his way. It occurred to him that Dr. Calderón was handing him all of the control. He found himself unsure of how to handle it, or if, in the final analysis, he even liked it.

"I'd like you to begin . . ." Dr. Calderón broke off and reached behind him for a file drawer. Stefan braced himself. " . . . By keeping a journal." He presented his patient with a blank tablet of lined paper. "Give it a title, write in it every day—what you are thinking, how you are feeling. Also, record your dreams, particularly any about your illness. All right?"

Stefan opened the tablet and scanned the blank paper with a sense of disappointment. A journal? He hadn't written in a journal since middle school when it was required by an English teacher.

"As I mentioned previously, Dr. Sandler will be working with you in concurrence with my therapy. He's an herbalist and certified in several body therapies. It's critically important that you follow his directives. You're exceedingly wasted, Stefan, and cannot afford to put anything into your body except foods from nature that contain super nutrition. You'll be dining strictly at the café." He glanced out the window at the park across the street. "You are to exercise in the fresh air every day. Walking your dog on the beach would be ideal. Be sure to take your shirt off in the sun if it's warm enough."

Stefan began to grow angry. The man was playing a game with him while building up to the real treatment. He suspected he was being offered some flimsy control with a journal while the doctor secretly plotted his actual therapy.

"Have you examined my X-rays?"

"Not yet. Those should be here by tomorrow. I'll have a careful look at everything, I assure you."

"I don't want any more chemotherapy or radiation. I've had enough."

Dr. Calderón nodded. "All right. In your case, those particular therapies failed to stop the destruction of body tissue, and considering the length of time and amounts already administered, they wouldn't be my recommendations either—not at this point."

Stefan remained motionless, a sense of relief filling him. But he grew puzzled, wondering what other treatment options remained. "What will you be doing?" he asked, studying the doctor's profile with the prominent aquiline nose.

"We'll be attempting to uncover the cause of your disease and address that," he admitted, casting him a quick glance.

Stefan sensed the doctor was holding back, waiting until the time was right. "You mean like diet and smoking cigarettes?"

"Those are certainly contributing factors. But many people smoke and eat improperly yet do not develop a terminal case of cancer by the tender age of twenty-seven." He looked away again. "There are many factors in the environment that can alter the genetic codes of our cells and trigger the uncontrolled growth we call cancer. But my primary focus, in your case, will be the connection of conflict and repressed emotions in the psyche and how that manifests in your physical and psychological health."

Stefan swallowed hard and began to rub his hands together. He noticed the doctor watching him engage in his favorite nervous habit and abruptly ceased the action.

"Let me see the incision." Rising up and walking over, Dr. Calderón assisted Stefan with lifting his shirt and stared at his back. The red line appeared angry and painful.

The doctor studied the red gash for what seemed a long time before pulling Stefan's shirt down again. He reached for his desk to grab a pad and began writing out a prescription for some medication.

"This is for pain relief. Follow the dosage carefully." Tearing the slip of paper from the pad, he eyed his patient thoughtfully. "I'm curious, Stefan. What did your former physician have to say when you discussed your dissatisfaction with his course of treatment?"

Stefan exhaled and rubbed a patch of hair, recalling that painful day. "He said if I discontinued my treatment with him . . . that all I had left was a hope and a prayer."

Dr. Calderón stood motionless for a moment, considering his patient's words. At last, he nodded. "Well, I've checked into your former doctors. Dr. Gambian is at the top of his field."

Stefan glowered, unimpressed. Dr. Gambian was the worst of them all—his particular all-time un-favorite.

Dr. Calderón continued. "Yes, he's legendary. I've never had the pleasure of making his acquaintance." He tossed the prescription pad back on his desk. "I have to leave now, Stefan. Please come back the day after tomorrow at the same time. We'll do a complete physical examination. Also, bring the journal. And one more thing. Draw me a portrait of yourself—just a simple drawing on a piece of paper."

Stefan stood up, clutching the journal. "Okay."

"We can arrange finances at that time as well. My receptionist has left for the day. Before you return to your motel, go to the café again for something to bring back with you for later tonight; and please stop down the hall at the second door on the right."

Stefan paused, momentarily disoriented. "What?" He'd assumed his appointment was finished for the day.

"On your way out, stop down the hall, second door on the right." He didn't offer any further explanation and began collecting some files to lock away in a cabinet.

With a shrug and feeling a trifle spooked, Stefan exited, still clasping the journal under one arm. In the hallway, he passed the first room on the right and paused before the second. After hesitating a moment, he slowly opened the door and peered inside. It was the hospital chapel.

The following evening, after taking the prescribed pain medication and drinking a "to go" smoothie purchased from the café, Stefan felt exhausted; and though it was only seven o'clock, he decided to climb into bed. While slipping off his shirt, he heard a knock on the door. Frowning in puzzlement, Stefan opened it a crack, assuming the interruption to be the management disturbing him with a triviality. He was startled to discover Samantha instead.

"Stefan? I'm sorry to bother you." She smiled, appearing like a beautiful angel within the confines of his dingy motel. Stefan stared sadly, reluctant to invite her in.

"Come in," he said at last, wishing he hadn't revealed to her where he was staying. "I was just going to bed." Samantha averted her eyes out of respect as her acquaintance pulled his shirt on again. He felt self-conscious of his body and didn't want her to see the hideous incision traveling all the way down the left side of his back. "Make yourself comfortable." Stefan motioned toward a cheap chair, the only one in the room. He seated himself on the edge of the bed.

"Do you need me to walk Rebel for you tonight?" Samantha asked, gazing down at his dog where Rebel lay curled up across the room. He thumped his tail against the carpet.

Stefan looked over at his dog. He'd been too preoccupied with his own problems all afternoon to pay any attention to him. He stiffened inside, resisting the need for her assistance. At last he sighed, realizing he was going to have to trust Samantha eventually anyway—in fact, he already had.

"To tell you the truth, I was busy with appointments all day."

"Well, it's no problem. Dreamer is in the car. That's the reason I stopped by . . . to see if you wanted to go for a walk together with the dogs; but if you're tired, I'd be happy to walk Rebel for you." After a good stretch, Rebel ambled over and sniffed her leg.

"Rebel, knock it off." Stefan frowned at the dog. "All right, sure. And thanks." The ambiance between them remained awkward; he possessed absolutely nothing to impress a woman with—a former tactical standby for him. The last thing he wanted in his present condition was a beautiful woman feeling sorry for him, and he felt forced into a friendship with her.

"All right. We won't be gone long." She reached for the leash on the nightstand and snapped it to Rebel's collar. Stefan attempted to smile in gratitude and sit up straight. "See you in a while, Stefan."

"Okay." He nodded. When the door closed behind her, he collapsed on the bed. Obligated to remain awake now, he eyed the blank tablet of lined paper lying on the nightstand. A journal! What could he possibly write in a journal? He needed to draw a picture of himself. That would be the day. An artist he was not. Stefan picked up the tablet and opened a drawer to locate his pen. Dr. Calderón said to give it a title. Ridiculous! *The World According to Stefan*, he wrote across the top of it.

Tonight a beautiful woman came to my door. I didn't know

what to say to her. Actually, I have no idea what to say to anyone anymore. I am still the same person I used to be; but now, in my present circumstances, I feel as though I must have been nothing at all. Take away the career, the condo, the status, and I find that I am, undeniably, nobody.

Stefan read back over his words, a strange feeling overtaking him. Having intended to write some sort of sarcastic diatribe, he had inadvertently recorded something honest. He quietly closed the booklet, his assignment finished for the night. He was not about to have a go at the portrait.

Stefan lay back on the bed, thinking. The pain relief seemed to be working; his mind was now free to contemplate, something he had not been able to do at length for a while. He thought back on his relatively short life—his elevated career, whirlwind lifestyle, and the blur of a million distractions. If only he hadn't smoked all those cigarettes!

Bored to tears, Stefan switched on the television and a sitcom appeared on the screen. When the show ended, there was another knock on the door; and he forced his weary body up to let Samantha and Rebel in.

"Hi." Dreamer was with her as well, and the dogs appeared pleasantly tired. "What a beautiful sunset. I wish you could have come. Did you see Dr. Calderón today?" she immediately zeroed in, although not unkindly. Samantha seemed to have little trouble relating to him.

He sank back on the bed again with a sigh, pulled the pillow under his head, and studied Samantha at length. She possessed such large brown eyes with curly dark lashes; it made one feel very pleasant indeed to look into them.

"Yes, I did. I went to my first appointment at his office." With reluctance, he tore his gaze away. "You were right; he's going to let me call all the shots."

Samantha nodded. "I remember my mother and Dr. Calderón argued a lot during her treatment. In the end, they reached a compromise. But first my mom insisted on doing it all her own way. She's the most stubborn woman on the planet."

"Did you work on your magazine today?" he asked, hoping to change the subject. A compromise! The crafty devil was obviously biding his time until the moment of desperation arrived, when the real decisions were always made.

"Yes." She smiled shyly, prettier than ever. "I . . . I had to work, too."

"Where do you work?"

She appeared embarrassed. "At The Town Grill. As a hostess."

"Really?"

"It's difficult to find a job around here. I moved back from the city when my mother was ill to help take care of her. I grew up in this town. Now I don't want to go back. I don't know. . . ." Her voice trailed off. "I just don't like all the crime and urban sprawl."

"I know what you mean." So she used to live in the city years ago. It was possible they had once dined in the same restaurant at nearby tables, unaware of the other yet destined to meet under desperate circumstances, at least in his case. He pondered that thought for a while, thinking of time passing, moments in one's lifetime, meetings, departures, and the irony of it all. If introduced, she would have discovered him puffing away on a cigarette, quite taken with his own image, probably more so than with any feelings of attraction to her. Her fledgling publication would not

42

have interested him either, hard as he had pushed himself working eighty hours a week at that time. But as he lay sprawled across the bed in his low-cost motel room, there was at last some time to spare—granted, not much—but more than ever before.

"And you're engaged now," he reminded her. He had never been engaged—not even close. He'd been married though—to his career and the cigarettes.

"Uh-huh." She smiled, but he thought she seemed a little sad. He always managed to put a damper on things.

"When are you getting married?"

"May fifth."

That was his birthday, ironically. It seemed so far away. A chill passed over him. According to his former doctors, he was not supposed to be alive to celebrate it. He would never be older than his current age: twenty-seven.

Stefan sat up. "Look, I'd offer you something, but honestly, I don't have anything. I'm eating at that granola-head café, and I threw away the coffee. Doctor's orders."

"Oh, that's all right. I should get going. You need your rest." She tugged on Dreamer's leash, preparing to depart.

He now regretted to see her leave. "All right. If I'm feeling up to it, would you like to walk the dogs tomorrow night at same time?"

She nodded. "Sure. That would be nice."

"Okay." He stood next to her. "See you then."

"All right. Goodnight, Stefan."

"Goodnight."

She closed the door behind her and paused for a moment out in the hall with Dreamer. Why had she agreed to do that? She and Richard already had a date to go bowling tomorrow evening with his pals from work. They found it difficult to coordinate their busy schedules and spent too little time together as it was. Her fiancé would be angry with her. But she felt sorry for Stefan, and he seemed very lonely. No one should end up alone at the end of their life.

Thinking it over in the hallway, Samantha decided that she wasn't being completely truthful with herself. Stefan interested her, and she wanted to know more about him—that was the real reason for her visit tonight. It would be problematic to grow too attached to him; he appeared very ill, and she would undoubtedly lose this friendship in the end. Her mother's dream occurred to her. Already she found herself sacrificing time with Richard. Samantha pulled on the leash and headed out into the night, resolving to think it all over in the morning when her mind was always clearer.

Stefan tossed and turned after Samantha's departure even though he felt reasonably well for a change. Some nameless anxiety tormented him, and he couldn't sleep. Lying awake in the shadows, he began to think about Dr. Calderón; and his eyes fell on the darkened nightstand next to the bed while recalling the instructions to record his dreams.

"Jeez," he muttered drily to himself in the darkness. Rebel wagged his tail against the carpet at the sound of his voice, apparently unable to sleep either. He didn't have dreams—none that he remembered anyway. Turning over and shutting his eyes, he tried to quiet his mind. Anxiety threatened to flood over him again, an unsettling agony that had no name. Why wouldn't it just go away? He lay awake in the dark for a long time, worrying and wondering.

"What?" Richard appeared shocked as he looked up from the fax machine behind his desk. Samantha had stopped in to see him at work the following day. "Samantha!"

"I agreed to walk Dreamer with him this evening. He has a dog too. I promised to take Rebel for him when he . . . when he can't take care of him anymore."

"You're taking his dog?" Richard sighed, appearing resigned. Samantha realized it would be Richard's dog as well, something she had failed to consider upon agreeing to adopt it.

"Well, I could always leave it with my folks." It was Samantha's turn to sigh, and Richard took her hand.

"Oh, all right. But we were all going out to Dave's place afterward to soak in his hot tub and have margaritas. Do you realize, Samantha, the last two times we'd planned to go out there you had other last minute obligations? Like the publication or a sick animal?" He shifted his stout frame in his office chair, a hurt expression etched into his rosy face. "I mean, I know the guy's in a bad way, but he should be with his family right now. And he's got hope-springs-eternal Miguel, don't forget." Richard grinned up at her.

Samantha appeared stony. "Yes, well. It's a walk on the beach. I'm not calling off the wedding."

"Samantha . . ." Richard grew appeasing, and reaching up, he pulled her onto his lap. "I said, okay. I admire you for wanting to do it. The guy is . . . well, he's bad off. Go for a walk with him, but Samantha, he's going to die. Try not to get too involved, all right? There is no way in hell he's going to come out of this—trust me—I don't care what Dr. Psychosomatic says."

"Don't call him that."

Richard rolled his eyes. "All right, if you insist. Hey, why not drive out to Dave's afterward? We'll be there late."

"Okay, I'll try." She stood up and he patted her rear end. For some reason, it annoyed her; she suddenly disliked the gesture. It had never bothered her in the past, but now it made her feel like an object. "Well, maybe I'll see you later." She kissed him on the forehead and waved goodbye.

After she left, his coworker Dave quickly closed ranks. "What's up?"

Richard grimaced at his computer screen. "Nothing, as usual. She can't make it."

"Bummer. A sick bird?"

"Nope. Homo sapien. On its last legs, too."

"You mean that guy at her mom's party? He's not going to be around much longer. She's a nice girl, Rich. You're lucky; you know that?"

"I know. But cripes, I wish she'd lavish a little attention on me for a change."

"Well, she will. Hey, we're going to cream you guys tonight, wait and see!"

Richard laughed, straightening his tie. "Yeah, right. Nobody ever beats me," he declared, losing himself in the screen. "And I mean . . . *nobody!*"

Tonight the beautiful woman came to my door again, and we went down to the ocean to watch the sunset. We talked. I tried to relax and be myself, but realized how much I've always striven to impress women—therefore, I've never really been me—so I

46

stopped endeavoring to be anything and just gave up. I can't brag about how intelligent I am, how far I've come, how much money I make, or feel that I'm attractive any longer . . . so I just surrendered to my irrelevance. It was a little like being a kid again, free to be nothing of significance at all. I'm not important anymore.

Dr. Calderón set the journal down on a table in his office the following afternoon and gave Stefan an encouraging look. The lantern clock on the wall ticked methodically in the quiet room; it was four-thirty. The waiting area had proved deserted today—with Stefan's name called right away, much to his relief. After a brief examination, they had retired once again to Dr. Calderón's office.

"Where is the portrait?" He turned back to the journal, thinking he might have missed it.

"I . . . I didn't do that yet. I can't draw."

"You can draw. Everyone can. I have a patient who is quadri-plegic—he drew that for me." He pointed to a framed pencil illus-tration of a clipper ship hanging on the wall.

"Uh-huh." Stefan shifted on the sofa. The incision was bother-ing him again.

"When you go down to the beach, you must expose your wound to the air and sun."

"I hate this thing! Why won't it heal?" Stefan asked, afraid of the answer.

"Your immune system is too compromised right now, but there are things you can do to help it."

"Yes, I know." Stefan furrowed his brow. "Dr. Sandler's filled me in."

"And what are your impressions of Brian?"

"I think he's more than a little strange."

Dr. Calderón laughed softly. "He'll grow on you."

"He said if I don't follow his instructions to the letter I'm out the door."

"It's a lot of discipline, but consider the alternative. I'd like you to practice meditation three times a day. Here are the instructions." He placed a small cassette player in front of him. "The tape is already inside. Let me know if you have any questions."

With a languid sigh, Stefan scooped up the machine. His stomach growled. He was on day two of Dr. Sandler's intensive liver cleanse.

"You didn't record a dream for me, Stefan." Dr. Calderón studied him pensively, his blue black hair reflecting the afternoon light slanting through the open windows.

Stefan set the tape player down again and shook his head. "I don't dream."

"We all dream. See if you can remember."

Stefan grew perplexed and then annoyed. "You . . . you mean right now?"

"Absolutely." The doctor nodded. Stefan frowned in disbelief and began to strain his mind. "No, Stefan, don't struggle. Relax. Look around the room for a minute."

Glancing around the office, he thought to himself about how absurd it all seemed. This mass in his chest was spreading, killing him inch by inch. Who cared about dreams? It was impossible! He couldn't remember.

"Stop thinking," Dr. Calderón scolded. "You head-trip too much."

Stefan smiled, despite his frustration. He looked around the room once more, his eyes resting at last on the sketch of the clipper ship. It was a captivating piece of artwork, to say the least, the rough ocean waves surrounding the schooner building up into a squall. He stared at the waves pounding against the side of the ship.

"I . . ." Stefan hesitated. "I . . . dreamed about the ocean," he admitted, growing astonished. "Yes," he nodded, remembering more clearly now. "Right before I woke up this morning."

"What did you dream about the ocean?" Dr. Calderón asked.

"I found something washed up on the beach." Stefan glowered, remembering. "And I went over to see what it was." So he dreamed after all. "When I arrived at the right spot, the water washed over it, and I stood there waiting for the wave to recede again."

"What was it?" Dr. Calderón prompted.

"It was a clarinet."

"Did you used to play one?"

Stefan turned away and glanced out the window. "I suppose."

"What do you mean, you suppose? Either you did or you didn't."

"Okay, I played one as a child. Didn't everyone?"

The doctor chuckled. "I suppose." His son Luis played the clarinet in the elementary school band. He remained silent a moment, reflecting on his patient's dream. "You couldn't see it initially though, the clarinet, I mean. It required hiking to the right place and waiting for the water to withdraw," Dr. Calderon said.

"Well, you're right. I do dream after all . . . asinine dreams."

Dr. Calderón handed the journal to Stefan. "I don't consider your dream silly."

Stefan tossed the tablet on top of the tape player. "Now I suppose you're going to tell me that my cancer has something to do with my upbringing. Well, I hate to disappoint you, but I had an incredibly average childhood." He exhaled with exasperation.

"I was afraid you were going to say that."

"Look, I know why I'm sick, all right? I'm sick because I smoked all those damn cigarettes."

"Yes, but why did you smoke?"

"Because I enjoyed it." His incision hurt when he leaned back too abruptly on the couch, and he winced in pain.

"Did you wake up in the middle of the night and light a cigarette because you enjoyed it or because you needed it?"

"I was addicted—I admit it. It's called nicotine, and it's highly addictive." He felt angry and tried to repress the feeling; he didn't want to give the doctor the satisfaction of seeing him squirm.

"Why did you stop smoking? You weren't sick then, or at least, you didn't realize you were."

It was beginning to anger him the way this man knew things. He had never told him that! How could he possibly have known? He felt like clamming up, shutting down; the doctor had no right to pass judgment. If anything, Stefan was better than most people. He found it extremely difficult at this point to look his doctor in the eyes.

"Stefan?"

He shook his head, rebuffing the question.

"Tell me why you stopped smoking."

"I quit because of a woman. I asked her out, and she turned me down. She said I smelled like cigarette ashes."

Dr. Calderón fell silent, as if deliberating this information. "What about after you quit? Did you try to ask her out again?"

"No. By then I'd found out. About the cancer."

"Did you find it difficult to stop?"

He shifted in his chair and covered his eyes. "I don't think I could ever convey to anyone how agonizing it was."

"You must have liked this woman a great deal."

"Look, what are you, a shrink? You know, I ought to start smoking again. Why not? I'm going to die regardless, and soon, too. I still feel like having a cigarette all the time, every day."

Dr. Calderón checked the time. "Follow Dr. Sandler's instructions to the letter. I will see you again next week on Tuesday at the same time. Is that convenient for you?"

"Yes." His entire life was free now; the only obligations remaining to him were to show up here, walk his dog, and dine at the café.

"And draw the portrait for me if you please. Also—your X-rays. My receptionist called your hospital and former physicians three times, and they still haven't complied with my requests. I really don't want to take anymore, considering the radiation you've already been given. Can you give them a call?"

"Sure." He nodded without enthusiasm. How typical. Having collected his last cent, they were now ambivalent about helping him.

Dr. Calderón stood up. He clasped Stefan's hand, and his patient was able to face him again. "Don't get discouraged, Stefan. During our next visit, we will be doing some blood work and begin discussing the unconscious process of repressing unmanageable fears and subsequent unexpressed feelings." He led his frail patient to the door.

"Sounds enthralling," was the patient's sardonic response.

"A good afternoon to you, Stefan."

Stefan turned for a last glance into the dark, even eyes searching his. He clutched his journal to his chest, feeling both frightened and uplifted.

5—*Los Médicos Buenos y Malos*

Stefan exhaled into the receiver when placed on hold again, and the soft rock music began to play for him as he held the phone away from his ear. This was his third attempt to make the call for a lousy packet of X-rays.

"Hello, records department."

"Yes, I'd like to have my X-rays sent to my new physician, please. My name is—"

"I'm sorry, but you'll need to come in and do that in person. You'll have to sign—"

"I can't do that!" Stefan closed his eyes, attempting to collect himself. His back ached today, and he'd vomited up his smoothie.

"I'm sorry, but it's our policy to—"

"I'm very sick! I can't make the trip."

"Well, do you have a relative who could come in and—"

"No!" Stefan struggled to hold onto his patience. If only he didn't feel so nauseated! It always made him short tempered. "I don't. Please, could you just send them? What does it matter anyway? Just send them!"

"Let me check on that."

The clerk placed Stefan's call on hold again and music flooded his ears. It made him furious. They had no right wasting his entire morning making him beg for something that rightly belonged to him and he had paid an arm and a leg for too! He hated that hospital. It was dank, ugly, and situated in a bleak, uninspiring district of the city. The sordid memory of his brief visit there came flooding back to him. He repressed the desire to hurl the phone against the wall in defiance of the place. Why did they have to keep putting him on hold? It was such a waste of time when he could be curled up on the bed resting, trying to bear this terrible pain in some kind of comfort. After what seemed like an eternity, the records' employee returned.

"All right. I'm not supposed to do this, but give me your name, please."

Stefan proceeded to give her his name, social security number, and date of admittance while trying not to be sick again. He blamed his nausea on the briny sludge Brian forced down him day after day. What he really needed was a good cup of coffee, but as luck would have it, he was too ill to even feel like drinking that. Now declining at an alarming rate, he would never be well enough to drink a cup of coffee again.

"I'm sorry, but we don't have your X-rays. They've been accessed."

"What does that mean?"

"Dr. Gambian must have them in his office. You'll have to try and call there."

Stefan remained silent on the other end of the line. Too weary to feel angry any longer, he yielded to an odd sense of defeat instead, as if the world were too much for him now. Having always prided himself with being able to handle a million things at once and remain calm under pressure, he now attributed his former capabilities to the cigarette that had perpetually dangled from his mouth and the perennial cup of coffee always close by to bolster his confidence.

"Could you give me that number, please?" he asked at last.

"I'm sorry; I don't have the information. I'll have to transfer you to—"

"That won't be necessary . . . goodbye!" Stefan tossed the phone down and hurried into the bathroom. Bending over the toilet a minute later, he felt a wave of dizziness pass over him. He leaned back against the wall and slid slowly to the floor, too exhausted to stand any longer. Another wave of pain was approaching—this time incredibly severe. He passed out on the bathroom floor.

Samantha waved to her neighbor from the top of the stairwell as she paused a moment with Dreamer. "Hello, Miguel."

The doctor looked over at her from where he was crouched at the edge of his property, staring at the ocean. He stood up and nodded in response. "Hello, Samantha." His youngest son, Mateo, played in the sandbox nearby with Toby, a terrier mix recently rescued from the dog pound.

Samantha smiled, feeling, as she always did, a flush of delight upon meeting her unusual neighbor. "How are you today?"

"Fine, thank you. And you?"

"Very well." She stood next to him, shielding her eyes from the setting sun. Dreamer settled next to Mateo and began cleaning the salt water from her paws. "It's a beautiful evening."

"Yes, it is."

"How is Stefan doing?" she asked, anxious for a bit of news regarding her friend.

Dr. Calderón grew pensive. "I can't really say for sure."

Alarm filled her. "He hasn't stopped seeing you?"

"Oh no," he said. "I meant that it's a little too soon to tell. His is not an easy case."

"I see." She didn't want Stefan to die. Her fondness for him seemed to increase with each encounter. "Is he under Dr. Sandler's care as well?"

"Yes, he is. He's about two weeks into the first month of Brian's program."

"That's good." Dr. Sandler's café was the subject of unrelenting controversy in Acantilado del Mar, but Samantha felt comforted by the iconoclastic herbalist taking Stefan under his wing.

"He's a complicated one," Miguel stated, as if something by way of warning to his neighbor.

She appeared puzzled. "What do you mean by that?"

"He came to us late . . ." Dr. Calderón brushed the residue of Mateo's sticky lunch from his shoulder. ". . . And you brought him. He didn't come on his own."

"But he agreed to treatment."

"Yes, he does as he's told well enough. But I'm hoping, at some point, that Stefan will uncover some passion for life again."

Samantha leaned closer, trying to understand. "You mean despite his pain and physical condition?"

He shook his head. "Not exactly."

"I'm not sure I know what you mean. He was a tremendous success before he became ill. Stefan worked as editor in chief for *Paradise Magazine*; did he tell you that?"

"Yes, a golden boy."

Samantha found herself taken aback by the cryptic admission. People were often offended by him, including her own mother, despite the help he had given her.

"I don't think there's anything wrong with being so accomplished at such a young age," she began. "He's a good person. It's terrible to see someone suffer like that."

Miguel frowned, considering her observations. "I'm not altogether sure his life was as wonderful as you seem to believe. And let me caution you, Samantha; it takes a long time to get to know someone."

Samantha attempted to read between the lines of his words. She found the last statement particularly ambiguous. Her curiosity aroused, she proceeded with trepidation. "Do you like Stefan?" she asked.

Dr. Calderón shrugged. "We've only just met."

She shielded her eyes from the setting sun, watching a wave crash against the jagged rocks below. "Well, I think Stefan is a nice person, and I hope you can help him. If only he hadn't smoked all those cigarettes. He smoked a lot of cigarettes—he told me—and everyone knows that it's injurious to your health."

"Yes." He fell silent, and Samantha sensed he felt she couldn't understand. It both intrigued and insulted her, and she grew quiet as well. "Yes, if only he hadn't smoked all those cigarettes," he replied at last. "Why do you suppose he smoked cigarettes, Samantha?"

"Well, people smoke for an image when they're young to look impressive. Unfortunately, they become addicted to the nicotine, and it can be very hard to quit."

"He could have stopped."

"Well, he doesn't smoke anymore. Maybe another surgery might help him," Samantha ventured, studying her neighbor with hope. He had once convinced her own intractable mother to undergo an unwanted operation—one that ultimately saved her life.

He shook his head. "Not if I can't get his consent." Alicia waved to him from the patio. He scooped up Mateo in his arms and whistled to Toby, preparing to leave. When he looked over at her again, he smiled, but his dark eyes appeared melancholic. "*Hasta luego*, Samantha."

Stefan sat slumped behind the wheel of his car and eyed the medical complex sullenly. Rebel curled up on the back seat, preparing to take a nap. He had survived another drive back to the city. Upon his departure two months earlier, the notion of ever returning seemed totally implausible; his plan at that time had been to face the end of his life in peace down on the beach. Now he was back to retrieve a bunch of depressing X-rays from a doctor he detested the sight of.

He felt better than yesterday when he'd passed out on the bathroom floor. The incredible waves of nausea had vanished, leaving him merely weak and breathless. But today his diaphragm was bothering him; it almost seemed as though a tree branch had been wedged up inside his chest. Whenever he moved, the mythical branches scraped around inside of him. The body was an odd phenomenon, he reasoned bitterly; when well, you felt nothing and took it completely for granted; and when sick, there seemed no end to the terrifying variety of pains one could find himself tormented with.

No longer able to delay the inevitable, he reached for the door handle and painfully eased his way out. "Damn!" he breathed as the tree branch moved about. Rebel glanced up in alarm. "I'll be right back," Stefan promised, pushing the door shut. He was so weak that his shove lacked enough power to close the door completely. He stared at the half-shut door almost wryly, remembering the days when he could stay on his feet while working twenty hours at a stretch with energy to spare.

With a sigh of utter hopelessness, he left the door ajar and limped toward the front of the building. He just wanted to get it all over with. The entrance door proved so heavy that he had to concentrate all his strength to open it. Why did grocery stores have automatic doors? Surely medical offices ought to as well. Following the eerie maze of hallways, he arrived at the place he dreaded.

Inside, he discovered the receptionist who used to greet him with the same uneasy smile. Upon spotting him, she looked as though she'd seen a ghost.

"I'm here to get my X-rays." Stefan stared her straight in the eyes.

"Just a minute." She smiled brightly. "I'll . . . I have to ask about that."

"Well, can you hurry? I have a long way to drive back tonight, and I need to leave right away."

She turned and disappeared into the back of the office. Stefan remained standing at the counter and refused to get too comfortable. The waiting room was crowded with forlorn-looking people pretending to be absorbed in magazines. The receptionist returned, but to Stefan's chagrin, she was empty handed. "I'm sorry; Dr. Gambian is with a patient right now, but if you take a seat, he will—"

"No, you don't understand. I don't want him, just the pictures. I'm not feeling well and need to get going. I know you have them; the hospital told me."

"Well, you see, I have to ask him first if—"

"They're my X-rays, okay? Not his. I have a new physician, and he wants the pictures. So please go get them." Stefan leaned against the counter for support, his expression determined. It was the first time since falling ill that he had actually stood up in defiance of the medical establishment, having previously put up with it all: the endless waiting; delayed appointments; thoughtless, unfeeling remarks; cold, hard talks about payment plans; and even eerie, triumphant little smiles out of some of the doctors when told how bad his condition was.

"I'm sorry, but I simply can't just hand them over without first informing Dr. Gambian."

"I'm not leaving this counter until I get them."

She shrugged and smiled, resettling herself behind her station. "Suit yourself."

Stefan began to sweat. What could he do? Once again, he was boxed into a corner with nowhere to turn. He felt sick again, and his head began to spin. If he were well and handsome, she would retrieve them for him. Slumped against the counter, he began to consider all of the people in his past, the beautiful women, friends, associates, and business contacts. It was over . . . gone . . . just like his health, his money, his appearance, and all his authority. It struck him square in the face with a frightening clarity how shallow and superficial his existence had been.

Another thought added to those crowding into his mind. If he were, by some miracle, able to recover his health again, would he be swallowed up in the same delusion? From this startling viewpoint came another sobering truth: He wasn't sure if he really wanted to go on any longer.

Stefan glanced over at the receptionist, the truths unraveling before him suddenly unendurable. She refused to look in his eyes. Why should she want to? He was completely ravaged and torn to pieces inside.

The inner door opened behind the work station and a nurse appeared, handing the receptionist a folder. "Excuse me," Stefan blurted, interrupting their whispering, "is Dr. Gambian finished? All I need are my X-rays. I'm not here as a patient; I have a new physician. Please, I really need them!"

"I already explained to him that Dr. Gambian—"

The nurse stepped over, recognizing Stefan. "I'll get them for you right away," she announced, concern flooding her. Stefan collapsed against the counter again in relief. At last! Someone who understood and could take action. The receptionist appeared annoyed and trailed away after her. Stefan waited, and true to her word, the nurse returned carrying a large envelope. The receptionist was not with her. "Here you are," she announced. "They should all be here."

"Thank you very much. I appreciate it."

"You're welcome."

The interior door opened once more, and Dr. Gambian himself stepped out, the pretty receptionist close at his heels. Removing his glasses and placing a patient chart down, he stared at Stefan. Clutching his X-rays protectively to his chest, Stefan turned to leave; but Dr. Gambian hurried out from behind the receptionist station, preparing to stop him short.

"Oh, no you don't . . . you just wait up a minute!" he insisted, his voice an angry hiss as he caught up with Stefan and glared at him face-to-face. "I want an explanation from you! Just where the in the hell have you been? Why did you leave the hospital like that?"

Stefan attempted to back away. "Because I decided . . ." He broke off, the old intimidation settling in. "I have another doctor now," he stated, wishing he could leave. All the patients in the waiting room, as well as the receptionist and the nurse, were listening, although they pretended otherwise.

"*Who?*" Dr. Gambian demanded, with the authority of one who knew he was the absolute best in his field of expertise.

"Dr. Sandler," Stefan replied, banking on the hope that the obscure young herbalist remained unknown to the renowned oncologist. For some inexplicable reason, he felt hesitant to mention Miguel. "He's up in Acantilado del Mar." He pressed his X-rays tighter against himself like a shield. "And . . . and . . . Dr. Calderón," he managed, his voice catching in his throat and barely a whisper.

For a moment, Dr. Gambian appeared puzzled by the names, possibly still experiencing shock that his former patient was seeing another doctor. But a smile of amusement crept to his lips as he continued to eye Stefan contemptuously. "I see." He nodded. "Yes, I've heard of *that* name before." He laughed. "Doctor Calderón . . . the *curandero*." He shook his head again. "You'll be back." He was still smiling. The smirk chilled Stefan's blood, and he turned to leave, unable to withstand anymore. "You'll be back!" Dr. Gambian called out after him in the hallway, well out of earshot of the others. "I guarantee it! You'll come crawling back to me, wait and see!"

Stefan hurried out the glass doors as fast as he could manage in his weakened condition, a feeling of horror overtaking him. He felt woozy again, and reaching his car, he leaned against it, attempting to pull himself together.

When he'd gathered a bit of strength, Stefan opened the door, slid painfully inside, and quickly turned the key in the ignition. Rebel lifted a paw and panted in greeting from the back seat. Pulling away, he headed north, the hot afternoon sun beating down on his sallow cheeks.

The man had no right! Stefan wanted to push the distress of the last few minutes out of his consciousness but found it impossible. He didn't have any more room for pain inside of him; every square inch was already taken. Pushing the accelerator to the floor, he resisted the impulse to fall even deeper into despair, attempting instead to concentrate on the now enormous task of driving a car. When safely out of the city at last, he pulled over at a rest area overlooking the ocean and, unlatching his seat belt, climbed into the back seat to lie down.

He was tired, so incredibly tired. Before this moment, he had never thought it possible to feel so completely shattered. The pain in his chest weighed down on him like an anchor thrown overboard from a boat, and the tree branch felt pushed up into his neck. Rebel appeared dejected and resigned. The dog knew what was coming, even if all the doctors were unwilling to admit it.

Stefan stared out the window at the swaying treetops, trying not to breathe too deeply. It didn't feel as agonizing that way. Although unbelievably fatigued, he couldn't sleep. He thought of the meditation techniques explained to him by Dr. Calderón. The doctor had implied it was to be practiced when rest eluded him. But he hated doing the meditation—it made him feel even more unwell when he attempted to. A great weight rested on his chest, crushing the life out of him. Stefan wanted to cry, but his heart felt ossified like a block of stone. Watching the canopies of foliage swaying above him while stroking the top of his poor dog's head, he lay back against the seat and suffered instead.

Dr. Calderón looked up from the paperwork on his desk as Stefan stepped into the office for another visit. His right hand was braced protectively against his hollow chest, the left clutched around a large packet of X-rays.

"Hello, Stefan. Don't tell me you managed to get those?" Dr. Calderón looked surprised. "How did you retrieve them so quickly?"

"I drove down there." He placed the package on the edge of his doctor's desk and turned for the sofa, sinking gratefully into its interior.

"You shouldn't have driven back to the city!" The doctor exhaled in disbelief. "You are in no condition for that." He shook his head and reached across the desk for the pictures. "You're lucky you didn't kill someone out on the highway," he continued to scold, removing the X-rays. "You'll have to excuse me for a moment. I need to step into the other room and have a look at these. Can I get you anything?" he asked, rising up from his chair.

Stefan shook his head. "No, thank you. I'm fine."

"I'll return shortly." Dr. Calderón walked into the examining room, closed the door behind him, and switched on the panel lights. Carefully arranging the X-rays, he studied the images at length, the reality of what he saw settling in around him like a melancholy pall. Another surgery was needed, but could he ever convince the young man who sat just beyond the door of that necessity? Even if it were possible to persuade him, could that frail, weakened body withstand the assault? Right now, he didn't think it could. Stefan's body was wasted away, the reserves of his youth no longer a resource to draw upon. In his mind's eye, Miguel saw a gap, an escape route, closing with increasing rapidity—soon all hope would be gone. Clasping the edge of the panel border, Dr. Calderón steadied himself, closed his eyes, and drew a deep breath.

Stefan glanced back at him when he re-entered the room. "Well, how long do I have?"

"No one can answer that," the physician responded.

"No more surgery," Stefan reminded him.

Dr. Calderón nodded. "All right." He was silent, settling himself next to his patient on the couch.

Stefan experienced trouble meeting his eyes, "But you think I need it, don't you?"

Dr. Calderón nodded. "Yes."

"But you said—"

"You need to regain some strength, Stefan. I wouldn't recommend another surgery right now anyway. You wouldn't survive it."

"I'm not undergoing another surgery! Not now, and not later, if there's even going to be a later!"

Dr. Calderón changed the subject. "Are you managing to hold down most of your food?"

Stefan sulked, annoyed that his doctor was like all the rest—a butcher. He shrugged noncommittally.

"Stefan?"

"I guess. I hate that food, though. It's compost."

"Is it?"

"I'm tired of greens. I'm turning into a rabbit."

"Is that what you dreamed last night?"

Stefan frowned. Here they went with the dreams again. "I dreamed . . . well, I wrote it all down." He handed the notebook to his physician.

I dreamed about a miserable place that I didn't recognize. There were other people there, and we were being held captive. I told another prisoner that I planned to make a run for it, and he said I'd never succeed. I didn't care. I'd been held in that place for a long time, but I wasn't going to put up with it anymore. There

65

was a way out that seemed easier, but I chose to run a different way instead, straight up a mountain through a forest. I knew if I took the hardest route, they'd never be able to find me to take me back; and if I didn't make it, I'd die alone in the woods. So I took off and ran with all my strength, straight into the forest, surprised by how much vigor I still possessed.

Dr. Calderón looked up from his reading. "Your impressions?"

Stefan shrugged, feeling rebellious. The doctor wanted to operate on him, probably from the minute he'd first laid eyes on him in the garden at Samantha's house. They just didn't understand what it was like to be mutilated like that! He scowled, remembering.

"Stefan?"

"What?" Stefan turned his frown on the doctor.

"What's wrong?"

"Nothing."

"You're irritated with me."

"No, I'm not."

"Yes, you are. You're upset because I feel that another surgery might be needed at some point. Why be indignant with me, though? Why be angry at all?"

Stefan shook his head. "Why be angry? You try being in my place. I wish you could feel what it's like!"

"Why don't you tell me?"

"They had no right. They laughed at me. Laughed! Dr. Gambian ought to be stripped of his medical license."

"Did you see Dr. Gambian yesterday?"

Stefan slumped back on the sofa, growing somber. "Yes."

"What did he say?"

"He said I'd come crawling back to him. After I told him that you and Brian were my new physicians."

Dr. Calderón placed his index fingers together against his lips, appearing almost amused. "When you strip away the professional veneer, you see people for who they really are . . . human beings, full of human failings."

"He's a doctor; he ought to know better. They wouldn't even give me my lousy X-rays. I had to beg."

"Well, we have them now."

"In his dreams, I'll come crawling back to him. I'd rather be dead than ever let him touch me again."

"He's that bad?"

Stefan glared, suspicious. Everyone knew doctors covered each other's back-sides. He suspected Dr. Calderón of poking fun at him. "He thinks he's great. So *legendary*. Top of his field. Well, big deal. He's nothing but a heartless jerk."

"What is bothering you so much about Dr. Gambian? He was rude to you when you retrieved the X-rays, but the world is full of offensive people. Why don't you tell me the real reason for your anger? He's the one who performed the surgery; isn't that right?"

Stefan nodded. "Yes."

"Is that what's bothering you? They must have explained the procedure to you beforehand."

"Yes."

"So, why all the resentment?"

Stefan grew quiet, refusing to cooperate. "I'm not that angry."

"How did he behave after the surgery?" the doctor asked, skillfully hitting the nail on the head.

"He stood in the doorway. He wouldn't even waste his time stepping into the room. During the surgery, I heard him and the other doctors talking."

"During the surgery? Don't you mean before?"

"No. I was supposed to be out, but I heard them. Dr. Gambian said the only way I'd ever leave the hospital was feet first. And he laughed."

"Perhaps he laughed as a defense mechanism against the agony he has to witness every day; did you ever consider that?"

"He's in it for the money and power—all of them are." Stefan paused, remembering his own impressive career. Did he feel irate because his former life, now stripped away from him, suddenly appeared as empty and shallow as that of Dr. Gambian's? The revelation seemed to tear a hole in him.

"Have you drawn me your portrait yet?"

"No." He shook his head. "I . . . I keep meaning to, but I tell you, I'm a terrible artist."

"It doesn't matter. Please draw it for me; it's important."

He nodded, resigned. "All right."

"I need to examine you now."

With a sigh, Stefan heaved himself up, preparing to walk into the other room. Once in the exam room, he lifted his shirt and slumped over on the table. Stefan breathed in and out a few times as the doctor listened to his respirations. The scar on his back hurt. He altered his position to relieve the discomfort.

"Is the pain medication working?"

"Yes."

His doctor focused on his heart now, listening to its rhythm. Next came the endless probing of the nodes. He hated having his body touched; he felt like a ticking time bomb, with another explosion about to go off at any moment.

"Okay, Stefan. Let me just have a look at the incision again." Dr. Calderón examined it closely, touching it lightly with his finger. Stefan flinched in pain. "Sorry."

"That's all right."

"You know, Stefan, your back looks better."

Stefan turned in surprise. "Really?"

"Yes, it does. Must be all the greens." He pulled his patient's shirt down again.

Stefan felt pleased. "Then, I'm not torturing myself eating that stuff for nothing? It's expensive too. A big rip-off."

"Breakfast pastries are a real bargain, aren't they?" Dr. Calderón was smiling now, and Stefan slid off the exam table. Breakfast pastries always did seem to have a coupon attached to them at the grocery store.

"Next time, bring the journal again. And the portrait."

Stefan attempted to straighten up and fool the doctor into thinking that he could still comfortably stand erect. A terrible fit of coughing rewarded his efforts. The pain felt so excruciating that he nearly passed out. Dr. Calderón grabbed ahold of him and, as the spasms gradually subsided, guided him into a nearby chair. Stefan collapsed onto it, his head in his hands.

The doctor held his shoulders. "Are you all right now?"

Stefan looked up, feeling weary. "Yes, I think so."

"Good. Come back into my office, and we'll finish up for the day."

Stefan followed Dr. Calderón across the hall where they seated themselves together on the sofa again. The physician regarded his patient with empathy. "How is the cleanse coming? Dr. Sandler told me you're beginning the second round."

Stefan sighed. "It's going okay." He was actually feeling somewhat better today. Still, if he made a little comeback, would that mean he'd be forced to undergo another surgery? He felt his trust in his doctor increasing, and it troubled him. At some point, he might cave and submit to Dr. Calderón's will.

"You existed in that place for a long time," the doctor began, referring to Stefan's dream. "Yet all of a sudden, you decided to leave."

"I told you, I was being held hostage."

"Why didn't you escape sooner?"

Stefan rolled his eyes. "Because that's where the dream began."

"See if you can recapture the impression of the dream's opening before you decided to run."

"I don't understand."

"Why had you put up with your circumstances for so long?"

Stefan allowed his psyche to drift back and linger in the vivid impression of his dream for a moment. "Because I kept hoping they'd be nice to me."

"You ran for the dark, nearly impassable woods. . . ." Dr. Calderón studied his patient a moment. It was a peculiar look.

Stefan exhaled slowly. "Yes."

"Why not take the easier way and improve your chances?"

"Because I never wanted them to find me again. If I could get far enough away, they wouldn't be able to follow me. I didn't ever want to go back to that place."

"But it included a terrible risk."

"Yes, and I didn't intend to go through the woods. But as soon as I took off running, I headed straight in that direction."

"What if you did make it?"

Stefan remembered clearly. "I'd be free."

6—Unos Temas de la Conversación

"Stefan!" Samantha smiled down at him from the top of a massive rock formation where she stood alongside Dreamer. Waving up at her from the beach path, Stefan shielded his eyes from the setting sun.

"Hello . . ."

She started down, careful not to slip on any loose rocks. Soon she stood beside him. "Are you going for a walk or just finishing?"

"Just beginning."

"Good. We'll come along too."

They started down to the beach together, the two dogs racing in front of them. Samantha noticed that Rebel was not so attached to his owner's side as previously had been the case. She sneaked a side-glance at her friend. Could it be her imagination, or did he seem to be looking healthier? With seriously ill people it could be difficult to tell. She recalled her mother's stint with cancer and the good days intermingled with the bad. He definitely walked with more energy.

"How's everything?" he asked.

"All right." They'd reached the oceanfront and Dreamer immediately took off running for a pelican perched on a rock. "Dreamer, come!" The agile dog shot back in their direction.

"You know, I'd be happy to give you and your friends a few tips on expanding your publication."

Samantha was delighted that he wanted to help her and felt overwhelmed with gladness. He must be feeling better if he offered his assistance. "That would be wonderful. I mean, if you feel up to it."

He shrugged. "I'm getting a little stronger. How about tomorrow?"

"Sure. We usually get together in the afternoon sometime since most of us work in the evening. How about two o'clock? We meet at Wanda's house—I'll call and give you the address. We have our entire operation set up in her garage."

"Okay, that would be fine."

They walked on in silence until she sensed he was growing fatigued. "Would you like to rest for a while?" she asked when they reached the spot next to the cave where they had once sought shelter from the storm.

Nodding, Stefan sank gratefully into the soft sand, resting his shoulders against a rock. Samantha sat next to him, and he adjusted his position in order to breathe easier.

"It's a beautiful sunset, isn't it?" she remarked.

"Yes," Stefan replied. The western horizon appeared magnificent, and as he studied the darkening sky alight with fiery bands of colors, he felt fragile, like blown glass.

"How are things going with Dr. Calderón?" Samantha couldn't help asking, though it seemed intrusive. She recalled the conversation with her neighbor up on the bluff some time ago.

"Okay, I guess," Stefan admitted, allowing some smooth, dry sand to slip between his fingers. It seemed unusually warm for a

November evening; a soothing breeze stirred against their faces. It made one think fleetingly of spring. Yet the memory was quickly followed by the realization that the deepest part of winter remained ahead. Fear threatened to steal into him as he remembered how close spring actually was, but for him, how impossibly far away.

"Is he giving you a hard time?" Samantha asked.

Stefan glanced up. "I'm not sure what you mean." He studied her for a moment. "Dr. Sandler does sometimes," he acknowledged. "He's a tyrant about getting me to swallow every concoction he comes up with."

"My mother couldn't get along with Brian and refused to go to his café. Dr. Calderón gave her a diet outline that she followed pretty carefully though."

"What didn't she like about Dr. Sandler?"

"She claimed he was insular."

"But she did okay with Dr. Calderón?"

She looked away. "Not always. Sometimes he made her angry. A few times, she declared she was finished with him and refused to go back. It started to seem like a bad romance after a while." Samantha laughed but Stefan grew troubled. His trust in Dr. Calderón continued to increase, and he worried about a bomb suddenly going off in his face. They lapsed into respective silences as the waves raced up the glistening sand and their dogs chased back and forth.

"Sa-mannnnthaaaa!" a loud voice called out from a distance away.

Samantha sat up and glared. "Oh, great. Here comes my mother."

Stefan glanced down the shoreline and spied the large woman rapidly closing ranks on them, her flowing muumuu flapping in the breeze. Walking behind her was a diminutive man who wore glasses and a look of uncertainty.

"There you are!" Maureen proclaimed, her eyes sweeping over the scene. "Hello, Stefan. How are you?" She shielded her eyes from the setting sun. Samantha's father remained silent.

Stefan looked up at her. "Still alive."

"I can see that!" She grinned at Stefan and then switched to frowning as she faced her daughter. "Richard's waiting for you at the house."

She looked up in alarm. "Is he?"

"Yes, he is. He said you were expecting him."

"I completely forgot!" Rising up, she brushed sand from her pants and sighed in distress. How could she forget that he was coming over?

"I should be going too." Stefan prepared to depart as well, whistling for Rebel to come. The four of them headed up to the beach path that wound its way along the bluff. Stefan struggled to keep up, beginning to feel the weariness of the day's end. When the foursome reached the trail, they encountered Richard, apparently searching for Samantha.

"There you are," he exclaimed, exasperated. "Sammie, I thought we were going out tonight!" His gaze rested on Samantha a minute before turning to Stefan.

"I'm so sorry, Richard. I guess I just lost track of time." Samantha pushed the dark curls back from her face, appearing guilty.

"You didn't have to track her down, Richard," Maureen scolded.

"We were bringing her back. Now you've got dust all over your nice shoes."

Richard exhaled and rolled his eyes. "Whatever."

"Well, hello, Miguel." Samantha's father nodded behind Richard to where Dr. Calderón now stood. The doctor had encountered the group while hiking from the other direction. Alicia and the boys waved in the distance, walking farther up the path toward home.

"Hello." He smiled at everyone, his eyes pausing a moment on Stefan.

Stefan found himself growing amused. He couldn't imagine encountering Dr. Gambian hiking along the dusty trail in an old poncho. Dr. Calderón removed his sweat band and pressed his dark hair back from his face.

"Hello, Doctor," Stefan nodded.

"Stefan . . ." Dr. Calderón returned the gesture.

"How's your practice coming?" Richard chimed in politely, eyeing the doctor and his patient with unease. The odd group that had assembled by accident made him uncomfortable for some unknown reason.

"Fine." Miguel regarded Richard and Samantha. "Is the wedding still on?" It almost seemed as though he asked the question with the expectation that it would be called off.

"Of course it is!" Maureen admonished. She glared with disapproval. "And you're getting an invitation; don't you worry."

"Why'd you ask that?" Richard wanted to know, his expression annoyed.

"Yes, May fifth at three o'clock," Samantha rejoined, edging Richard out.

"It's a nice evening we're having, isn't it?" Samantha's father offered, hoping for takers.

"You're going to come, aren't you?" Maureen studied the doctor with determination in her steel blue eyes.

Dr. Calderón didn't answer right away. Out of the corner of his eye, he discreetly studied Stefan's shallow breathing. "That's a long way away yet to be making plans," he said, glancing at Samantha.

Stefan thought of his birthday. When he lay six feet under, the group gathered on the bluff would be celebrating a wedding together.

Richard exhaled impassively. "Well, it's been nice chatting. Time to shove off now."

"Richard . . ." Samantha began, wondering if he appeared rude.

Stefan suddenly felt tired and, gathering Rebel to his side, prepared to leave. "See you later, Samantha."

"Bye, Stefan." She waved, turning to look behind once more as Richard led her away.

"A nice evening to everyone," Dr. Calderón replied, clasping Maureen's hand in farewell.

Maureen cheered considerably. "Thank you. You too, Doctor. See you later, I'm sure." With a nod they were off, leaving Stefan and Dr. Calderón standing at the junction in the path. Soon they were alone.

"Where are you headed, Stefan?" The physician stood next to him in the darkness as the waves pounded invisibly behind them.

"Back to my motel. My car is parked just up the hill."

"I'll walk with you."

They started out in silence, each waiting for the other to speak. The stars were visible by now and the crickets chirped in the dry grasses along the footpath. Stefan could tell the doctor was listening to his respirations as he walked. He made no effort to conceal that he was laboring for breath. "I had a terrible dream last night," Stefan related, as they continued walking.

"What did you dream?" Their feet crunched in the gravel on the path.

"I dreamed I was better, handsome again. But as I admired myself in the mirror, I noticed that all my teeth were missing." He paused to catch his breath. "I felt shocked. All I had were these tiny nubs." Stefan grew silent again.

Dr. Calderón rested for a while, considering. It was very dark now, almost too dark to see. "That is not a terrible dream, Stefan."

"It isn't?"

"No, not at all. It means you are undergoing a transformation. You're getting your second teeth." They turned up the curve in the trail, continuing on their way.

"I don't feel well." Stefan clasped his hand over his heart in the darkness. It seemed an odd admission from one who was terminally ill, but Dr. Calderón accepted it as if he were expecting it. The dark leaves of the ghostly trees rustled around them.

"Are you still vomiting?"

"No, not anymore."

"Good."

"I dreamed about Dr. Gambian last night, too." The trail ended at the parking lot. "I dreamed he gave me a video cassette. He said it was the truth because *National Geographic* put it out. It was written on the back. He handed it to me and I took it. Then I realized it contained all animation, cartoons. They were all over the cover. I knew it wasn't any good, that it couldn't be true."

They reached his car. Opening the door, Stefan motioned to Rebel and the dog jumped onto the back seat and settled down.

"I hope you can trust me, Stefan."

"I've been coughing up all this junk."

"Your body is trying to get rid of accumulated poisons."

"I've got acne. I've never had a pimple in my life, not even when I was a teenager."

"It will pass."

"I have this sore on my back."

"Let me see it," Dr. Calderón said, trying to get a good view under the street lamp. He lifted Stefan's shirt.

"On the left side, toward the center of my back," Stefan said.

There was a bulge filled with pus. "That must be bothering you. Stop by tomorrow and I'll have the nurse take care of it. It might continue to fill and drain for some time. Don't worry about it, though."

"All right, I won't." He positioned himself behind the wheel. "Thanks."

"Goodnight."

"Goodnight, Miguel."

Dr. Calderón hesitated a moment before starting back down the trail. It was the first time his patient had ever addressed him by his first name.

Stefan stood in front of the bathroom mirror and surveyed his reflection with interest for a change, running his palm against one cheek. His appearance had definitely improved in just the past few weeks. The medication prescribed by Dr. Calderón was working; the chronic pain felt manageable. Best of all, his energy level had increased dramatically after just two months of treatment with his new physicians. Having accepted his downward spiral as inevitable upon his arrival in Acantilado del Mar, he now felt unsure of what to do with his small rebirth.

"Come on, boy, time for our exercise." Rebel leaped up and he snapped on the leash. On the way out, he stopped by the front desk.

"Yes, can I help you?" The desk clerk looked up from his comic book. He wore a nervous smile that Stefan had grown accustomed to receiving from almost everyone.

"Yes, I want a different room if possible. One with a kitchenette. When I first checked in, you told me you had a few."

Glancing down at his manifesto, the clerk shrugged. "Sure, there'll be one available tomorrow. I'll pencil you in."

"Thanks."

Stefan felt so good he decided to walk to the beach. Rebel appeared surprised when they bypassed the parking lot. He hiked the four long blocks to the oceanfront quite easily. Once down on the boardwalk, he paused to rest a moment and released Rebel. He glanced up and down the shoreline for Samantha, but the beach appeared deserted this picturesque autumn morning.

The waves lashed spectacularly against a rock formation out in the water as he settled himself on his favorite rock. The initial intensive cleansing finished, Dr. Sandler was introducing more foods into his diet; and Stefan felt the change. He'd been informed that he no longer needed to eat his meals at the café and been given a juicer to take back to his motel. Now all he needed was a small kitchen.

"Rebel, get over here!" he scolded, noting his dog playing with something. Rebel glanced his way a minute and proceeded to ignore him. Forcing himself up, Stefan walked over. It turned out to be a bird huddled against the rocks, its wings held out in warning. One of them appeared out of joint.

"Great . . ." Stefan muttered, shaking his head and studying the bird. An idea occurred to him. Samantha cared for injured animals like this. Slipping off the flannel shirt he wore over his T-shirt, he knelt down and draped it over the bedraggled creature. Rebel wagged his tail. "Easy now . . . easy . . . little guy." The bird struggled under the shirt and succeeded in popping its head out. Afterward, it seemed to calm down. Stefan laughed, and Rebel trotted around him, anxious to be of help. "C'mon, boy, this way."

He started down the beach, cradling his precious cargo. Upon reaching the stairs ten minutes later, he glanced up. With any luck, she would be at home. It surprised him how quickly he ascended the steps, hardly needing to pause for breath. At the top, he turned for Samantha's house, the bird beginning to struggle in protest again.

As he rounded the curve in Samantha's driveway, he spied Richard and a few other men lounging around their trucks, gathered for an outing. They glanced at him and Stefan forced himself to walk over, feeling silly about his mission. A stereo blared music, and their gazes felt obtrusive.

"Stefan, hello!" Richard smirked as he hopped down from the back of the truck bed. The other men nodded in acknowledgement. "Whatcha got there all wrapped up?"

"A bird. I think its wing is broken. Is Samantha home?"

"A bird!" Still grinning, Richard peered at Stefan's bundle as if concerned, but his interest left Stefan uneasy.

The front door opened and Samantha stepped out, clasping a beach bag and thermos. Spotting Stefan, she hurried over. "Hi, Stefan!" She gave Stefan a smile and he quickly returned it. Without a word, she took the bird from him, expertly handling the tiny creature and examining it with concern. "The wing is a little crushed . . . I wonder how that happened?"

"I don't know. I just found it on the sand. It didn't even try to get away."

"It's very weak. Probably been hurt for a while."

"Do you think it will be all right?"

"Gosh, do you think it will?" Richard asked, and Stefan felt himself stiffen. There was a quality about this man he was beginning to actively dislike.

"Oh, I'm sure it will. It needs attention though, right away."

"Samantha, we have to go now." Richard's voice was firm. "We're already late."

"Just let me call Wanda. She'll do it," Samantha replied. Her fiancé sighed and shook his head, staring at the ground. "C'mon, Stefan; we'll put it in back." Samantha led Stefan around the side of the house.

"Who the heck is that?" asked one of Richard's friends, studying the two retreating forms.

"Samantha's latest project."

"What's the matter with him?" Cooper's face looked grave.

"He's sick. He's going to croak." Richard stared grimly after the departing duo.

Dave stood next to them, running a hand through his blond hair. "Is it my imagination or does he . . . does he actually look better than the last time I saw him? That day at the party, he could hardly walk. Now look at him. And that was only a few months ago!"

"Yeah, well. He's got that herbalist pumping him full of his crazy tinctures and seaweed. I've seen Sandler picking it up off the beach late at night. And damn it, Samantha's getting attached to Stefan. It's going to be really hard on her."

Dave exhaled in sympathy. Cooper shook his head. "Think we should, you know, invite him to come along fishing with us?"

"No way." Richard winced. "The last three times I've asked her to go someplace, she had to do something with him." His expression grew determined. The sick guy would just have to turn out to be some former hotshot editor who could help Samantha with her new publication. It all added up to lost time between them, and he had to work sixty hours a week besides.

Back around the other end of the house, Samantha motioned Stefan toward a cage. "Let's just set him in here," she said, placing the bird down. There were several other cages, but they were empty. She poured some water into the cup hanging on the side of the cage. "I just have to run inside a minute and call my friend Wanda. She's studying to be a vet."

"All right." Stefan glanced over at the bird for a moment and then at Samantha again. "Go ahead."

She hurried away and he stayed put. The last thing he felt like doing was hanging out by the trucks. Even if things had been as they were before, he would have avoided the men. He wondered what Samantha saw in Richard. It was unfortunate that they were here today; now he wouldn't have an opportunity to chat with her, an increasingly happy pastime for him. A minute later, Samantha returned.

"She's coming right over. Thanks, Stefan, for bringing it and everything." She paused, looking down at the bird. "I'm . . . I'm sorry I have to leave now. We're fishing out by Esperanza Point. Would you like to come along?" she offered graciously.

"No thanks, I can't." They smiled at each other again. Despite his initial resistance to their becoming friends, she had been persistent in developing the relationship. It was difficult for him because Stefan felt like he had so little to offer, but eventually he had grown comfortable and learned to accept it. "I have a doctor's appointment this afternoon."

"Oh, well. Maybe another time."

"Samantha!" Richard's voice boomed out from around the other side of the house.

She ignored him. "If you have time later, stop by and see how he's doing. I'll be home this evening."

"Sure. Maybe I'll do that." With a wave, he started down the path in the opposite direction of the gang. Samantha returned the gesture, watching him depart.

Stefan arrived early for his appointment, so he leafed through a magazine in the waiting room. The freckled, peeling-nose boy was back, and he sidled over, in the mood to chat.

"Hi. My name is Daniel."

"Hello. I'm Stefan . . ." he replied, setting down his magazine. To his dismay, he noticed Daniel was missing patches of his red hair. "How's it going?"

"Good! I'm seven years old. How old are you?" He squinted at Stefan.

"Twenty-seven."

"That's old! Do you have a little boy?" he asked, picking at a chip of skin.

"No," Stefan admitted, casting his younger friend a look of regret about the matter. "I'm not even married."

"Oh. Well, maybe when you get married . . . after you're all better . . . you might have a boy." He smiled, holding one arm out for emphasis, his palm cupped in the air.

Stefan chuckled at the innocent gesture, studying the boy with admiration. "Maybe," he agreed, growing sadly amused. "Maybe I'll name him Daniel."

"That'd be good. My hair's growing back. Dr. Calderón said to imagine it growing back and it will."

A small laugh escaped Stefan. "Really?"

"Yeah." He nodded enthusiastically. "And it has. It's a good thing, too; I get sunburned real easy. I donwanna get sunburned on the top of my head!" He burst out laughing again, holding his

84

arms out to his sides in a silly way. "My mom's calling me. I have to go now." He tagged after his anxious mother, casting a smile back at Stefan. Stefan felt his mood darken and a gloom settled in around him. Twenty-seven. It was old when you contemplated the tender age of seven.

Musing over this for the next forty-five minutes, he found himself in an even lower state of mind while the nurse drew blood and recorded his vitals. The abscess on his back had nearly healed, and after changing the bandage, she updated his paperwork. Finally, he entered his physician's office.

"Hello, Stefan," Dr. Calderón acknowledged, looking up from where he was scribbling something at his desk.

"Hello."

"How are you?"

"Just jolly." He grimaced and handed the doctor his journal.

Dr. Calderón flipped through it, his expression displeased. "Why haven't you drawn me that portrait yet?" he asked, holding up the booklet.

Stefan lapsed into an insulating silence, feeling wary of his doctor friend.

The doctor seemed agitated himself this afternoon. He opened the journal again and held it up. "What is this?" There were no recent entries of any kind.

Stefan stared straight ahead, refusing to answer. He didn't have to take this. In another minute, he was going to walk out of here.

"Did you record any dreams for me?"

"Uh . . . no, not really," he admitted.

"Why not?"

Stefan twisted in his seat and began biting his fingernails.

"Stefan? Answer me, please."

"Because you and I both know . . . this is all hopeless."

"No, it's not hopeless. You are wrong!"

"It's delaying tactics. I'm a goner."

Miguel tossed the journal onto his desk and propped his head up with one hand. "You don't believe in your treatment, then?"

Stefan shook his head, smiling wryly. "What treatment?"

"Well, if it's not sufficient for you, let's discuss a possible surgical option. I'm very concerned about that mass in your chest. You've gained weight, your incision has begun to heal, your hair is growing in, and your energy level is up. But this course of treatment may not be enough. We could run out of time; your condition is advanced, and—"

"No, no, no! No surgery. I can't go through that again. No more!" He shook his head emphatically, a shadow falling across his face. "I don't know why I ever came here. I don't believe I'm ever going to come back from this. I don't believe in miracles."

"Do you want a miracle?"

"I know what you're thinking . . . you think I don't want to live." Stefan glanced out the window, awaiting his doctor's response. They'd been over this ground before, and Stefan could feel Dr. Calderón closing in on him.

"I think you're conflicted about it."

"I've done everything you've told me . . . followed Dr. Sandler's protocol to the letter. I've done his lousy cleanses three times!"

"You're good at following instructions."

"And what's that supposed to mean?" Stefan shot back in exasperation. There was simply no pleasing the doctors. He had been completely compliant in every regard, and yet he still felt like he was coming up short. "If I didn't want to live, why would I subject myself to Sandler's colonics? It would be a lot easier to just give up."

"You mean go back to the pastries and coffee?" Dr. Calderón arched his brows.

Stefan chuckled in spite of himself. "Well, truthfully, I thought they were good for you. They advertised as much . . . that they had vitamins in them and everything."

The doctor frowned. "Yes, I suppose a lot can be chalked up to people's ignorance. But you knew smoking was harmful."

"I planned to quit. I didn't think it would hurt me if I didn't smoke for more than a couple of years. I started right after I graduated from college, so I wasn't smoking that long. I didn't deserve to get cancer. A lot of people smoke for decades."

"And die of something else?"

"Yes."

Dr. Calderón was silent a moment, fingering a small, misshapen clay pot on his desk—a present for his fortieth birthday from Luis. When he spoke again, he gazed straight into his patient's eyes. "Smoking most likely didn't cause your cancer, Stefan; although I'm sure it was a factor in the disrupting the subtle functional order of your physiology."

"Brian is supposed to be repairing my immune system."

"Yes, addressing environmental factors is essential to success. But in your case, I strongly sense that we need to uncover the psychosocial aspects of your disease if you are to make a permanent recovery."

Stefan clasped his hands together, and Dr. Calderón noted his shallow breathing. He wondered if his patient had ever breathed normally—even as a young child.

"Okay, Stefan . . . last time we talked about your dislike for your position as editor in chief for *Paradise Magazine*. I'm curious to know if there is a job you might possibly enjoy. Have you ever given that any thought?"

Stefan sat on the edge of the sofa, his expression resolute. "I don't have to think about that anymore."

Dr. Calderón paused, absorbing the revelation. "Well, I'm not at all convinced you're going to die."

It was Stefan's turn to remain silent.

"Surely your former position was not the only option you ever considered?"

Stefan shifted in his seat. "It's just all the workplace politics and bowing and scraping. There's no avoiding it."

"This world is replete with discomfort, isn't it?"

"There's just a bit too much of it for my taste."

"Well, you certainly could avoid dealing with it anymore by dying."

"It's the same wherever you go. You can't escape it."

"You could fight against it . . . change the status quo."

"If you say anything, it just gets worse."

"Then, why not simply be uncomfortable? If you don't resist it or smother it with a cigarette, you might find it's manageable after all and that life has a lot to offer."

"When I allow myself to feel anxious, I start getting irate."

Dr. Calderón shrugged. "Is that so terrible?"

"Whenever I got angry, my mother used to tell me I should count my blessings."

"No, Stefan . . . you have a *right* to be angry when people mistreat you. I think your sensitivity to the world's rough handling is wearing away what strength you have left. You can't afford to do that. Your state of intactness has crumbled away, and you have completely disregarded yourself."

"I feel guilty when I get angry."

"What's happened in your past has amounted to abandonment, Stefan. It's not unexpected to uncover anger."

"I don't like angry people."

"It bothers you to see your anger. You want to be dead because your discomfort will end."

Stefan studied the drawing of the clipper ship. He began wringing his hands, his favorite nervous habit.

"Are you afraid of making mistakes?"

Stefan nodded, still looking at the picture.

"Don't be afraid of honest mistakes. You're entitled to them."

"Tell that to my former employer," Stefan replied sarcastically.

Miguel opened the journal to a previous entry on dreams.

I dreamed that I saw an owl passing by my window at night. It was flying, but it had no wings. It made me sick to see it. The owl caught something—a small bird, like a sparrow. The bird began to scream. It was agonizing listening, so I covered my ears. I could still hear the cries of the bird though, and I fell down on the floor. I wanted the sound to stop, for the bird to finally die, but it just went on and on. . . .

Dr. Calderón looked up from the journal. Stefan was staring out the window, his expression staid. "Why do you suppose the owl had no wings?" he asked his patient.

"Because it was another pointless nightmare, I suppose. I have a lot of them."

89

Miguel set the journal aside. "Wings are the expression of the aspiration of the soul to attain freedom."

"Well, it didn't fly. It lurched instead."

"Did it remind you of anyone you know?"

Stefan was silent and remained immobile.

"How about your stepfather?"

He closed his eyes, resting his head against the back of the sofa. "Not him again."

Dr. Calderón proceeded with caution. "What does your stepfather look like? Is he broad in the shoulders?"

Stefan shrugged noncommittally.

"Is he—"

"All right, it was him!" Stefan sat up to face his doctor. "He was a terrible stand-in father; I admit it. Can the rotten dreams about him stop now? I'm tired of them!"

"I think you still have some grieving left to do."

"Oh, yeah? How so?" He accepted his journal back, anxious to leave.

"It's a shattering, life-altering experience to lose your father at the age you did. And though you say you can hardly remember him, I'm beginning to suspect he was a very caring individual."

"Well, how am I supposed to grieve for someone I can barely remember?"

"You will, Stefan."

"I'm sick and tired of all this."

"In the dream . . . did the bird finally die?" Dr. Calderón seemed to already know the answer but wanted to make the point to his patient.

Stefan looked him in the eyes while clasping the journal. "No, it didn't. I could still hear the screaming when I woke up."

Miguel nodded, pressing his hair back from his eyes. Darkness appeared to be closing in around Stefan, and he sensed it would be helpful to end their appointment today on a positive note.

"Why did you get a dog?" he asked, a pleasant subject change.

Stefan pondered the question a moment. "I don't know. I went to the shelter one day with someone from work and noticed Rebel sitting there all alone."

"Do you like having him around?"

Stefan nodded. "Yes, it happened to be one of the few intelligent decisions I ever made. And it was completely out of character for me. I had something else to think about besides that stupid magazine."

"Dogs can be a lot of trouble."

"He turned out to be a lot of trouble in the beginning." Stefan smiled but then quickly frowned. "That's what bothered me the most when I found out that I was sick. I worried about what would happen to him, that he would feel abandoned again." Samantha would take good care of him if it came to that, but Stefan knew Rebel would deeply mourn his passing.

"I suppose that's why people have three dogs sometimes," Dr. Calderón mused.

"I can't afford it." Stefan laughed, his face lighting up. "But I'm beginning to think that most things worth having in this world are a lot of trouble."

"You mean like your health?"

Stefan didn't reply. Their time together had come to an end, and rising up off the sofa, he nodded goodbye.

"Don't forget," Dr. Calderón reminded him.

"I know . . . the picture."

Dr. Calderón leaned back in his red Mission rocking chair and adjusted a book in his lap. It was past midnight, and although exhausted, he wanted to remain awake until Luis' fever broke. The boys had been sick with a virus sweeping through town, and while Mateo and Roberto were now both on the mend, Luis remained listless, his fever returning at bedtime. Placing his hand against his son's cheek, Miguel frowned, unable to shake an uneasy feeling.

Alicia slept in the next room, worn out from caring for their children, and after checking his watch, Dr. Calderón rubbed his eyes. The soft, rhythmic sound of his son's breathing calmed him, and he found himself relaxing despite his resolution to remain awake. Several more minutes passed, and he drifted off to sleep.

He dreamed that they were living in the city again. Alicia came to him crying, completely distraught. "I can't find Luis," she sobbed, tears streaming down her cheeks. "I've searched everywhere for him!"

Fear seized Miguel's heart. He hurried outdoors, looking around. "Luis!" he called, scanning their fenced backyard. The gate to the back alley was open, and he ran toward it. "Luis!" Luis knew better than to leave the safety of the backyard!

"Luis!" he shouted again, racing down the alley, searching as he went. Terror gripped him. His middle son, the sensitive dreamer, was missing!

Filled with trepidation, Miguel thought of the house five doors down. A rundown, ramshackle place, the owners were criminals constantly in trouble with the authorities. Sprinting quickly in that direction, he scanned the cluttered yard strewn with debris in desperation. Surely Luis would not have come here! *"Luuuiiisss!!!"*

Awakening with a jolt, Miguel bolted upright in his chair, his heart pounding in his chest. He experienced difficulty recovering his breath. Relief flooded through him when he realized it was only a nightmare and that Luis still slept peacefully several feet away.

Reaching over, he touched his son's face to reassure himself that everything was all right. The fever had broken. The racing of his heart gradually subsided, and Miguel slumped back in the rocker again, utterly spent. Closing his eyes, he drew a deep breath, the sound of his desperate cries in the dream still reverberating in his ears. He opened them abruptly, surprised by a sudden revelation. Although calling for Luis in the dream, he had actually been shouting "Stefan."

"Stefan!" Samantha waved from across the street where she stood with several friends in front of the restaurant La Mariposa. "Over here!"

Stefan looked up in surprise from the shrubbery along El Camino Hermosa, and upon spotting her, he started over. Tired from another restless night, the sight of Samantha and her friends cheered him. "Hi, Samantha." He nodded politely to Wanda and Shelly.

"Hi, Stefan." Samantha took his hand in hers. "What have you been up to lately? We're going to stop in here for lunch and discuss the first draft of next month's newsletter. Feel like joining us?"

"Sure." He smiled. "But I doubt I can eat much of anything."

"That's okay, Stefan. We'd love to have you, eating or not." Samantha laughed.

"All right."

Once inside the popular restaurant, they were seated in a booth next to the front window. The girls ordered margaritas and Stefan, mineral water. He scanned the menu. His regimen was still being meticulously monitored by Dr. Sandler, and he was required to turn in a weekly diet sheet recording everything he'd consumed.

"Can I have the garden salad?" he asked the waitress moments later. "And no dressing, please."

"All right." The waitress flipped open her notepad and recorded their orders.

"When will you be able to eat . . . you know, like everyone else?" Shelly asked, sipping her margarita.

"When Dr. Sandler says I can, I guess," was Stefan's response.

"Oh, you mean never, then." Wanda cut loose with a boisterous laugh.

Stefan chuckled too, despite his somber mood. The noon sun streamed through the windows and the sky blazed an azure blue above. He liked Samantha's friends and it felt good to be sitting in the booth with them even though he was denying himself alcoholic libation and hearty food.

"He's a strange one," Wanda commented, dipping her chip into the wooden bowl of salsa placed at the center of the table. "I saw him behind me in the grocery store checkout a while ago, and we struck up a conversation. He said nothing I had in my cart even qualified as food."

"What was he buying?" Samantha asked curiously.

"Toilet paper." Everyone laughed.

"He told me he lives out in the valley with Whitney, that old grandfather of his, and grows all the organic food for his café. He said what you eat reflects who you are and whether you love life or not."

"I almost ran over him on his bicycle the other day," Shelly remarked. "The next time you see him buying toilet paper, you ought to tell him to stop at stop signs since he loves life so much." Everyone laughed again, and Stefan started on his salad.

"How's everything going with Dr. Calderón?" Samantha asked Stefan.

He shrugged. "Okay."

"What's soul retrieval?" Wanda asked, studying Stefan curiously.

"What?" He looked up, startled.

"That's what someone told me Dr. Calderón does."

"I thought he was an M.D. over at the medical center," Shelly remarked.

"He is," Samantha said, wiping her face with a napkin. "He graduated from Duke University. He an oncologist, but he also does adjunct therapies."

"Wasn't he your mother's doctor?" Wanda asked.

"He advised her," Samantha said. "But she was actually a patient of Dr. Benson's. And she absolutely refused Brian's therapy altogether after the two of them got into a screaming match out on the sidewalk in front of his café."

"Really!" The girls appeared shocked and amused.

They turned to Stefan. "How do you get along with Dr. Sandler?"

He rubbed his neck. "I don't have a problem with him."

"Did you know that Miguel and Alicia are expecting another baby?" Wanda asked between bites of cheese enchilada.

Samantha looked surprised. "Really?"

"I bet they're hoping for a little girl this time."

After they'd discussed the newsletter and finished up their lunches, Stefan sneaked a peak at his watch. His biweekly appointment with Dr. Calderón was in a little over an hour. After weaving their way through the crowded lunchroom, the group lingered out on the sidewalk.

"I've got to get going, Samantha," Stefan said.

"Do you need a ride?" she asked.

"No." Stefan squinted across the road. "My bicycle is stashed in the bushes over there, if no one's stolen it yet."

Samantha held onto his hand. "See you later, Stefan." He smiled fondly in return. Shelly and Wanda grew quiet, their expressions pensive.

"Thanks, Brian." Stefan pushed his way out the glass door of the café with a bag of medicinals under one arm and was greeted by the winter sun. Sea birds circled overheard, their cries heralding the approach of a late afternoon storm on the horizon, one that mirrored the tumult beginning to brew in Stefan's soul.

After dropping his things at the motel, he bypassed his car in the parking lot and stopped again at the shed, dragging out the old bicycle that the manager had given him. He loved riding the bike—it freed him and cleared his head. Swerving back through the bougainvillea intertwining overhead along El Camino Hermosa, he headed downtown for his appointment.

"You can go right in," the receptionist assured him with a smile. "He's been waiting for you."

"Thanks."

Stefan slipped into his physician's office and collapsed on the sofa. He no longer leaned forward to better catch his breath. His curly hair almost reached his shoulders and his large dark eyes were clear. But something was troubling him this late Monday afternoon, and Dr. Calderón, nursing a dour mood himself after a night of virtually no sleep, began peeling an orange while regarding Stefan silently.

"How is the hydrotherapy going, Stefan?" he asked at last.

"I hate those horrible baths of Sandler's." Stefan cast his doctor an irritated look. "They're giving me nightmares."

"What did you dream, Stefan?"

"I keep dreaming I'm living with my parents, or I'm working at that damn magazine again. Last night, I dreamed I was back and all this garbage was going down . . . deadlines, people getting upset, and I kept rushing around trying to keep it all together. I felt exhausted. Then I went outside to do something, I don't remember what. Another responsibility, I suppose. I turned and saw this rundown garage with nothing in it but a dirty old cage sitting right in the center. I went to investigate and found a baby inside."

"A baby?" Dr. Calderón sat up straighter in his chair, his orange forgotten.

"Yes." Stefan nodded.

"What did you do?"

"I got it out of there as fast as I could. It was freezing outside."

"Then what did you do?"

"I started to carry it back inside. The baby felt cold and didn't move, but it wasn't dead. Not yet, anyway. I felt terrible, like it was my fault. But I couldn't figure out how it happened. The dream terrified me so much that I couldn't go back to sleep afterwards. I had to get up and sit in a chair for the rest of the night."

Dr. Calderón frowned, watching his patient. "It sounds as though the baby was dying of neglect and exposure."

Stefan's face looked pale. "It was dressed in light, worn-out clothing, and it seemed really cold in that horrible garage."

"Did you feel the baby would survive?"

Stefan shook his head. "I didn't know. I held it to my chest, trying to warm it back up; but it was cold and not moving. I felt sick and anguished."

"Did you feel better after you woke up?"

"No . . . I told you, I couldn't fall back to sleep. I was too angry."

"What were you so angry about?"

"I felt anger toward God for allowing me to dream that in this first place . . . for making me feel so much fear that I couldn't sleep."

"How old did the baby appear to be?"

Stefan stood up and turned away, his expression annoyed. "How should I know? I don't know anything about babies! I hate this damn world. I'm suffering all the time—in constant pain. I feel like even God is out to get me and tortures me in my sleep at night."

"Why was the baby your responsibility?"

"How should I know? I don't even know how he got there!"

"He?"

Stefan whirled around to face his doctor. "I know what you're thinking!"

Dr. Calderón remained silent.

"That wasn't me!"

"Stefan . . ."

"It wasn't me!"

Miguel arose and walked over, standing next to his patient. "I think it was."

Stefan closed his eyes a moment, recalling the dream. "Then, what's the use?"

Dr. Calderón placed his arm around Stefan's shoulders. "That baby wasn't dead yet."

9—La Playa Fantasma

Stefan stood next to Rebel in the beach parking lot the following morning when Samantha waved and started over. Looking away, Stefan suppressed a twinge of annoyance. He didn't feel like facing anyone today, especially someone sure to quiz him on his medical profile. He wanted to be by himself, alone with his dog on the sand.

"Are you leaving?" she asked, removing her sunglasses. The wind blew her dark curls across her face, and he nodded in response. His own black ringlets were growing back, and he ran his fingers through them possessively. It was a relief to have all his hair in place again, and he shook his head with a sad grimace. Thanks to Brian Sandler, he wouldn't be going to his grave as bald as a cue ball.

"What's the matter?" Samantha appeared sympathetic.

Stefan shrugged. He wasn't about to tell her. She'd be sure to gush with empathy and then turn right around and beg him to go under the knife. "Nothing. Besides the usual, I mean."

"Oh." She grew silent, feeling pushed aside.

Stefan began to feel guilty. Why was it necessary to be so civil to everyone all the time? He wasn't in a polite mood and needed to be alone. Still, Samantha had been nothing but kind and understanding to him. Why take it out on her or anyone else for that matter? "I'm sorry," he said, looking her in the eyes.

"That's okay."

"I don't know. I'm in a bad mood or something. I don't even feel like walking on the beach. Nothing makes me happy right now." He scowled and looked out over the vast expanse of moving water.

She tried not to laugh, feeling touched by his admission. He was beginning to remind her of a little boy now that he didn't appear so ill. "I know how you feel. Everyone feels like that sometimes."

He sighed. "I suppose." Yes, he used to feel like that "sometimes." He'd handled the disquiet in the past by smoking an extra cigarette or indulging himself with some expensive distraction until the feeling went away. "I suppose we're all in the same boat if you really think about it."

"How's your treatment going?"

He knew it! "Fine," he lied. He thought of the portrait. He ought to draw it just to get the doctor off his case. What was the big deal about a picture anyway? He'd probably draw something— *anything*—and the doctor would immediately exclaim that he needed to operate based on some uncanny aspect of the image.

"What are you thinking about?" Samantha asked gently, her expression concerned.

"Nothing." He proceeded to shut down inside, anxious not to reveal anything. Sighing again, he relaxed. Samantha wasn't like Miguel; she couldn't read his mind. "I just feel . . . nervous."

"Maybe it's a side effect of the pain medication you're on."

He laughed, studying her with amusement. "I don't think so. Who knows, though? Maybe my liver's shot. The medication is supposed to destroy it eventually. Maybe you feel nervous when your liver is about to stop working. You know, a subconscious, subliminal sort of thing because you're about to die." He smiled, feeling silly.

Samantha frowned, unable to discern the humor in the situation. Stefan removed a packet of sunflower seeds from his pocket and tore them open, scanning the long stretch of beach below as if expecting someone.

"Want some?" he offered. Samantha shook her head. "I don't blame you. They're raw and there's no salt on them. Meanwhile, I'm on some toxic drug that's overloading my liver." He laughed again, feeling almost giddy over the irony.

"Would you like to drive up the coast?" she offered, hoping to distract him. "There's a gorgeous view up ahead about ten miles."

He exhaled and shrugged his shoulders. "All right . . . sure. Why not? C'mon, I'll drive."

"Dreamer!" She clapped her hands, and Dreamer ran up the path toward them, leaping into the car when the door was opened for her. Rebel stood up on the back seat and wagged his tail, realizing he wasn't going to be trapped in the motel room all afternoon. Samantha slid into the front seat next to him, and he turned the key in the ignition, casting her a dubious look. "A really gorgeous spot, you say? You mean it's not so beautiful around here?"

She giggled as he turned down the road. "Oh, sure it is. But this place . . . it's unbelievable. It's called Playa Fantasma. Just wait, you'll see."

As they drove along, she noted the way he handled his car. Even in his weakened state, he exuded a certain ease and confidence; and she wondered what his life must have once been like. Recalling Dr. Calderón's words, "a golden boy," spoken in a rather uncomplimentary fashion, she contemplated whether or not she would have even liked him.

"Playa Fantasma? I don't think I like the sound of that." He grinned again, beginning to feel more comfortable.

"Well, don't let the name put you off. I don't know why they ever called it that anyway. It ought to be called 'Playa Cielo.' "

He grew intrigued. "Really? Now I've got to see it." They were silent a moment as the car sped along the scenic coast highway, each lapsing into their own thoughts. Stefan thought of heaven. It was not an easy thought to contemplate; it filled him with uneasiness, perhaps because, if there even was such a place, he felt as though he didn't deserve to go there.

"Turn on the next side road," she instructed him a while later, and upon reaching a gravel road on the left, he turned. "You have to park down here and hike up," she explained, pointing to a bare spot where a few cars could fit. There was a sign nearby with "Playa Fantasma" carved into it. He pulled up in the dirt, and after releasing the dogs, they started up the path.

"It is beautiful here," he remarked, gazing about. How unfortunate it now seemed to him that he had never journeyed north before while residing in the city. When he tore himself away from the magazine, it was never to come to a place like this but always something business related—contacts in another city, or some grand scheme to ace out the competition. There were the times he went on trips with friends, mostly to drink and gamble.

"Wait until you see the ocean," she reminded him, smiling in anticipation. "You won't believe it."

They hiked up to the crest, and feeling out of breath, Stefan frowned, anxious to see for himself. At last, they rounded a curve in the path and came upon a magnificent view of the sea.

Stefan's eyes widened with awe, taking in the resplendent sea-scape. It appeared so unspoiled and completely pristine, tears threatened to well up in his eyes. What a beautiful world it was after all.

"Are you all right?" Samantha lowered her sunglasses a moment, noting how emotional he seemed. He merely nodded, too broken up inside for words. "C'mon down here, Stefan; there's a place to sit and rest."

Below rested a low bench in the shape of a square, and they seated themselves, still taking in the view. Black rocks jutted out of the sapphire water, and the glittering waves lashed over them again and again. A minute later, the surf pounded against the sand below, sending up a cascade of fragranced sea mist, and birds of all kinds sailed against the deep blue sky above.

Finally, he felt able to speak. "You're right, Samantha, it is truly special . . . really something. It ought to be called Playa Cielo. I agree."

She smiled. It seemed like a foretaste of heaven, especially to have Stefan by her side enjoying it with her and apparently not so close to the grip of death as in the past. For once she was happy, completely happy, the sadness and sorrows of the troubled world forgotten. "I love this place," she said. "I wish we could stay right here like this forever!"

He studied her almost bashfully. "You'd miss your wedding."

She laughed, growing embarrassed. "Oh, you know what I mean!"

"I know." They sat in silence for a while longer until Samantha reluctantly checked her watch. "You know, Stefan, we should head back now. I have to work later this afternoon."

"All right." Rising up, he whistled to the dogs, and they trotted back to them. He turned to look out over the ocean a final time. He reached for Samantha's hand. "Thank you, Samantha, for suggesting we come here."

That evening, Stefan stopped in at the café for his meal. After finishing his dinner, he still felt hungry. That was a switch; normally, he struggled to finish his food. Stefan studied his empty plate thoughtfully. Perhaps he should order something else. Thinking the better of it, he paid the bill and bundled up in his black windbreaker, deciding to walk around downtown instead before heading back to the motel. That was another first. Usually by this time of day, he felt too weary to do anything but collapse on his bed.

It was a windy, unsettling evening, and he studied the billowy clouds in the dark sky as he passed by the well-lit shops. He used to walk with determined steps, anxiously stepping around anyone who threatened to hold up his life. Now he walked leisurely, bent over to one side in order to breathe easier to be sure, but unhurried. He passed by bars with men and women perched on stools, conversing loudly. He felt sweet, alone.

The ocean, now obscured by nightfall, appeared mysterious. He looked out over the shadowy, swirling water, remembering the beauty of Playa Fantasma earlier that day. "I love the ocean," he murmured aloud to himself, almost surprised by this admission. Was that the reason he had landed in Acantilado del Mar? As far as he knew, he'd never felt any affinity for the ocean in the past. A foghorn sounded out by the point, far away in the darkness, mournful and serene. He sighed, growing tired at last. Walking back to the car, he pulled his collar up tighter and shivered. His recent weight gain of ten pounds still proved insufficient to keep him warm.

Back in the motel room, Rebel curled up on a dingy throw rug with a contented grunt and drifted off to sleep. Stefan observed him almost enviously. If only sleep would come so easily to him. Crawling into bed minutes later, he lay awake in the darkness, his mind anxious. It was like this lately when the lights went out, and everything grew quiet. He switched positions, hoping sleep might come; but it proved even more painful when he lay on his left side. His chest seemed to bother him no matter which way he turned, and Stefan thought of the hideous thing growing inside of him. He forced his mind to not consider this, but the anxiety increased. Once plunged into this state of mind, he knew there was no way out; and it would be another terrible night.

His chest felt heavy, and he wondered whether the sensation originated from the tumor or perhaps his heart, which felt very much like a stone. Stefan stared forlornly at the flashing motel sign out his window, and after suffering through a miserable hour in this fashion, he drifted off to sleep.

He dreamed he was at Playa Fantasma again, but this time without Samantha. The sun shone brilliantly in the sky above, and he hiked up the dusty trail with great anticipation, anxious to see the view once more. Stefan rounded the curve and reached the summit, staring out over the immense expanse of open sea. He could not believe his eyes! Staggering forward, he crumpled to the ground and rested his face in the dust. After a moment he pulled himself back up by the square bench, and while still prone, looked out at the water, unable to fathom the wonder of it all. The entire ocean appeared completely clear, as distinct and visible as anything he had ever seen. He could see everything . . . every living creature, rock, shell—even the tiniest pebble in the sea. The enormity of it overwhelmed him, and he could not tear his gaze away. He awoke with a start and found himself back in his motel room again, the sign still flashing.

The following week, Stefan grew anxious as he filed in for his appointment. There was no doubt about it now—his doctor wanted to operate. Dr. Calderón studied him with a guarded expression as Stefan seated himself. Stefan returned the look, bracing himself for another lecture.

"How are you today, Stefan?"

"All right." He reclined comfortably on the couch. The incision had healed at last; it felt wonderful to be able to sprawl again. Now the doctor wanted to cut him open in the front! He shook his head as he pondered this irony.

Dr. Calderón sat forward and smiled uneasily, feeling both pleased and alarmed. Stefan appeared to be laboring slightly for breath and leaning to one side—an ominous sign. On the other hand, his hair had grown back, the bald patches now replaced with shiny dark curls. He watched Stefan run his fingers through it, fluffing up the dark waves. It appeared at this point that Stefan enjoyed his locks. Indeed, he had never allowed it to grow so unkempt before. In years past, his hairstyle had always been ultra-conservative.

His skin tone looked more normal; nearly gone were the green cast to his complexion and sallow cheeks. Glancing over at him again, Dr. Calderón noted that Stefan's dark eyes appeared luminous. His patient was now a strange concoction of renewed life and impending death. With a long sigh, he reached for some paperwork lying on the desk. "I have the results of your recent blood work. Things are looking somewhat better there. How is your pain level?"

"My chest still hurts, but I feel much more relaxed and don't seem to mind it as much. I'm getting used to it, the pain, I mean."

Dr. Calderón nodded. "Yes, one can get used to almost anything if plagued with it long enough."

"I'm no longer eating solely at the café. They gave me a juicer and told me I'm ready to do it on my own. It's not so expensive that way."

"Great." His patient possessed initiative and was penny-wise. Penny-wise and pound-foolish.

"Overall, I'm feeling pretty good."

Dr. Calderón placed the test results aside. Stefan was now strong enough for the surgery, yet it was impossible to convince him to undergo another operation. The doctor attributed his patient's stubborn refusal to his previous ill treatment at the cancer treatment center. Miguel cleared his throat, treading judiciously.

"Was there anything positive that you can recall regarding your former treatment at the medical center?"

Stefan frowned. "What do you mean?"

"Can you remember anything about it that you felt helped you, gave you hope?"

"No!" His tone was emphatic.

"There must have been something," Dr. Calderón persisted, "that place has one of the best reputations in the country."

"No, it was all depressing. Not one hopeful moment. They condemned me the first moment I set foot in the door."

"How so?"

Stefan recalled those dark days. "They said they could buy me time; that was all. If I'm going to die, why do it there running up a pile of bills I couldn't afford? Near the end of my treatment, I decided to leave and hawked everything I owned. I just took off and drove until I ended up in Acantilado del Mar. The ocean drew me in, and I decided to use the last of my resources to hole up and drop dead here." They were both silent for a long while, lost in their own thoughts.

Stefan cleared his throat. "Actually, now that I think about it, I did find one thing there that gave me hope. I'd nearly forgotten it."

Dr. Calderón glanced up. "What was that, Stefan?"

"On the way into the chemotherapy room, I used to walk by a bird aviary where a little yellow finch always watched me as I passed. I would whistle to him, but he'd fly away to the other side of the cage. That day I left for good, I whistled one last time." He laughed, remembering. "But in this instance, he perched right on the other side of the screen and sang back to me. It was the most beautiful sound I'd ever heard."

Dr. Calderón leaned back in his chair and tapped his chin reflectively with the eraser of his pencil. Reaching for the journal, he flipped it open.

I do not even know how I feel anymore. I am disconnected from myself. I have a lot of fear and guilt. I've ruined my life by this disconnection. The world seems unfriendly, and I don't trust people. I've been lied to all my life, but I admit I'm also paranoid. Last night, I couldn't sleep again. I felt oppression and anger to-

111

ward people from the past. I feel totally alone but realize my life has always been like this. My relationships were tenuous frauds, and you really know it because people show you in passive ways. People are only nice to a point. The problem has not been people's treatment of me but my delusion of "relationship" with them. I finally fell asleep but awoke at four a. m. with the dreads and a pall. I have lost all confidence in myself as a human being.

"Are you still waking up a lot at night?"

Stefan made a face. "I usually don't have trouble falling asleep anymore," he admitted. "But now I'm awakening about four in the morning in a sweat. A pall comes over me, and I keep seeing these horrific sights."

"Are they about the past?"

Stefan was grim. "Yes."

Dr. Calderón continued reading:

Barely slept last night. The terrible pall returned, almost unbearable, and lasted for hours. There is a spirit in the world that loves to take people down. I saw how tremendously unloved I've been for years . . . the indifference and clandestine abuse. I see how mistreated I've lived and wore a smile for a mask. To see the extent of it . . . I'm lucky it doesn't finish me off. Life is no joke. The truth will set you free. I feel like it's going to kill me instead.

Yesterday I remembered an incident from the past where I was berated by a teacher at school for absolutely nothing. She claimed I wasn't applying myself when I truly was. Yet another person totally incapable of realizing how hard I was already working to please the world. Then my stepfather really let me have it when I got home. My nights have become a grisly battle to the death for the truth. As I lay all alone in my room last night, I wished I could have another cigarette to finish myself off.

"What did it feel like when you stopped smoking?" Dr. Calderón regarded his patient quizzically, awaiting the response.

"Lousy. I could barely function. I almost lost my job. I felt constant fear and panic. Even the most inconsequential decisions became laborious."

"You must have always felt like that, but your addiction kept the discomfort at bay."

"I don't know why, but I never felt like I deserved anything. Every nice thing I possessed, I felt like I didn't deserve, even though I worked eighty hours a week to get it."

"What do you feel you merit?"

"Nothing. Just a threadbare existence like I have right now at the motel."

"People must have considered you very talented. You made a lot of money."

"Even in school, I didn't feel I deserved the good grades I received."

"Why not?"

"I don't know. I've always doubted myself."

"Did you always earn good marks?"

Stefan paused, recalling the years gone by. He grimaced. "No, I used to be quite average, now that I think back. It wasn't until about the eighth grade that I really began to excel."

"What caused the shift? Did you become more interested in what you were being taught?"

Stefan winced. "I doubt it. I don't remember studying anything that interested me that much in high school."

"Yet you earned perfect grades. You received a scholarship to the university of your choice. How did you manage it?"

Stefan blew air out of his cheeks. "I worked hard."

"What were your marks on your last imperfect report card; can you recall?"

Stefan's countenance suddenly altered. He did not appear happy. "Yes, I remember. I received three Cs and three Bs. It was in the middle of the 8th grade."

"Did that bother you?"

"No."

"It must have. You changed after that." Dr. Calderón refused to let the subject rest.

"My mother didn't like it."

"Did she tell you that?"

"No. She picked me up from school one day. I don't remember why. She rarely did that. Usually, she made me walk even though she had the time. I was sitting in the back seat, and she asked me if I had received my report card that day. I told her yes, and she asked me what my grades were. I said three Cs and three Bs."

"What did she say?"

"Nothing." Stefan looked out the window. "She just sighed, like she was disappointed in me, and started driving home."

"What did you think about it?"

"I thought I was another disappointment to her. She always seemed depressed."

"No, I mean before that. Before your mother's reaction. How did you feel about your report card?"

Stefan stared his doctor in the eyes and remained silent a long while. "I felt okay with it. It didn't bother me."

"They reflected something, didn't they, Stefan?"

"Yes, they did, now that I think about it. They spoke volumes. That's who I really am. I'm three Cs and three Bs. That's the real me." He laughed.

Dr. Calderón smiled. "They reflected a genuine interest level in your subjects."

"I suppose." Stefan felt his mood lighten. "Three Cs and three Bs . . ." He laughed again, louder this time. "What was I thinking?"

The following Monday, Stefan's car wouldn't start, so he took the bus into town for his appointment, not wanting to risk running into inclement weather on the bicycle. A winter storm was forecast for later in the day, and staring out the sooty window as the bus lurched its way along, he watched the ocean play hide and seek all the way downtown. Upon arriving at his destination, it began to rain.

"How old were you when your father died?" Dr. Calderón asked, broaching the subject with a certain reluctance, owing to how particularly frail his patient appeared this late stormy afternoon. Lightning flashed across the sky followed by a crack of thunder. Stefan was in the middle of a three-day fast. He appeared pale and introspective.

"I was four years old."

"Do you remember him?"

Stefan nodded. "Yes, I remember him."

"What was he like?"

Stefan reclined on the sofa, gazing up at the ceiling. "Well, I was very young. I suppose I idealized him. I remember what he looked like. He was tall and thin. His hair was dark and curly, like mine."

Dr. Calderón was silent, contemplating the matter. "How long was it before your mother remarried?"

"She married my stepfather when I was seven. By then I had nearly forgotten my real father."

"Did you miss your father?"

"I suppose."

"Let's step into the other room a minute and finish up with a quick examination."

In the next room, Stefan slipped off his shirt and eased himself up on the table with an expansive sigh. He remained thin, but there was evidence despite the fasting that flesh was beginning to fill in around the bones.

"How would you describe yourself in the grand scheme of things?" Dr. Calderón queried offhandedly, glancing through Stefan's latest test results after finishing the check.

"What do you mean?" Stefan grimaced as he slipped his shirt back over his head.

"How do you feel you fit into this world?"

They walked back into the physician's office, and Stefan scratched his head. "I don't know. Sick and unemployed, I guess."

"Apart from your present circumstances, how do you see yourself?"

Stefan squinted, attempting to ascertain to what his physician was referring. "I don't think I understand."

"Well, you stated previously that you didn't feel you deserved anything. That's why you prefer your cheap motel so much."

Stefan chuckled. "That's partly true. I guess I like my motel because it's uncomplicated."

"Is that the only reason?"

He shrugged. "I like the vine outside my door. In the past, I never would have noticed something like that. My condo was professionally landscaped. But for some reason, I noticed this vine growing in a patch of empty soil. I don't think anyone planted it. It just came up by itself."

Dr. Calderón gazed out the window. Stefan was no longer the hotshot magazine editor whose head was always in a whirl. He had become a youth again—and a markedly sensitive one at that—in need of emotional nurturing.

"There's an old deck outside my room. Late at night, when I can't sleep and it's getting colder, the wood starts to contract; and it makes a strange sound like a harp." Stefan fell silent, thinking. "I see myself as an unwanted creature in this world. And not because I'm broke and sick. I've always felt that way. Even at the top of my game. Sometimes I wonder if I wasn't *born* estranged from life."

"That's how you fit into this world?"

"Yes." Stefan nodded. "I was always an unwanted creature who got in the way. Now I'm a *broken*, unwanted creature who gets in the way."

Dr. Calderón leaned back in his swivel chair, placed his chukka boots on top of his desk, and folded his hands behind his head, regarding Stefan speculatively.

Stefan couldn't resist a smile because his doctor, not unlike the contentious herbalist, definitely marched to the beat of a different drum. "I would just like a simple life," he added, closing his eyes and resting his head against the back of the couch.

"That sounds wonderful," Dr. Calderón responded. "But life has a way of becoming complicated despite our best efforts that it doesn't."

"I don't want to feel ungrounded anymore. My life has been like the Lost Dutchman's Mine."

"The Lost Dutchman's Mine? What's that?"

"When I was about eight years old, we went on vacation; and I remember an amusement ride through a cave. I sat in a miner's cart that careened into complete darkness. Gruesome monsters popped up when you least expected it. It was supposed to be fun."

"Who do you consider to be a monster?"

"Dr. Gambian, for one. They all start out concerned and nice, and then . . . boom! Out pops a monster."

"Did the ride scare you?"

"It terrified me. But I never let on. My stepfather constantly accused me of being a crybaby."

"Perhaps it reminded you too much of your life."

"Yeah. When I really stop to think about it, even way back then, my life was full of monsters."

The sun shone directly overhead as Stefan strolled barefoot along the shoreline with Rebel. Waves raced up the glistening sand and washed over his feet, as cold against his skin as the sun was warm upon his face. At this point, he found himself making his way down the cliff multiple times a day, enjoying the solitude of the pristine shoreline. Between the emotional palls and dreadful insights, he was beginning to experience a tenuous, fragile peace. The immense ocean was spread out before him, deific and mysterious, and he existed all alone before it. The rest of the world toiled away elsewhere, hard at work. Now that Stefan had been granted a reprieve from it all, the day was his to do whatever he liked with it.

The water around him glittered like a million diamonds in the sun. They were jewels no one could labor for; indeed, gems no one cared about at all—phantoms, here one minute, gone the next, as the water moved in the iridescent sunlight. They were simply to be appreciated in a moment of peace. Rebel ran like the wind, as joyful as the day itself; and Stefan breathed in the salty air. He no longer thought about the future.

A stranger waved to him from the rocks above. "Hello, down there!"

"Hello!" Stefan waved in return, having seen him before, usually walking alone with a dog and a boogie board.

The man scrambled down. His dog ran over to Rebel, and they began to play along the water's edge. "Nice day, isn't it?" His long, scraggly hair was bleached blond from the sun.

"Yeah, it sure is." Stefan extended a hand. "I'm Stefan."

"Handy." He clasped Stefan's hand with enthusiasm. "Nice to meet you." Handy smiled through crooked teeth. "Seen you around here a lot."

"Yeah." The waves crashed against the rocks behind them, sending a spray of sea water high up into the air. A colony of sea lions barked up on the rocks as gulls swooped down from the bluff and landed nearby.

"Not many people on the beach during a weekday," Handy commented, squinting down the coastline.

"Nope." Stefan looked around as well. They appeared to be the only two people in sight.

"I work in the evening," Handy said, "So I spend all day down here."

"Where do you work?" Stefan asked. The man obviously had a good thing going.

"I clean the mall."

"Oh." Stefan nodded. "I've never been there."

Handy laughed, staring at the horizon. "Lucky you."

Stefan followed Handy's eyes, taking in the beautiful morning a final time before preparing to depart. "Well, sure wish I could stay all day myself, but I have to go to the doctor."

"That's a bummer." Handy whistled to his dog. "I never go to the doctor."

"Lucky you . . ."

"Tell me more about your stepfather," Dr. Calderón requested as he lifted Stefan's shirt and placed the stethoscope against his back later that afternoon. "Do you like him?"

"No," he replied flatly. Gone were the days when the patient hemmed and hawed, avoiding questions and playing hide and seek with his doctor and his own soul.

"Why not?"

"A cold wind blows off of him."

Dr. Calderón nodded. "You mean like the kind that blows off Richard?"

Stefan chuckled. "Uh-huh."

"Your mother?"

"She was preoccupied with her appearance and all her problems."

"Is your mother attractive?"

Stefan nodded. "Yes."

"So you were cared for in a rather utilitarian way?"

"My stepfather is quite wealthy, but he refused to help me with my education. He insisted I do it all on my own. At the time, I convinced myself that he cared about my welfare and didn't want to spoil me."

"How long has it been since you've seen your parents?"

Stefan thought for a moment. "They visited me a couple of times while I was undergoing treatment. But even during those trips, they ran around a lot. I'd sit out on my patio alone."

"How about a girlfriend?"

"Things just never seemed to work out."

"That girl you mentioned previously in our conversations together . . . the one you liked so much. What was she like?"

"I don't know. Different."

"In what way?"

"She reminded me of someone."

"Who?" Dr. Calderón asked curiously. The admission caught him by surprise.

"My best friend in the first grade—a girl named Christine."

"So you had a heartfelt friendship after all." The doctor smiled.

"The other children avoided me because I was such a crybaby, especially the boys. But she befriended me and we played together every day."

"What was she like?"

"A million freckles and a vivid imagination. But best of all, she liked me. She truly did. There's nothing else in this world that can equal that." Stefan looked out the window, his expression wistful.

"That must have been a lovely interlude in your life. What happened to her?" Miguel sensed that this light in Stefan's past had been extinguished.

"She flunked the first grade."

Dr. Calderón shook his head. "I didn't think that was possible."

"She refused to pay attention."

"Did you ever see her again?"

"No. Her parents withdrew her from the school after that. I don't know whatever became of her."

"But you must have had other friendships."

"None like that one."

Dr. Calderón nodded. "Those years you were in high school and earning perfect grades . . . can you recall a memory that to this day really means something to you?" he asked, replacing his stethoscope on the wall.

"I'm not sure what you mean."

"Something you can remember that was poignant . . . lifted your spirits."

"Poignant . . ." Stefan echoed with a sigh.

"Yes, anything at all."

They were back in Dr. Calderón's office. Stefan sat on the sofa and contemplated the matter at length, his gaze coming to rest at last, as always, on the clipper ship. "I don't know. I suppose there were lots of things, but I just can't remember them anymore."

"You received numerous awards during those years. You were voted most likely to succeed by your senior class. How about a family vacation or a special friendship?"

"Why is this so important?" Stefan asked, leaning forward and beginning to glare. "Who cares? I hate remembering those days. My childhood was awful. I admit it now, for all the good it does me."

It was the doctor's turn to be silent as he sat immobile and stared at the floor.

Stefan continued to grimace, feeling spent. It was obviously tough going for the old clipper ship, he reasoned to himself, still staring at the drawing. The ill-starred artist who'd fashioned it— had he survived the squall? It seemed to Stefan that the ship symbolized the illustrator, and the ocean, "existence."

"I can't believe there isn't a single consoling memory that remains with you from those days." Dr. Calderón refused to accept it.

Stefan felt himself relax, still considering the drawing. "Okay, I do remember something."

Dr. Calderón looked up. "What?"

"Well, you know how it gets rather drab in November, and the weather begins to change?"

The doctor nodded. "Yes, it can be quite melancholic."

"Those years in high school . . . by November a sort of depression had always set into me. But I recall, planted by the front walkway of our house, a purple mum plant that used to bloom about that time."

Dr. Calderón listened spellbound, staring at Stefan.

"Every year, it just sort of appeared and bloomed beneath everything else that had already gone dormant."

"That sounds enchanting." Dr. Calderón turned away from Stefan to conceal his heartbreak.

"The discovery of it every year reassured me somehow. It made me feel like things weren't so bad after all."

They both stood up, the appointment drawing to an end. Dr. Calderón squeezed Stefan's shoulder and smiled. "I'll see you on Friday."

That evening, Stefan found himself down on the shoreline again, watching the tide come in. Rebel ran in and out of the raging surf, chasing the gulls. Contentment washed over him like the waves rushing up to meet the shore, a sweetness hovering in his chest. Rebel no longer paid such close attention to his commands; instead, he tore around the beach with gusto, casting his master a guilty look or two when he didn't obey the first time around. Even the dog was finding renewal and happiness.

Stefan picked up a piece of driftwood and tossed it to his dog. Rebel bounded after the stick, and after catching the object, tossed it back into the air again. Stefan laughed. The wind blew his hair, and he brushed the long curls back from his face. His skin was tanned, even in winter, from spending so many days down on the sand.

The western sky was alight with fiery ribbons of color. He was all alone on the beach, alone in the world, with a feeling of peace and ease within him. As he played on the shoreline with his dog, he felt somehow beyond the reach of time. There were no more yesterdays and tomorrow did not exist. There remained only a beautiful evening to be cherished.

"Stefan?" someone asked. A group of people stood down the beach a way, watching him frolic with his dog. Squinting into the distance, Stefan recognized Richard and his entourage of friends.

"Hello." He felt his mood darken. So he wasn't alone in the world after all.

The gang moved in closer, chatting easily and dragging fishing gear. As he approached, Richard continued to study Stefan with interest, apparently having trouble believing what he was seeing. While still thin, Stefan no longer appeared old. Now, strangely enough—with his halo of dark curls and radiant eyes—he appeared younger than his years, like a teenager again. He stood facing the group of men a minute later in silence. No one seemed to know what to say. Finally, Cooper spoke up.

"How are you doing, man? You look good," he added.

"Fine . . . a lot better," Stefan admitted, tousling Rebel's ears self-consciously.

"That's good," Dave chimed in, rubbing his chin. It seemed extraordinary. He recalled the afternoon at the garden party. The man had looked only days from death at the time.

"Catch anything?" Stefan asked, running his fingers through his curls.

"What?" Richard appeared startled. "Oh, no . . . Cooper caught something, but it got away. The fishing just isn't as good around here as it used to be. Too many people, you know, moving in all the time."

"I see." Stefan grew amused. There were people who lived in beautiful places who, by some strange destiny conjured up in their minds, were allowed to be there because they had somehow arrived before an imaginary date when "other people" had appeared and ruined everything. He laughed a little under his breath, pondering this contrariety.

"What's so funny?" Richard asked, experiencing a twinge of annoyance. Yes, he knew . . . He was supposed to feel sorry for the poor little lad, like Samantha did, because he was so bad off. The trouble was he didn't *act* so sick. Underneath that ailing countenance lurked a razor-sharp mind, a jump ahead of his. And now, this eerie, otherworldly quality. Stefan was beginning to remind him of the crazy herbalist.

"Nothing." He guarded himself carefully, feeling no need for one-upmanship.

"Then why'd you laugh?"

"Richard, chill out, man." Cooper glared at him, adjusting the fishing pole over his shoulder.

Rolling his eyes, Richard started up the beach. "Nice bumping into you, Stefan. Later."

Stefan made no reply. Cooper nodded to him. "Sorry to leave so quick. We're going to try fishing up at the point before it gets too dark. Later, man. And you're looking real good. I'm happy for you."

"See you, Stefan." Dave nodded as well, and the men started down the shore after Richard. Once out of earshot, Dave hurried alongside his friend. "Rich, what's the big deal? You didn't have to act like that. The guy's got it bad enough."

Richard shook his head and glowered. "Look, why is it that just because a person's sick, you have to like them? I mean, if he were well, then could I detest him without everyone getting on my case about it? What's the difference? He's still the same person—sick or not!"

"Why do you dislike him so much?" Dave asked, puzzled.

"Why do I need a reason? I just do. He's strange. And he's getting stranger. No wonder, when you consider who he's got for a mentor."

"Well, I think the person you really don't like is Brian. Right, Rich?"

"Bingo," Dave replied.

"Listen, you guys. Just buzz off, okay? Me and about a jillion other people don't like that charlatan. He's a joke. That so-called café is going to be shut down, wait and see. And his patients croak all the time, just like everyone else's. He capitalizes on hopeless cases even worse than all the rest of them. He holds up some spirulina and cashes in. Know what he had the nerve to tell me the other day?"

"What?" Cooper asked.

"I was downtown with my boss buying a couple of corndogs from that new vendor . . ."

"Those are awesome," Dave interjected.

". . . And he peddles by on his bicycle and calls our lunch 'death

127

on a stick!' "

Cooper laughed. "That's hilarious."

Richard waved his friends away, weary of the conversation. "Oh, never mind. It's a big waste of time to even talk about it. But I'll guarantee you one thing—Stefan's going to die. Brian's managed to revive him temporarily, but he's still a goner. Know what Samantha told me?" Richard swung his gaze around the group almost accusingly. "The guy had Dr. Gambian before all this. You know, the one written up in the paper a while back. You remember. Well, if *he* couldn't do anything . . ." His voice trailed off and he shook his head. "Enough said. If there's one thing in this world I can't stand, it's people who give false hope."

Stefan watched the group depart down the beach and experienced a twinge of annoyance with Richard. Frowning, he looked out over the ocean. He must be truly feeling better. Starting up the beach, he signaled to Rebel, wondering if Samantha might be home. It seemed unlikely. If she were, she'd be tagging along with Richard, but he decided to hike up and check anyway.

Reaching the beach stairway, he glanced back out over the sea. The sunset looked unusually intense. He watched the sun as it slowly slipped behind the horizon. A green flash suddenly appeared. The green flash! It was incredible. How many times had he watched the sun set from some overpriced bistro, dragging on a cigarette while wearing a jaded expression, hoping to see it?

Feeling gladdened by the sight, it almost seemed as though the world was not such a treacherous place. The wind began to blow, stirring the dry grasses that grew in the crevices along the slope; and he started up the steps for the cliff above. The dark shapes of tiny birds flitted in and out of the wild roses, deepening his peace as he walked. He experienced the sensation of time standing still. Inside him was the loveliest feeling he had ever known.

He reached Samantha's house and noted her leaning over a cage in the shadows near the side of the house. She filled a small container with water, and hanging it on the side of the cage, peered inside.

"Hello, Samantha."

She turned around and bumped the cage, spilling the water inside. "Stefan," she said, surprised. Slowly standing up, she studied him under the porch light.

"I'm sorry. I didn't mean to startle you. Here, let me help you with that." Kneeling down, he retrieved the cup and refilled it, neatly dabbing up the spill with a cloth. He attached the container to the side of the cage and smiled. "How is the little guy doing anyway?"

"Fine." She wiped her hands on her pants, still gazing at her friend. How could he appear so well? She glanced away, not wanting to stare. He had been getting better all along, yet suddenly, the transformation was nothing short of miraculous. For some strange reason, she felt uneasy. "I'm . . . I'm going to let him go. Very soon, as a matter of fact."

"Oh, good." Stefan nodded, pleased. "Birds should be free," he added, appearing almost angelic under the light.

She thought of her mother's dream of the little bird flying up into the tree. "Yes, that's what I think, too. I would never keep a bird in a cage for long . . . not even a parakeet."

"A bird in a cage will forget how to sing."

"Well, sometimes you can't help it," Samantha replied, straightening up her things for lack of another way to hide her discomfiture. "Sometimes animals are too disabled to ever be returned to their natural habitat; then you have to take care of them for the rest of their lives."

"Yes," he admitted, not at all uncomfortable with himself for a change. "It's such a shame, though. They weren't meant to live that way." Stefan glanced over at the house next door. Miguel and Alicia had appeared with the boys, and he watched the doctor swing Luis up into his arms.

Samantha was silent, observing Stefan's long stare across the garden. She decided to change the subject. "What are your plans for Christmas Eve, Stefan?" she asked, not wanting him to be alone, and also hoping to be able to spend the day with him. Christmas was only ten days away.

He shrugged. "I don't know. I don't really have any."

"Well, why don't you spend the evening with us? It's going to be very quiet . . . just a few friends and maybe my aunt and uncle."

"Gee, I don't know." He shook his head. "That's very nice of you. Can I get back to you on that?" He didn't relish the idea of spending Christmas Eve listening to Richard and possibly a few of his sidekicks.

She resisted the impulse to feel insulted by his uncertainty. Their relationship was undergoing a metamorphosis. She no longer knew quite what to say or expect from him. The tables seemed to be turning. Now it almost seemed as though it was she who needed him. She wanted him to come. He wasn't sure if he felt like it. Again she thought of the little bird flying up into the tree and struggled to revive her loyalties to Richard, but strangely enough, they eluded her. Recalling his generosity, all the thoughtful gifts and kind things her fiancé had done for her, she tried to feel appreciation. Instead, she felt herself drawn to Stefan's presence.

"Well, I hope you can come." She smiled, feeling sad.

The feeling proved contagious. A silence followed that stretched into minutes, and Stefan turned at last to look out over the cliff. His gaze floated back to Dr. Calderón's house. It was almost dark, but he could hear the boys playing with Toby in the garden.

"I'll let you know," he said at last, reaching out to touch her curls. She looked up, startled by the gesture. He smiled. "All right?"

She returned the smile. "All right."

"See you later."

"Goodnight, Stefan."

Christmas Eve arrived with crystal clear skies and a sudden dip in temperature. Studying his reflection in the bathroom mirror later that day, Stefan laughed to himself. He ought to cut his hair! Not too long ago, his head had resembled a cue ball. Now, his curls were back in place and thicker than ever before. He noted Rebel sitting behind him, waiting patiently for his dinner.

"All right, boy, let's eat." After pouring some dog food into Rebel's bowl, he prepared a pot of tea for himself—a concoction of five different herbs that were supposed to flush out the toxins left in his system from the chemotherapy ordered by Dr. Gambian.

Sipping the beverage in a reflective mood, he decided the taste was quite pleasant once you became accustomed to it. The aroma reminded him of damp summer grasses after a rainstorm. Stefan recalled how he used to explore and play in the fields of vacant lots as a child. He felt like that person again—the boy—and not the man. The successful magazine editor, the hotshot whose life was always in a commotion, seemed a stranger to him now.

"Oh, how the mighty have fallen," he confided to his dog. Rebel looked up at him from his bowl, dog food dribbling down on the worn carpet. Stefan's condo in the city had boasted a white wool rug and ultra-deluxe décor, complete with all the latest technologies. His only possessions at present were a lumpy bed and a tacky chair, and technically, he was renting them.

He prepared a meal of salad greens, lentils, and vegetables. Having finished his bowl of food, Rebel sat close by and proceeded to stare. "Get real," Stefan remarked, pulling his plate closer. "There's hardly enough for me. You're out of luck."

He finished his dinner in silence, growing even more contemplative. The phone jangled, and reaching over, he answered it. "Hello?"

"Stefan?" It was Samantha.

"Hi, Samantha."

"Are you coming over?"

He exhaled slowly. "Well, I . . . I don't know." It proved difficult for him to make up his mind. He enjoyed Samantha's company but felt reluctant to spend the evening being antagonized by Richard and Maureen.

"Oh." She tried not to feel insulted. Sick and alone, he had no place to go on Christmas Eve, yet he remained uncertain over the invitation to her festive house. "Well, are you feeling all right?" she faltered, trying to understand.

"Yes, I feel fine." Why couldn't he decide? It used to be that he made snap decisions, twenty at a time, his mind as sharp as a razor. The trouble was that he had become the boy again, playing in the field, unable to decide whether or not to listen when called to come in for dinner.

"Do you have other plans?"

"No." He sighed and grew quiet. All he really wanted to do tonight was walk on the beach with Rebel. He felt like asking her to come along but knew it would be impossible for her to abandon her fiancé and family in exchange for a Christmas Eve with him. "Okay, Samantha. Maybe I'll stop by later. I'm just in a really strange mood tonight."

"Oh." It was her turn to sigh. "Well, all right. But I hope you will come. It's not good to be all alone on Christmas Eve, Stefan."

"I've never been alone on Christmas Eve before," he replied. There had always been parties, beautiful restaurants, clubs, and places to play. Now he wanted to sit on the sand and watch his dog romp along the water's edge. It felt like a miracle that he had survived long enough see this Christmas Eve at all.

"Well . . ." He cleared his throat. "Maybe I'll join you later."

"Okay. Goodbye, Stefan."

"Goodbye."

Replacing the receiver, Samantha shook her head in dismay, glancing around the beautifully decorated home with an unhappy expression on her face.

"What's the matter now?" her mother demanded, the little bells on her corsage jingling accusingly. "Isn't he coming?"

"He can't decide."

"He can't decide?" Maureen appeared astonished. "Well, what else does he have to do?"

Samantha shrugged, feeling hurt and rejected. The truth was that he didn't want to come. After all she had done for him—begging him into treatment with Dr. Calderón, inviting him over, agreeing to take his dog, walking with him on the beach, and listening to all his troubles. Why, if not for her, he wouldn't even be around to celebrate any longer! Now, out of kindness, she had invited him to her home to be part of the merriment—to which he would undoubtedly arrive with absolutely nothing—and he couldn't decide if he wanted to come!

"Well, Richard is coming over." Her mother glared, noting the statement failed to cheer her daughter. She took another swig of her gin and tonic, shaking her head and remembering. The little bird was preparing to spread its wings and fly up into a tree. "Samantha?"

"I know he's coming over." With a sigh of exasperation, she forced herself up to get some eggnog, even though she didn't feel like having any. The doorbell chimed. "I'll get it," she said. "It's probably Richard." Opening the door a minute later, she discovered Richard, his older brother Duke, and Dr. Calderón standing out in the front entryway together. Richard and Duke appeared slightly pained while Dr. Calderón wore a grin, and Mateo peeked out from under his father's coat.

"Richard, Duke . . . Miguel, please come in."

"Merry Christmas, Sammie." Leaning over, Richard kissed her cheek as he passed, handing her a white envelope. Duke, taller and leaner than his brother, slapped her shoulder in greeting.

"Merry Christmas, Samantha." Dr. Calderón presented her with a plate of dried fruit.

"Dr. Calderón, how good of you to come!" Maureen gushed, clasping his hand warmly.

Richard rolled his eyes and leaned closer to Samantha. "Especially since he wasn't even invited."

"And you brought Mateo! How are you, little one?" Maureen squeezed his cheek, and Mateo buried his face in his father's shoulder.

"Well, I can't stay. I only stopped by to wish you a Merry Christmas."

"Are you sure? How about a quick drink? Don't tell me you have to go to the hospital tonight?"

"A drink would be nice. Anything would be fine, thank you."

Maureen hurried off to fetch him something, and Samantha showed everyone to a nearby sofa where the four of them seated themselves. "Is Stefan coming by tonight?" Dr. Calderón asked, studying Samantha. Richard's expression immediately grew dour.

"I don't know. I invited him, but he can't seem to decide." Samantha placed her hands in her lap. "He . . . he seems like he's in a strange mood or something."

Richard laughed lightly. "Well, let's hope he works it all out and everything."

"He is looking so much better though," Samantha added, ignoring her fiancé and gazing at Dr. Calderón. "It's amazing. It seems to have happened so quickly, too."

Dr. Calderón offered Mateo a toy from his pocket. "He is looking better."

"Here you are!" Maureen exclaimed, placing a frosty glass down on a coaster next to him. She served drinks to Richard, Duke, and Samantha as well.

"Thank you." Miguel held up his glass. "Cheers."

"Cheers," they replied, lifting their glasses in return.

"What's in the envelope, Sammie?" Maureen wanted to know, her sharp eyes zeroing in on it.

"Well, I don't know," Samantha faltered, glancing over at Richard. He clapped his hands together enthusiastically.

"It's your Christmas present. Go head, open it."

"Gee, all right." Smiling self-consciously, Samantha unsealed the envelope and removed the contents. Inside she discovered an itinerary for a trip to a new resort up the coast—Summerwood.

"Summerwood," Maureen exclaimed, peering over Samantha's shoulder. "How extravagant, Richard. I hear the golfing and dining there are superb."

"You bet they are!" Richard grinned.

Dr. Calderón's expression darkened as he cast his eyes on Samantha. "You're going to Summerwood?"

"You bet!" Richard repeated, clasping his hands together and studying the doctor.

"The developers of that resort are directly responsible for damage to the local ecosystem up there."

"Now, Dr. Calderón!" Maureen eyed her neighbor with amusement.

The doctor studied the group. "They're amassing a fortune while paying their employees starvation wages. Those golf courses were constructed right next to a protected area and require vast amounts of water to maintain. They've created a water scarcity."

Samantha felt on the spot. She attempted to smile but failed miserably. She tried in vain to think of something to break the awkwardness of the little scene.

Richard, however, appeared triumphant. "It'll be a blast. You have no idea how hard it was to get those reservations."

"I heard you and Alicia are expecting a baby," Samantha interjected, hoping a subject change would calm the storm.

Dr. Calderón nodded. "Yes, that's right."

"Congratulations," Samantha added.

"Another baby?" Maureen appeared surprised. "Wherever are you going to put them all?"

Samantha cringed while Richard and Duke chuckled. Miguel's

smile vanished and he quickly gulped his drink, probably anxious to leave, Samantha surmised.

"Actually, we're planning to move to Valle Escondido next year," Miguel responded graciously, but his expression remained strained.

Duke leaned forward with interest. "Really? Have you found any property out there?"

The doctor hesitated. "Yes . . ."

"Where? Debbie and I have been looking for over a year now. Nothing has even come up for sale."

"Whitney Sandler has offered us some property."

"*That's crap!*" Duke exploded, rising up off the couch. "He's bought up that entire valley!"

"He doesn't want it developed," Miguel attempted to explain.

"Then why do you get a piece of the pie?"

"There's a house already in existence along the western border. We're going to renovate it."

Duke's face flushed with anger. Maureen waved him down. "Now Duke . . . it's Christmas Eve. Let's all just try and get along for one evening of the year!"

The doorbell chimed again, and Samantha jumped up to answer it. Upon opening the door, she discovered her cousins. "Hi, everyone. Come in."

"Thanks. Hey, Richard!" They waved, and Richard started over. Maureen hurried off to retrieve some refreshments, and Dr. Calderón set his empty glass down and stood up to leave. Failing to spot the hostess, he went off in search of her.

"What a hypocrite!" Duke continued, once the doctor was out of earshot. "Objects to you going golfing because it ruins the environment, but he moves his brood into Whitney's bird sanctuary!"

"Chill, Duke." Richard placed his arm around Samantha. "Whitney has to be in his nineties by now. It'll all be partitioned off when he passes."

"Yeah, right!" Duke exclaimed. "He'll probably leave it all to that crazy grandson of his, and he'll run up and down the hills cramming weeds into pouches until he's ninety-nine, like his big shot grandpa in the fedora. What a quack—why do people even call him a doctor?"

Samantha sighed. No wonder Stefan had refused her invitation tonight. She didn't even want to be here.

Dr. Calderón discovered his neighbor in the kitchen. "Goodnight, Maureen. Thank you for the drink and your hospitality."

"You're leaving so soon? Well, thanks for coming by. Merry Christmas." They embraced. "Goodnight."

On the way out, he glanced back at Samantha. She tore herself away from the gathering to see him to the door. "Goodnight, Miguel."

"Goodnight, Samantha."

"Please, Dr. Calderón, let me apologize for everyone in there. Please don't associate me with their thinking in any way. And thanks for helping Stefan. I'm just so glad that he is going to be okay."

"I hope you have a Merry Christmas, Samantha." He adjusted Mateo in his arms and held out his hand. "And Stefan is far from well. He needs surgery but refuses."

Dazed by his admission, she accepted his hand, but he did not shake it. He simply held on, staring into her eyes. "That's . . . that's terrible," she stammered. "He never told me that. Perhaps if I talked to him, it might help."

His dark eyes looked away and searched the expanse of ocean in the distance. "No, Samantha, I doubt it. What will become of Stefan, I can't say."

Stefan pulled his car up to the curb in front of Samantha's house and switched off the ignition. Rebel slept curled up on the back seat. After studying the exquisitely lighted home for a moment, he sighed. The beauty of the darkness cast a spell over him as he studied the twinkling array of Christmas lights. It felt peaceful and warm in the car, with the only audible sound the soft breathing of his dog.

He noted Richard's truck parked across the street just as he knew it would be. What in the world did Samantha see in the man? He felt tempted to grow disapproving of his angel of mercy—to criticize her lack of good judgment. But what had he ever seen in the women he once pursued? Worse yet, why had they been attracted to him?

He closed his eyes a moment. With yet another sigh, he opened them again and allowed his gaze to rest on the house farther down the street. Instead of Christmas lights, luminarias lined the garden walkways leading up to the front door. A light glimmered deep in the grove of Torrey pines, and he felt an impulse to go over and wish the doctor a Merry Christmas.

Opening the door, he slid out and started down the sidewalk, hoping no one would spot him and drag him inside next door. It was very quiet as he wound his way up the pathway of luminarias in secret, the moon shining through the dark silhouettes of trees in the frosty winter sky. He passed a *nacimiento*, lit with paper lanterns hanging from the boughs of a nearby tree. The loveliness of the night took his breath away. He knocked on the front door.

Roberto peeked out and grinned. "*Hola*, Stefan."

"Hello, Roberto." Stefan returned the smile. "Is your father around? I just wanted to wish him a Merry Christmas."

Alicia appeared in the doorway, holding Mateo. "He and Luis just stepped out to visit the Christmas party at the pediatric ward. They should be back soon. You're welcome to wait for him here if you like."

"Thanks, but I'll go see if I can find him." Stefan nodded and smiled.

She took his hand in hers. "*Feliz Navidad*, Stefan."

"Merry Christmas, Alicia."

With a wave, he started away, anxious to get back to his car. Once inside, he glanced over at Samantha's house again before turning out on the icy street and driving into town for the hospital.

He parked in the visitors' section and walked up the front steps, breathing a sigh of relief that he wasn't spending tonight, of all nights, locked up in the miserable place. With a shudder, he thought of the children there.

"Yes, where is the pediatric ward?"

"Third floor."

"Thank you."

In the elevator, several nurses and a doctor wished him a Merry Christmas. On the third floor, he located the children's wing, and though crowded with parents and staff, he spotted Dr. Calderón and Luis seated at a table.

A moment later, Stefan stood over the two of them, feeling amused.

"Doctor! A donut? And is that coffee you're drinking?" Stefan grinned at Dr. Calderón.

Dr. Calderón glanced up, appearing pleased. "Stefan! This is certainly unexpected. Please join in the festivities." He pulled out the chair next to him while taking another bite of his donut. "Merry Christmas."

"Merry Christmas." After seating himself, Stefan glanced around the room and studied the milling parents and their children. Most of the patients gathered around tables, but a few were too ill and had to be tucked into wheelchairs. To his shock, he discovered Daniel close by with his parents and an older brother. Daniel's head was bandaged, and upon catching Stefan stare, he started over.

"Hello, Stefan." He appeared subdued, but his blue eyes looked clear.

"Hi." Stefan tried to smile.

"Are you having a nice time, Daniel?" Dr. Calderón turned to study his patient with affection.

Daniel went over to Miguel and allowed himself to be pulled up onto the doctor's lap. "Yeah. I wish I could be home though. This is the first time I've never been at home before at Christmastime."

"Yes, the hospital just isn't the same, is it?" Dr. Calderón adjusted Daniel's bandaging.

"No . . . hospitals are too bright," Daniel complained. "I don't like these lights. They hurt my eyes." He rubbed them tiredly.

"You'll be home soon. How is your brother Robert?"

"He's good. *Robert!*" he shouted, his voice surprisingly commanding for one so ill. Robert trudged over, smiling self-consciously. "Dr. Calderón wants to see you," Daniel explained when

Robert stood next to them.

"Hi, Dr. Calderón."

"Hello, Robert. This is Stefan."

"Hi." Freckled and red-headed like his brother, Robert appeared about three years older than Daniel. He was not nearly so childlike and uninhibited, however, and glanced around the ward uneasily, much like Stefan had earlier.

"Daniel, your father wants to speak with you." Dr. Calderón set him down and motioned toward his waiting parent. After Daniel scurried off, Dr. Calderón turned all his attention to Robert. "Daniel will be home by New Year's Eve."

"That's good." Robert appeared resigned.

"What's the matter?" Dr. Calderón asked, offering him a Christmas cookie.

Robert accepted the treat out of politeness. "Nothing."

"Do you miss Daniel?"

"Yes." He looked sad.

"He'll be home soon. Don't worry."

Robert remained quiet, his expression glum.

"I know you miss him, but he has to be in the hospital right now. We need to keep a close eye on him."

Robert nodded and hesitated a moment before speaking. "Why did he have to get so sick? I want everything like it used to be . . . before."

"I know, Robert. But your brother is doing considerably well."

"I wish he wasn't sick," he repeated.

"Yes, but that's not how this world works, Robert. As you grow up and live your life, there will be many things that come along like this. You've discovered how much you love your brother.

143

When he returns home, you'll always know how much he means to you."

"Yeah." Robert managed a smiled and waved goodbye. "My family is leaving now."

Dr. Calderón finished his cup of coffee. Stefan watched him, deep in his own thoughts. He wondered what his life would have been like with an older brother around. His mother had not wanted more children. Would his brother be with him now— waiting at doctors' offices and visiting him in the hospital? If his brother lived across the county, would he call him in the evening to check on his progress? Dr. Calderón seemed to read his mind.

"A brother might do you a lot of good right now."

"Really?"

"Yes."

"How so?"

Miguel turned to study his patient. "Daniel didn't want the surgery. Robert bribed him with one of his toys."

Stefan smiled, despite feeling ill at ease. "Yes, but it was all a ploy. They'd have done it anyway whether he'd liked it or not."

"Yes, but this way it was his choice, and he went into it with a positive attitude. That can really make a difference in the recovery phase."

Stefan fell silent. He'd already been through enough. There was no end to the poking and prodding by the medical establishment except, of course, when your insurance ran out. Then they'd rip the IVs out of the patients in intensive care to cart them off to the county hospital. "Well, I should get going. Rebel's out in the car."

Dr. Calderón nodded, rising up and motioning to Luis to wait for him. He walked with Stefan to the elevator. Stefan extended his

144

hand. "Merry Christmas, Miguel."

"Merry Christmas, Stefan." The doctor clasped it firmly and held on. The elevator opened, and after Stefan was released, he stepped inside, careful to conceal his feelings. He knew in that moment that Miguel cared as much about him as any brother ever could.

"Stefan?"

"Yes?" Stefan held the button, clamping down the emotion deep inside. He hadn't cried since he could remember and didn't want to start again now.

"Draw me that portrait."

When Stefan awoke two weeks later, he couldn't shake an ominous perception. He felt besieged by a distinctly "unwell" sensation, although his appearance revealed nothing amiss upon further inspection in the mirror. But the previous few days had proved unsettling, leaving him weary and empty in the aftermath, like a desert filled with nothing but sand. Stefan found himself avoiding Samantha. He felt weary of talking even to her. It seemed disappointing, coming so soon on the heels of his former exhilaration and peace of spirit.

Later that day, he drove up to Playa Fantasma alone with Rebel and sat on the square bench again, recalling—with melancholy—his dream of the crystal clear ocean. The gray, uneven water matched his mood, and he stared out at it, expressionless. Even the rocks, so visible on the day of the visit with Samantha, eluded him today.

Dr. Calderón was continuing his relentless quest for further testing. Stefan could now feel the tension and desire of his doctor to push the surgery on him the minute he walked into his office. He thought of that huge, unfeeling machine peering into his afflicted body and delivering more bad news.

How he had once loved machines, gadgets, and technology in

general, but now he preferred the salty ocean air and birds soaring overhead. They shared a similar destiny—cast to the four winds, his future as uncertain as their own as they scurried about, worrying about a tenuous existence one moment at a time. The sea birds didn't concern themselves with dwindling bank accounts or funeral plans. They merely searched for their next scrap of food, keeping a sharp eye out for impending death, trying to scratch out one more day of life down on the sand.

It again seemed a likely possibility that the tumor in his chest would defeat him in the end, but that depressing reality hardly troubled him as he stared spellbound into the spiraling gray water. He no longer held any fear of his own mortality. By far, that was the greatest benefit he'd received from his treatment with the doctors.

It began to rain, but he scarcely noticed. The sprinkling of misty droplets obscured him like a burial garment. He could not take his eyes off the swirling, choppy water. Rebel crawled under the bench and laid still, his head resting between his wet paws.

The night of the incredible dream had left him with an inexplicable feeling of hope, but now he was sinking into an ever deepening vortex of gloom. He recalled events and circumstances from the past that revealed his true motives as being calloused and self-serving. Was the hotshot boy wonder, who knew how to charm the world in order to get anything he wanted, capable of doing anything right? The rain soaked into him, but he couldn't stop staring over the slate gray water, remembering.

Miguel sat alone in his office, deep in thought and awaiting his first appointment for the day. Upon his arrival earlier, he'd discovered a note on his desk from Brian. Picking it up again, he reread the cryptic message.

Woke up with a strange feeling . . . watch out today.

He glanced out the window and spied a robin singing in a cedar tree located near the middle of the courtyard. The doctor walked over to the glass for a closer look, and the bird abruptly stopped its song and flew away. A moment later, it reappeared on the window ledge directly in front of him. Miguel watched the robin in surprise, and the diminutive creature looked back into his eyes. It began tapping on the glass over and over. He stared in silence until it ceased the action and glided across the square.

The ensuing workday proved stressful but not out of the ordinary. Four-thirty arrived, his final appointment for the day; and he reclined back in his desk chair while listening to the ticking of the lantern clock. The door finally opened, right on time.

"How are you, Stefan?" Dr. Calderón smiled at him.

Stefan headed right for his usual spot on the sofa. "All right." He coughed into his sleeve. "I've drawn you that picture."

Dr. Calderón felt shocked. "Really? Let me see it, please."

Rising up, the patient reached into his back pocket and walked over, handing his doctor a folded piece of lined paper. He reseated himself, his impassive stare focused on Dr. Calderón.

Miguel unfolded the paper and held it out in front of him, frowning handsomely as his dark hair fell across one eye. He brushed it back impatiently. Along the bottom of the page, the name "stefan" appeared, written faintly in pencil with the "s" not capitalized, though the actual drawing was done in ink. It was a sketch of a cigarette butt, bent slightly in the middle, as his patient often did in order to breathe easier. Thin, spindly arms projected out on each side and the funny looking face wore an expression of amused stupidity. Cigarette ashes fell from the top of the head, and squiggly stink lines rose up from the drawing in general.

Dr. Calderón could not seem to draw his eyes away from the illustration. "So this is how you see yourself?" he managed at last.

"Yes." Stefan nodded emphatically. "That's me exactly. I'm glad I waited to do it. I don't think I could have captured myself and done the portrait justice if I'd tried to draw it the first time you asked me." After a deep sigh, Stefan allowed his gaze to float around the office, studying the paintings on the walls and coming to rest on his favorite: the clipper ship. "Well, anyway . . . I'm seeing a lot more clearly now."

Dr. Calderón swallowed hard and cleared his throat, still clasping the drawing. "Yes, but remember, Stefan, you will not always see yourself like this." He flipped open the journal and turned to the most recent entry.

I dreamed I was playing my clarinet at a concert. During the middle of the piece, I performed a small solo. After it was over, my stand partner told me to go over to the edge of the stage and take a bow. I didn't want to and refused. Finally, I got up to do it, just to get him off my case. But partway there, I tripped and fell on the floor. I noticed that my shoes didn't fit; that's why I stumbled. I tried to pull myself upright again on a pillar, but it took every ounce of strength in my body. Everyone watched me as I struggled. I went to the edge of the stage and bowed to the audience. There was absolute silence. Not a single person applauded. I just stood there, listening to the silence and staring out at all the people.

Dr. Calderón looked up at Stefan. "How old were you when you stopped playing the clarinet?"

Stefan exhaled, trying to recall. "I guess I was about twenty-two."

"Twenty-two?" Miguel leaned forward in surprise. "You mean you played while you were at the university?"

Stefan nodded. "Yes, that's right."

"I thought you only played as a child," Dr. Calderón remarked, increasingly uneasy about the dream.

"Nope." His face was expressionless.

"You must have enjoyed it."

"Not really. I did when I was younger, and it was still fun. I liked being in band because it got me out of class."

"Why did you keep playing?"

Stefan shrugged. "I excelled at it. I practiced a lot and took private lessons."

"Yes, but . . . you were earning a degree in journalism."

"True." Stefan stared at Dr. Calderón in silence.

"Then why keep doing it?"

"They wanted me to."

"Your parents?"

"Who else?"

"But, why?"

"Because I needed the money!"

Miguel startled at the anger in Stefan's tone. Brian's premonition crossed his mind. When he spoke again, it was with hesitancy, as he recalled that Stefan's parents, although wealthy, had refused to support his education. "You mean for college?"

"Yes! If you were in that damn marching band, you received a tuition voucher!"

Miguel turned away to hide his discomfiture and, breathing deeply, attempted to collect himself. After a moment, he turned in his swivel chair to face Stefan again. To his shock, he discovered his patient on his knees, his complexion blanched and his features rigid.

"Stefan?" He jumped up in alarm. "Stefan!" Rushing to his patient, he clasped him by the shoulders and gave him a shake. Although still conscious, he appeared unresponsive. "Stefan . . . speak to me!"

The color returned to Stefan's face and he pulled himself free, crumpling partway to the floor. "*I hate them . . . I hate them all!*"

Dr. Calderón knelt beside him, his eyes wide with astonishment.

"*I hate tightfisted, stupid people! Stupid, clueless people . . . who are hypocrites and legends only in their own minds! I hate them and their inane blathering! I wish they'd all go to hell where I wouldn't have to hear the sound of their idiotic voices! I hate listening to them! Shut up, stupid!*" He covered his ears with his hands. "*I said, shut up! I hate you because you're a clueless idiot, okay?*"

Dr. Calderón grabbed Stefan from behind in an attempt to steady him, fearful his patient might slip into catatonia again.

"*You treat me like forgotten dirt!*" He began pounding the floor with his fists. "*I am not forgotten dirt! You make me want to vomit, get it? Shut up! Go talk about yourself to the mirror! But shut the door first, so I don't lose my appetite for dinner because you make me so sick I can't eat! Do you hear me? I can't eat because of you! You think I suck as an editor? No! I'll tell you what sucks! Working for people like you, sucks! I hate people like you!*"

151

All of you! You make me sick! You made me sick!" He collapsed on the floor and began to cry—racking, heartrending sobs. *"Come back,"* he wept, as he buried his face in his arms on the carpet. *"Oh, please come back! Don't leave me! Don't leave me . . . all alone."*

Miquel held on to him, shocked by the depth of the grief he was witnessing.

The nurse opened the door and peered inside.

Dr. Calderón looked up at her. "Please . . . go get Brian."

She turned to leave, but not before noticing tears in the doctor's eyes.

At the insistence of his doctors, Stefan returned the following day for another appointment. Dr. Calderón sat on the edge of the sofa, waiting for him. When Stefan entered the room, the expression on his face appeared composed. Recovered from the tumultuous events of the previous afternoon, he seated himself next to his doctor.

"How are you feeling today, Stefan?"

"I feel much better." He leaned back on the sofa and regarded his doctor frankly. "I really do."

"Did you sleep last night?"

"Yes, I did," he assured him. "I slept better than I have in years. I'd like to go back to my motel," Stefan insisted, having spent the night out in the valley under the watchful eye of Whitney Sandler.

"Whitney said you could stay with him for the duration of your treatment if you like."

Stefan actually grinned. "I appreciate that. I truly do. But I'm okay."

"All right, Stefan. You can go back to your motel." It was Dr. Calderón's turn to smile, relief filling him. "You're making excellent progress. But I have to say . . . at this point, I absolutely must emphasize that further surgery is indicated in order to buy you more time for your emotional healing process. I've conferred with Brian and even he agrees. Your illness is a complex phenomenon that requires an intricate approach of different modalities. My associate, Dr. Benson, is an excellent surgeon. I have every expectation that—"

"I don't want the surgery." He shook his head.

"But, why not?" Dr. Calderón could no longer contain himself. "*Why* won't you agree to it? We've made such excellent progress with the psychotherapeutic process. You're much stronger. Your chances would be so much better now. Really, Stefan, I didn't think you'd come back like this. I knew there was hope, but you have truly surprised me. I just wish you would let me help you!"

"I'm not changing my mind."

"Let me at least schedule an MRI." Perhaps he could ease his way in behind the wall with an incremental approach.

He shrugged. "I don't know. . . ."

Dr. Calderón looked out the window at the birds gathering in a nearby tree. "I need to schedule an MRI. It's been a while since the last one."

"I told you; my insurance capped. Those things cost a fortune."

"Don't worry about the money."

"I don't anymore. Believe me."

"Well? Will you agree to the MRI?"

"When?" he asked.

"Let me try and schedule one now. I'll be right back. I'm just going to step into the other room for a moment."

"Fine." Stefan sighed, tiring of the conversation.

Dr. Calderón disappeared down the hall and picked up the phone, dialing the hospital. "Yes, connect me with extension 364, please."

"One moment."

The phone rang twice on the other end before it was answered. "Radiology. This is Angie. How may I help you?"

"This is Dr. Miguel Calderón. I need to schedule an MRI."

"All right. Let me see . . . I have Friday open at 3:00. We had a cancellation."

"No, that's not soon enough. What about tomorrow?"

"That's impossible."

"The day after tomorrow."

"That's not possible either."

"It's an emergency. Schedule it for tomorrow evening."

Angie frowned. Dr. Calderón had never been demanding in the past like the other doctors she was forced to contend with on a daily basis, but today proved to be an exception. "All right. In that case, it will have to be administered in the hospital. Is seven-fifteen all right?"

"Yes, fine." He proceeded to give her the patient information and medical details, turning to glance behind him to make sure Stefan hadn't overheard him lean on Angie to get the appointment.

"All right. Tomorrow at seven-fifteen."

Thank you." Replacing the receiver, he walked back across the hall to Stefan. He discovered his patient lounging comfortably on the couch. "Okay, Stefan, I've scheduled you for tomorrow at seven-fifteen."

Stefan sat up in surprise. "Tomorrow?"

"Yes, tomorrow night."

He considered this for a moment, beginning to feel unsure. That was fast. Usually it took days, even weeks, to schedule tests. "What floor?"

"The eleventh. Be there a little early."

Stefan grimaced, growing glum. Another date with a machine. For them you always had to be on time.

"Come into the next room, Stefan. I'd like to do a quick check."

Stefan followed him into the examination room and removed his shirt. His back had healed and Dr. Calderón was able to place the stethoscope over the scar without inflicting any pain. He listened to the intake of breath. "Exhale," he instructed, and Stefan complied. Dr. Calderón frowned. Something didn't seem right, but he could not detect a problem. "Again." He listened carefully, unable to dispel his apprehension. The MRI would be able to tell him what he needed to know. Stefan had gained noticeable weight in just the past week, and his skin tone looked vibrant. "How's your appetite?"

"Good, much better."

"Great. Wonderful." After they finished, the doctor noted how easily Stefan slipped his shirt over his head, no longer requiring his assistance. He spotted Stefan's untied shoe and knelt down to tie it.

"Thank you, Doctor."

Dr. Calderón straightened up and smiled, wishing he could shake his troubled feeling.

Stefan cleared his throat. "I know you're not supposed to discuss your other patients, but how is Daniel doing?"

"Fine. He's been home for a while now." He wanted to emphasize how quickly his young patient had recovered from the surgery but sensed it would push Stefan farther away, not draw him closer.

"Children are my favorite patients," he confided, his expression serious. "Initially, it was a terrible shock to work with children so gravely ill. But I quickly realized that they often possessed more inner resources to draw upon than most adults. A sort of ignorant innocence, so to speak, which works wonderfully in their favor. Daniel is resilient and optimistic." Dr. Calderón laughed. "He's also obnoxious. He screams that I'm killing him sometimes, and the entire waiting room can hear."

Stefan chuckled. "That must be unsettling."

"Only at first."

"Well, I'm glad to hear he's doing all right." He glanced at the clock on the wall. Their time was up for the afternoon. "I should get going. I have to go to the store. I'm out of food."

"Okay, Stefan. And I should have the results of the test by Friday. Can you call and arrange an appointment for some time later in the afternoon on that day?"

Stefan nodded. "Sure, I'll see you Friday."

"Goodbye, Stefan."

After his patient's departure, Dr. Calderón picked up the portrait again and studied it soberly. There was something about the simple, lined face that captured him—the amused stupidity. He noted the name again, "stefan," not capitalized and written in pencil. Dr. Calderón decided to ring up the lab and order two tests in addition to the scan. He knew Stefan would resent it, but his authority as a doctor and affection for his patient for once overrode his sensitivity towards intruding too deeply into his patients' lives.

Stefan drove back to his motel, deep in thought. He had agreed to the test against his better judgment. What did it really matter anyway? He was doing it more to please Dr. Calderón than anything else. Having forgotten his checkbook, Stefan wondered if he should skip eating tonight, even though he felt hungry. He was too preoccupied with his own apathy to eat. However, the patient now held a new responsibility to his body and felt unable to neglect it, despite having abused and misused himself for so long in the past.

Back at his motel, Stefan retrieved the checkbook, whistled for Rebel, and headed for the food co-op across town. As he pulled into the cramped lot next to the store, it started to rain again, increasing his gloom. The store turned out to be crowded, especially the organic sections. Stefan didn't stand out in the crowd any longer, he appeared too well on the outside; and as he scanned the long aisles of food, he felt overwhelmed by his indifference to the vast selection. Standing in front of the coffee display, he recalled Dr. Calderón promising to take him into town for a cup when he felt better. That had never happened. He was better now . . . or was he? Either the doctor had forgotten or he didn't really consider Stefan truly on the mend. Dr. Calderón seemed to recall everything in minute detail; nothing eluded him, so Stefan decided it had to be the latter.

Paying for his groceries moments later, he studied the remaining balance in his checkbook. His resources were shrinking at an alarming rate. The test would clean his savings out. He'd be broke. What would he do then?

After he had eaten at the motel, Stefan walked Rebel in the alley for a minute in the soaking rain. He felt as disappointed as the dog that he couldn't walk down on the beach tonight. When he returned to his room again, he began shaking from the cold and huddled up to his wall heater. Chilly, long, and dark, January was his least favorite month of the year.

His journal lay on the nightstand across the room, but he didn't feel like writing in it. He hadn't recorded any entries for some time now, perhaps because what he was experiencing seemed beyond any words. The phone rang. Reaching up, he grabbed it.

"Hello?"

"Hi, Stefan." It was Samantha.

He smiled, no longer weary of her. "Hi, Samantha."

"How are you?" She sounded so sweet and kind tonight.

How could he ever explain how he was? "Bummed out. I feel like going for a walk on the beach."

"Oh, me too. The rain's really cold though. It's very cold tonight."

"Yes, it's probably the coldest night of the year . . . tonight."

"Well, it's supposed to get even colder."

"Really?"

"Yes, we could have a severe freeze."

"Oh." He fell silent, considering this.

"Yes, it's always so terrible when that happens. All sorts of plants and things die. They can't live through a heavy frost."

"People shouldn't have planted them."

"What's that, Stefan?" She seemed not to have heard him.

"The things that die in the deep frost. It's silly to even plant them in the first place. Why not just grow what really belongs here? That's what I think."

"Oh. Well, I suppose because they are so beautiful . . . the flowers and things. That's why."

"Well, I don't agree. It looks artificial and contrived . . . all the lush, constant blooming. What I really like are the cliffs that run down to the beach. Everything looks like it belongs and is so beautiful, too. It's sort of a ragged, wild beauty that can survive anything that comes. You know, the waves breaking over it and the cliffs giving way. It all comes back, regardless. I love to sit on those rocks in desolate places. It's very restful."

Samantha laughed lightly. When she considered it, she felt exactly the same way. The flowers and cliffs appeared so fragile and picturesque, yet they survived everything. "Yes, I like the cliffs, too."

"So what are you doing tonight, Samantha?"

She smiled to herself as the wind whipped the branches against the windowpane of her bedroom. The cadence of his gentle voice gladdened her somehow, despite the fact that she always had to call him instead of the other way around. Conversing with Stefan or reposing up on the cliffs seemed one and the same—enjoyable and relaxing. "Nothing. Just sitting around. If it stops raining tomorrow evening, would you like to go for a walk together?"

"I can't. I have to go to the hospital for a test."

"Oh." She felt crushed with disappointment.

"How about the next night?" Stefan ventured.

"I can't. I have to work."

"Oh." That wouldn't work either. "How about your next day off, then?"

"I can't. I have a date with Richard."

"Oh." He grew silent, thinking it over. "Did you ever let that little bird go?" he asked, very curious to know.

"Yes, I let it go."

"That's good."

"He did remarkably well, too. He hurried right off and went back to his life just like nothing had ever happened. I watched him fly away. He flew perfectly."

Stefan smiled, feeling satisfied. "Where do you suppose he is tonight?"

She laughed. He reminded her of a little boy sometimes. Richard wouldn't have speculated about a gray bird's whereabouts on a stormy night in a million years. "He's someplace safe and dry, I'm sure."

"I never thought about it before . . . where all the birds go on nights like tonight. I bet he's in that cave, you know, the one where we hid the first time we met when it started to rain."

She was quiet, remembering that day. It seemed like a long time ago. "Maybe he is."

"Well, Samantha . . . I have to hang up now. I'm supposed to write in my journal. Doctor's orders."

"Really? He has you do that?"

"Yes. But he hardly ever reads it anymore. He's more interested in charts, scans, and tests."

"Oh." She pondered Stefan's refusal of an additional surgery. If only she could convince him, but Samantha sensed that Dr. Calderón's assumption had been correct. She knew in her heart that she couldn't persuade Stefan to change his mind, and there would be no point in even trying. "Well, goodnight, Stefan."

He remained quiet for a moment on the other end of the line. Finally, he spoke. "Goodbye, Samantha," he replied softly and hung up the phone.

The final week of January in Acantilado del Mar began with an unrelenting downpour that threatened to last for days on end. Hurrying down the rain-soaked path leading to her neighbor's house,
Samantha attempted to cover her head with her hands in a futile
attempt to stay dry. Upon reaching the protection of the alcove,
she took a moment to collect herself and then knocked. Toby
barked furiously from inside the sunporch, but no one answered
the door. Samantha leaned on the doorbell. With a sigh of dismay,
she stared out at the wet trees, water dripping and running in tiny
rivulets seemingly everywhere.

Stefan had not answered his phone for two days, and Samantha
was unable to shake an ominous feeling regarding his absence. A
terrifying thought kept occurring to her. In an attempt to eradicate
it from her mind, she convinced herself that he must be either out
of town or no longer living at the motel. Samantha rang the bell
once more in hope that Dr. Calderón might have the answer, but
except for a frenetic little terrier, the house appeared to be deserted. Racing back down the garden path, she burst through her
own front door and grabbed her purse.

"Samantha, where are you going?" Her mother hung over her
reprovingly. "Don't you dare drive anywhere in this downpour!

Wait until the rain stops."

Samantha suppressed her irritation with the constant barrage of interference she was forced to endure. "I *have* to!"

"Well, where are you going?"

"I'm trying to find Dr. Calderón."

"Dr. Calderón?"

"Mom, please. I'm in a hurry."

"Why do you want to see him? Is something the matter with Stefan?"

"I don't know. I can't reach him. I've been trying to get ahold of him for days, and I'm getting really worried."

"Samantha . . ."

"Mom, I just know something is wrong. Please, just let me—"

"Well, then use the phone for heaven's sake. Try calling his office. Here, I have the number." Flipping open her personal address book with lightning speed, Maureen propped the phone under one ear and punched the number.

"Yes, I need to speak with Dr. Calderón. It's an emergency."

"Mom!"

"I'm sorry," a receptionist responded, "He's not available right now. He cancelled most of his appointments for this afternoon."

"What?" Maureen appeared astonished. "Well, where in the blazes is he? He can't be out on the golf course in this weather!"

Samantha turned into a weary statue, waiting for it all to be over.

"He may be at the hospital. Would you like me to try and reach him for you there?"

"Yes, immediately!" Maureen waited, eyeing her daughter with a knowing look. "These doctors . . . taking the afternoon off. Imagine your father deciding not to go to work and cancelling on all his customers. We'd be out on the street!"

"I'm sorry, but he's not answering."

"What?"

"Would you like to leave a message? I'm sure he'll be checking in soon. I could also connect you to one of his associates if you like."

"No, that wouldn't be any good." After Maureen proceeded to give the receptionist her contact information, she slammed the receiver down. "The lady said he's in the hospital somewhere, but he doesn't bother to come when he's paged."

"I'll go look for him."

"Samantha, it's silly. You have to leave for work in an hour."

"I don't care!" Tears welled up in her eyes, and she turned away to conceal them from her mother. "I'm going anyway. Stefan could be there."

"Be sure to check the physicians' dining room," her mother called out after her.

The rain drenched the windshield in sheets as Samantha squinted through the swiping wiper blades, hoping the traffic would be light. At times she had to crank down the window and poke her head out to be certain the road was clear. Before long she reached the hospital and pulled into the parking lot.

"Yes, I need you to page Dr. Calderón for me," she managed a minute later while standing in front of the admitting clerk.

He appeared doubtful. "Dr. Calderón? He's not usually around this time of day. He's over in his medical office seeing appointments."

"He cancelled them. His receptionist said he was here. I'm trying to locate friend of mine who is a patient of his. I'm very concerned about him. Could you check to see if a Stefan Campeau has been admitted? Dr. Calderón is his primary physician."

"Let me verify that one way or another." He began tapping on his keyboard. "No, I'm sorry. We have no one admitted by that name. Do you still want me to try and page Dr. Calderón?"

"Yes, please!"

"Dr. Calderón to admitting, please."

Samantha began chewing on her fingernails. Where in the world could they be? If she was able to locate at least one of them, she might have an answer.

"Dr. Calderón to admitting, please."

The clerk's phone suddenly beeped and her heart jumped. He picked up the receiver. "Yes? Okay, thanks." He glanced up at her again. "That was Dr. Andrasz. He said that Dr. Calderón has not been in since this morning when he did his rounds and is not expected to return. He took the afternoon off."

Samantha turned for the front entrance again, wondering what to do next. Checking her watch, she realized there was now barely enough time to get to work. She drove across town, but instead of backtracking for The Grill, she swerved her car in the direction of the Budget Motel. Hurrying to his room, she banged loudly on the door. She held her ear against it, listening for Rebel. If Stefan were inside, Rebel would surely bark. There was only silence, and now she would be late for work. She thought of the beach, oddly enough, but no one would be down there in this weather.

Collapsing on the dingy carpet in the hallway, she felt utterly defeated. If only she could find Dr. Calderón! Worry wore away at her, and after catching her breath for a minute, she forced herself back up and walked across the hall to the pay phone. She fished a quarter out of her purse and pushed it into the slot. After checking the number in the phone book, she dialed the hospital again, this time requesting Dr. Andrasz.

After a long wait, he answered. "Dr. Andrasz."

"Hello, Dr. Andrasz. I'm calling about Dr. Calderón in regard to one of his patients—a friend of mine. You said earlier that he took the afternoon off. Do you know where he might be?"

"No, I don't. Do you have his home number?"

"I live next door to him. He's not at home."

"Have you tried his office?"

"He's not there either."

Dr. Andrasz searched his memory. "Well, I know he didn't leave town. Oh, hold on a minute. Now I remember; he's attending a service at Star of the Sea for one of his patients—an elderly gentleman who passed away on Sunday. That's where you'll find him."

"Thank you!" Sighing with relief, she replaced the receiver and started back for her car, neglecting to call The Grill. She drove to the historic district of town and wound her way up a hilly road, on top of which stood an old church. A towering masterpiece of architecture, the building was barely visible in the gloomy downpour. Alongside the road, dark, twisting trees lashed back and forth in the storm.

Cars were beginning to pull out, the service apparently over. She careened into the lot, switching off the ignition and hurrying up the long stairwell leading to the entrance. Once inside the foyer, she looked around. Should she go inside or wait? With some hesitation, she pushed her way inside. The interior of the church ap-

165

peared dark except for the glow of a few remaining candles. Incense lingered in the air as the rain pelted against the stained glass.

"Samantha?"

After an initial startle, Samantha was flooded with relief to see the doctor. He appeared surprised and concerned to see her.

"Miguel . . ."

"Are you all right? What is it, Samantha? Is it your mother?"

"No." She shook her head, her voice barely a whisper. Tears filled her eyes and fell down her cheeks. "It's . . . Stefan." She felt so overcome with emotion that she could hardly speak. She wiped away the tears. "I can't find him."

"Do you feel that something's happened to him?" He led her out to the foyer.

She nodded. "Yes, I'm scared."

Dr. Calderón nodded in understanding. "Don't worry; we'll find him. I doubt he's left town. He has an appointment with me later this afternoon after I receive the results of his tests. I had to cancel an earlier appointment we had today because of the funeral."

She shook her head. "He's not at his motel. I checked."

"Is his car there?"

She had neglected to look. "I don't know."

"Let's go check it out." They stepped outside under the awning. "It's possible that he could be in his room, unconscious. Thank you for tracking me down, Samantha."

"I knocked, but if he were in there, Rebel would have barked. I didn't hear a sound."

He nodded. "We'll get the manager to open the door. Then we'll see." In the parking lot, he held his car door open for her. She eyed her own vehicle, but he waved her concerns away. "Never mind, we'll come back for it later." They headed back down the road, which was now flooded with running water. "He seemed fine the last time I spoke to him."

Samantha stared out the window, feeling desolate. "I'm worried sick. I keep thinking about what you said on Christmas Eve."

"I shouldn't have worried you." He now regretted the indiscretion. "Unfortunately, it's true. He has to have the surgery. The trouble is he's so stubborn. It's very possible he's just collapsed somewhere. I should have checked up on him." He was growing unsettled as well, his dark eyes filled with apprehension. "Let's just hope he's in his room."

When they'd reached the Budget Motel, Dr. Calderón swerved into the lot and immediately spotted Stefan's car. "There it is." He pointed to it.

Hope filled her. Perhaps he'd only just arrived home and was now in his room with Rebel. "I'll show you his room."

"Good idea. We'll knock first." Upon reaching his door, they knocked loudly. There was no answer. Dr. Calderón knocked again, this time even harder. "Wait here," he requested of her. "I'll go and find the manager."

He disappeared, and Samantha chewed away at her nails, her heart heavy in her chest. She felt paralyzed with worry and fear. Dr. Calderón returned with a motel employee trailing after him.

"Here's the room. Please open the door for us."

"I can't. I've tried to tell you, I could get into a lot of trouble."

"There might be a very sick man in there that needs immediate medical attention. I'm his doctor. Open it up, please!"

"I don't know. . . ." The employee shook his head.

"If you don't open the door, I'll break it down!" Miguel threatened.

The motel employee reached into his pocket to retrieve the key. He unlocked the door and pushed it open.

Samantha and Miguel rushed inside but discovered the room empty. "He's not here," Samantha lamented.

The employee appeared disgusted. "I never should have let you in. The guy has a dog. If I knock on the door when he's around, it always barks."

Dr. Calderón looked about for a clue. The bed appeared neatly made and the room tidy. He checked the bathroom, but it appeared undisturbed as well.

"What are you doing?" The employee poked his head in. "I think you should leave."

Back out in the main room again, Dr. Calderón spotted the journal lying on the nightstand. Grabbing the booklet, he opened it. The motel employee disappeared to find his supervisor.

"What is it?" Samantha asked, watching the doctor's eyes widen as he scanned the latest entry from two days ago.

In my mind's eye, I see a beautiful place. It's late autumn in the woods—a deserted spot. Under the blue sky, there's a bed of dry leaves in the middle of a grove of trees. It's the last warm day of the year when the sunlight, for a brief interval, shines with perfect warmth. I lie down in the leaves and they cover me like a burial shroud—my face basking in the rays of the sun. After a rest in the radiance and leaves, I slip away and never see the light of day again.

Shock registered in Samantha's face as she read the entry over the doctor's shoulder. "He's killed himself!"

"No, Samantha. He hasn't killed himself. But we have to find him."

"Where could he be?" She collapsed on the bed, feeling spent.

"How about the leash? Is it gone?"

Looking up a moment, Samantha looked around the room again. Together they began opening drawers and checking cabinets. After a careful search, they gave up. "He must have gone off on foot with Rebel," the doctor surmised. "For all we know, he may be at your house by now."

They walked out into the rain again and slipped back into the car. Dr. Calderón's pager went off. "We'll go to your house. I can make the call from there." He pulled out and drove quickly up the street.

At Samantha's house, Maureen was astonished to discover her daughter again. "Samantha! The Grill is frantic! Where have you been?" She paused to study Dr. Calderón in surprise.

"Never mind, Mom. We have to find Stefan. And Dr. Calderón needs to use the phone."

"May I?" He stood questioningly over the receiver.

"Go ahead!" she exclaimed. He dialed the hospital. "Did you check at his motel?" Maureen wanted to know, asking the obvious and irritating her daughter.

"Yes, Mom, we did. He's not there and Rebel's leash is gone."

"Well, honey, it's probably nothing. Why are you both so upset? He's most likely just walking around downtown or something."

"In the pouring rain?"

"Well, he got caught in the rain, then. He's under an awning someplace, waiting for it to stop."

Dr. Calderón replaced the phone, his expression grave. Glancing over at Samantha and Maureen, he shook his head. "Stefan has pneumonia. I sensed something amiss the last time I examined him."

Samantha's anxiety increased. He had pneumonia and a partially functioning lung from his previous surgery, not to mention a cancer about to kill him. Where could he have gone? She racked her mind, trying to think.

Dr. Calderón pondered the same thing. "When was the last time you spoke to him, Samantha?"

"I talked to Stefan on Monday. I called him at his motel."

"Yes, that was the day of his last appointment as well. Did you speak to him in the evening?"

"Yes."

"Uh-huh." He considered the situation a moment. "My receptionist called Stefan on Tuesday to reschedule his appointment for this afternoon. When did you try calling him after that?"

"Yesterday. Early in the morning." She'd phoned to ask if he'd like to join her for a walk on the beach when the rain finally quit, perhaps that night if she could get off work early enough. "I tried all day yesterday and today. I never got an answer."

Dr. Calderón frowned and ran his fingers through his hair. "When you spoke with him on Monday evening, what did he say? Can you recall?"

"Well, nothing, really. We tried to arrange an evening to get together but couldn't. He mentioned his appointment for a test on Tuesday. I was working the next day. After that, I had a date with Richard."

"Did you talk about anything else?"

She thought of the cliffs, the possible freeze, the plants, and finally the little bird. "He asked about a bird he'd found . . . if I let it go free or not. He found it on the beach a while ago with a broken wing. I fixed it up and released it last week."

"Oh." The doctor nodded sagely.

"He wondered about it because it was raining really hard that night too." An unsettling thought occurred to her. She shook her head. He couldn't be there!

"What's the matter, Samantha?" Maureen moved in closer, sensing a change had come over her daughter. "What is it?"

"I don't know. There's this cave down on the beach."

"So?"

"We hid there once the first time we met. It was raining that day too, so we went inside until it stopped. "That's where he said the bird probably was . . . inside the cave."

"C'mon, let's go." Dr. Calderón rose up, pulling his jacket closed and zipping it.

"That's absurd!" Maureen declared, growing alarmed. "Why would he be down there in this weather?"

"Show me where it is, Samantha. And hurry!"

"Put these rain coats on at least," Maureen insisted, pulling two slickers from the closet. Samantha and Dr. Calderón grabbed the coats, slipping them on. Hurrying out into the rain, they headed for the stairwell in the distance. "This is craziness!" her mother shouted after them, barely audible in the driving rain.

The two of them ran down the staircase, quickly reaching the beach. Sprinting along the firmest part of the sand, they worked their way toward Esperanza Point.

"There's the cave." She pointed up near the cliff. To her shock, she spied Rebel peering out from the entrance. "Look!"

Dr. Calderón had seen as well. He maneuvered around the rocks, desperate to reach his patient. They found him inside the cave, curled up on the sand and lying very still. Dr. Calderón knelt over him anxiously as Samantha stood by in a state of shock.

"He's breathing, but I think he's unconscious."

"Oh, thank God." She collapsed with relief but then grew fearful again, wondering how bad Stefan might be.

Stefan opened his eyes and stirred under the doctor's touch. Dr. Calderón slipped off his rain coat and wrapped it around Stefan, preparing to stand him up. "We're going to help you, Stefan.

He shook his head. "No . . ."

Tears streamed down Samantha's cheeks. "Stefan, we have to take you to the hospital!"

Dr. Calderón turned to her in alarm, but it was too late. Stefan grew agitated and began to thrash. "No!" He shook his head and tried to struggle free, nearly hitting his head on a rock.

"Stefan, we're going to help you!" She grew more desperate, attempting to calm him. "You need to be in the hospital!"

"No, Samantha!" Dr. Calderón waved her quiet. She backed up in confusion. "I won't take you to the hospital, Stefan," the doctor promised. "I'll bring you back to my house. You'll be all right there, okay?"

Stefan writhed in pain and nodded his consent. "Okay."

Dr. Calderón hoisted him up, motioning for Samantha to assist him in a two person carry. "We'll be there in no time."

"Samantha?" Stefan glanced at her.

"What is it, Stefan?" She leaned close to him.

"Rebel . . . he's hungry."

15—*La Discordia y la Angustia*

"Samantha! What in the world are you doing?" Maureen thought she was seeing things. Only moments earlier, her daughter and neighbor had rushed off in the pounding rain to check inside of a dank beach cave for their friend. Now, Samantha stood in the utility room, pouring dog food into a bowl.

"We found him, Mom. This is for Rebel. He's hungry."

"You found him? Well, is he all right?"

Samantha wiped her tears away with a dish towel. "No, he's not. He's slipping in and out of consciousness. We had to practically drag him up from the beach."

"He was in that cave?" Maureen seemed unable to believe it. "What . . . I mean, *why*?"

"I don't know."

Maureen hurried to the window and peered through the curtain. "Is an ambulance coming, or did Dr. Calderón already take him to the hospital?"

Samantha shook her head. "No, Stefan's not going to the hospital. He's at Dr. Calderón's house. He got mad at me when I suggested it." She still felt bruised by the doctor's exasperation with her.

"What?" Maureen appeared baffled and more astonished than

ever. "Who got mad at you? Stefan?"

"No, Dr. Calderón."

"Dr. Calderón? You're kidding me! If Stefan's that bad, he should be in the hospital."

Samantha held the towel away from her face a minute. "I know. But he doesn't want to . . . be in the hospital, I mean."

"Well, so what?" Maureen's tone sounded emphatic. Long since fully recovered, she had conveniently forgotten her own stubborn, irrational behavior during her illness.

"I have to get over there."

"Well, wait a minute. I'm coming with you!"

They hurried next door in the rain. The torrents of water falling from the sky were now easing up; the storm would soon be over. Samantha didn't bother to knock and barged right in, quickly discovering Stefan propped up in a bed in the first bedroom down the hall. Dr. Calderón stood over him. Turning around in surprise, he hesitated a moment upon seeing Maureen. He placed his arm around her shoulders and steered her back out into the living room.

"Let him rest," he instructed Samantha over his shoulder.

"Now listen," Maureen immediately launched in. "She's worried sick! You've got to get Stefan to the hospital!"

"Maureen . . ."

"I'm dead serious. And if you don't listen to me, he's going to be just plain dead." She jabbed a thumb in the direction of the bedroom.

"I'm not going to stand here and argue with you."

"Well, just what do you plan to do for him?"

"One of my associates is on his way over with some medications

174

for Stefan." He rubbed his eyes. What good would anything do Stefan right now? The man down the hall was most likely hours from death despite anything he could offer, or anything the hospital could supply for that matter.

Samantha reappeared and stood in front of him with red, swollen eyes. "How is he, Dr. Calderón?"

"He's gravely ill, Samantha."

"Why is he unconscious?" she continued. "Shouldn't he be in the hospital?"

The doorbell chimed, and Dr. Calderón stepped aside to answer it. "Hello, Marek. Thanks for coming by so quickly."

Dr. Calderón made the introductions. "Maureen, Samantha . . . this is Dr. Andrasz. Marek, these are my neighbors." They all shook hands. "He's down the hall. Excuse us for a moment." The doctors disappeared into Stefan's room and closed the door behind them.

Samantha sank into a nearby chair, completely devastated. What were they doing in there? She suddenly found herself besieged by doubts regarding Dr. Calderón. It was true that initially he had helped Stefan. But now at this critically important juncture, he was choosing to allow his patient to die.

"What are you thinking about?" her mother asked, studying her daughter closely.

"Nothing." Samantha shook her head.

Dr. Andrasz reappeared, his expression grave. With a curt nod, he showed himself out. Dr. Calderón returned as well, regarding Samantha evenly. He walked over and seated himself next to her.

Maureen joined them. "How is Stefan doing, Doctor?" she demanded, her eyes sweeping across Miguel's face.

"He's asleep."

"Well, didn't Dr. Andrasz think he should be in the hospital?" Maureen asked.

Dr. Calderón nodded, noting Samantha's anxious expression. "Yes, he did."

"Well, then—"

"Maureen, I already told you that I don't want to argue. He doesn't want to be in the hospital."

"That's crazy!"

"Don't you think I'd like to have him in the hospital? He doesn't want to go!"

"So now he has a choice?" Maureen shook her head, unconvinced.

"What do you mean by that?" he exclaimed in frustration.

"You're opposed to sabotaging one's health, yet you allow this! What's the difference?"

Dr. Calderón stared at his neighbor, astonished. "Do you think I want to see this happen? Do you think I *want* this? He's not going to survive the night! But putting him in the hospital now is not going to make any difference. He needed the surgery but refused."

"You should have *made* him do it," Samantha declared, breaking her silence. "That's your job! Instead, you had him write in some silly journal!"

Dr. Calderón turned away, his expression pained. "I did try to talk him into it, Samantha," he replied. "But he was shut up in a fortress."

"What does that mean?" Samantha exclaimed, increasingly mistrustful.

Even Maureen seemed to be turning against him. "That's nonsense! He had one of the best physicians in the country before he ended up here."

Dr. Calderón looked away, refusing to respond. Alicia and the boys were due home at any moment. His house would be no place for a dying man. He'd have to make other accommodations for his family. Turning away from the window, he caught Samantha's cold expression. He cleared his throat. "I need to go into the other room and make a few calls."

"You have to phone work," Maureen reminded her daughter.

"I know." She didn't want to call work. She didn't care about The Grill anymore.

Her mother stood up. "All right, dear. Tell you what . . . stay put if you like. I'll go home and call for you. I'll phone Richard, too."

"Richard?" Samantha looked up in alarm. "Why do you want to call Richard?"

Her mother appeared surprised. "Why do I want to call him? Samantha, you're going to need him. He should be with you right now."

"I don't need him bothering me," she declared, her dark eyes flashing.

"Samantha!" Maureen studied her daughter in alarm. "Well, I'll call him anyway. He'd want to know." She collected her purse and disappeared out the front door.

Samantha continued to sit immobile with her head in her hands. The only audible sounds in the house were the ticking of a clock nearby and the soft patter of rain against the windowpanes. Tears began to fall down her cheeks again, and she buried her face in her arms, grief-stricken by the realization that today would be Stefan's last day on earth.

"Stefan?" Dr. Calderón held his patient's hand and observed him closely. Stefan began to stir and opened his eyes, appearing lucid despite his fever and pain.

"Miguel?"

"You're in my home, Stefan. Look." He pointed to the window across the room which displayed a beautiful view of the sea. "I have some diluted juice for you. Try to drink a little."

"All right." Stefan sipped the liquid. After that he resumed staring out the window at the ocean. "How beautiful," Stefan acknowledged. "It's a beautiful day."

Dr. Calderón pulled up a chair. "I love the rain."

"Is it raining?" he asked, despite the fact that drops were running down the glass.

"Yes, it is. I've given you something for your pain."

"Okay." He attempted to move into a more comfortable position. He was an old hand with an aching body at this point, knowing when and where to shift to obtain relief. He looked back at his doctor. "I'm sorry, Miguel."

Dr. Calderón shook his head. "Don't be sorry, Stefan."

"I didn't listen to you."

"Rest, Stefan. Don't worry."

Stefan continued staring, his dark curls like a halo around his head against the pillow. "Everyone has to die, though."

Dr. Calderón remained silent, staring at the floor.

"What's the matter?" Stefan asked.

Dr. Calderón glanced back at him, reluctance in his eyes. "I don't think it's your time yet."

Stefan grew tired and, after a long sigh, drifted off to sleep. Dr.

Calderón adjusted the coverlet around him and dabbed his perspiring brow with a cold cloth. After rising up and leaving Stefan's bedside, he was surprised to discover Samantha still sitting out in the living room.

"Samantha?"

She turned in his direction, startled. It was obvious that she had been crying. "Yes?"

"Would it be possible for you to sit with Stefan for a while?"

"All right." She scrutinized the doctor's expression. "How is he?"

"He's asleep. Just stay with him, and I'll be back shortly. A nurse is coming by. She should be here at any time now."

"Will you be back soon?" she asked, anxious at the thought of being left alone with Stefan.

"I have to drop a few things off at my mother's. Alicia and the boys will be staying there tonight."

"Will you return after that?"

"Yes." His expression remained grave.

Samantha turned away. She wished Stefan were in the ICU. There were machines there that could do things to help keep him alive. Stefan needed to be with a team of doctors and nurses, administering to him day and night.

"People die in the hospital, Samantha."

She stiffened. It felt eerie in the room—beyond time. Dr. Calderón disappeared upstairs to collect a few items and afterward closed the front door behind him.

Sitting in Stefan's room next to the bed, she hung onto every labored breath as if it were his last. It was a heartrending sight to witness. How much longer could his terrible pain continue? As

179

much as she loved him, she wished it would come to an end. How long had she witnessed him ailing? His suffering had begun long before their friendship's inception, that much was certain.

Taking his hand in hers, she recalled their first meeting and her recoiling at his touch. The memory of that moment cut her heart like a knife. Maybe it would have been better if he had chosen another to take his dog. Now her entire life was turned back to front: her relationship with Richard, her admiration for her neighbor; indeed, all her plans for the future. Her life had ended up a shambles—in complete disarray.

"Dr. Calderón?" His expression looked tormented.

She grew panicky. "Stefan, don't worry. Dr. Calderón is coming right back. He'll give you something more for your pain!" Rising up, she glanced around in dismay, and he slipped back into unconsciousness.

Samantha sat in the chair next to the bed again, watching a trickle of perspiration run down his face. Picking up a cloth, she gently wiped it away, her racing heart quieting. She felt helpless and alone. Unable to witness his distress any longer, she gazed out the window and watched the surf breaking against the rocks below. Her heart felt frozen with grief as she stared at the deserted shoreline, realizing that she and Stefan would never be together there again.

"How is he doing, Doctor?" Maureen asked as she offered him a cup of hot tea. Samantha's father, Richard, Maureen, and Samantha were grouped together in their comfortable living room later that evening when Dr. Calderón stopped by. A nurse was staying next door.

Dr. Calderón sat across from the gathering and studied them guardedly. "He's about the same."

"Well, can I please—"

"No, Samantha." Dr. Calderón shook his head. "He needs to rest, and he seems to want to be alone right now."

"You can't leave him alone," Maureen protested. "He has no idea what he's saying in his condition."

"He's lucid enough."

"He's on pain medication, isn't he?" Richard questioned, holding Samantha's hand in a comforting fashion.

"Yes."

"I just can't stand to see him suffer like this anymore," Samantha blurted out, her expression agitated. "He can hardly breathe!"

"Can you put him on a respirator?" Richard wondered. Samantha looked hopeful.

"Yes, that might be a good idea," Maureen agreed. "And he is in terrible pain. I can tell."

"Is it possible to increase his medication any further?" Samantha's father ventured, concerned for Stefan and his daughter as well.

"If he's in so much agony, why not give him something to make him unconscious?" Richard asked, crossing his legs and sitting back farther on the couch. "That would be a mercy if you stop to think about it."

"The minute he asks for it, he'll get more morphine."

"Well, what about the respirator?" Maureen persisted, her hands clasped together in front of her.

"It would only make matters worse."

"But—"

"Samantha—"

"You're not trying everything you could!" she accused him, her expression fatigued.

"I'm trying to do what's best for him, Samantha. But he has a right to make his own decisions. Against my strong recommendation, he decided to forgo the surgery. He can beat the pneumonia if he still has enough strength left to fight it, but the cancer is another story."

"He should be in the hospital," Richard insisted, for the umpteenth time.

"He doesn't want to be in the hospital."

"He doesn't want to be in the hospital?" Maureen countered.

"Look, Samantha." Dr. Calderón turned to his neighbor, hoping to clarify. "Why do you think he went down to that cave? He was afraid he'd be discovered unconscious in his motel room and dragged off to the hospital. He's told me time and time again that he doesn't want to die in the hospital."

"He doesn't know what he's saying," Maureen replied, shaking her head. "He's deathly ill."

"We've got to respect his wishes," Dr. Calderón insisted, beginning to regret that he'd stopped by. He turned to Richard. "And knocking him unconscious is a heartbeat away from simply killing him."

"So you'd rather he just suffered?" Richard returned the stare.

"What are you saying, Richard?" Dr. Calderón set his empty cup on the coffee table. His demeanor had changed.

Samantha's father rose up. "Please, can I get you anything else, Doctor? You must be completely worn out."

"What I'm saying is if it's all so hopeless and he's in such terrible pain, why just let him suffer?"

"It's not within my control."

"Aw, don't give me that! It's within your control, and you know it!"

Samantha shifted on the couch, watching her neighbor's face. Dr. Calderón seemed increasingly taciturn. She wished Richard would be quiet. There had always been a surreptitious friction between the two of them, and no discreet pinch or slap on the wrist was going to stop what was coming now.

"Richard . . ." she warned, knowing it was useless.

"I'm not going to cheat him out of his last moments if that's what you are suggesting. He has a right to them. Why don't I sedate you unconscious to keep you from suffering?"

Richard frowned, startled by the strange statement. He shook his head. "What are you talking about? I'm not suffering."

"Yes, you are. We all are . . . I assure you. Samantha, you're angry because I didn't force him into an operation to try and save his life, but we all choose death every day of our lives. It's just that we don't see the immediate results, like we do in Stefan's case."

"What are you talking about?" Richard demanded, shaking his head again, this time in disbelief. "You're crazy!"

"I do not choose death," Maureen retorted.

"You do when you drink to the extent that you do."

"How dare you say something like that to me in my own house!" Maureen objected, her face an angry mask.

"I say it for your own good because I care about you."

"You're a pompous ass," Richard declared. "Just some condescending, holistic fraud who takes the easy way out by blaming everyone for their own illnesses, just so you don't have to lie awake at night worrying about your own incompetence!"

Dr. Calderón stood up, his expression maddened. "I've done everything I possibly could for Stefan. That all of you fail to recognize that is unfortunate."

Richard waved him away. "We've had enough. If you ask me, you ought to just put the poor man out of his misery. What you and Brian put him through was completely unnecessary and cruel. You gave him false hope!"

"I want you to leave, Dr. Calderón." Maureen was furious. Her affections for her former physician were unable to override his abuses. He had crossed the line with her.

"I'll leave if that's how you feel."

"That's how we *all* feel," Richard assured him.

"Miguel . . . wait!" Samantha attempted to follow him, anxious not to be cut off from Stefan.

"Sammie!" Richard pulled her back, his neck flushing with anger.

"Let go of me!" She tried to wrench her arm away.

Dr. Calderón turned to watch in alarm. Samantha's father stood up as well, growing uncertain. "Samantha . . ."

"Oh, just *leave me alone*, all of you!" she shouted, bursting into tears. She ran down the hall to her bedroom and slammed the door closed behind her.

Richard walked over to the front door and held it open for the doctor. "*Adios*."

Samantha's father tried to calm the waters. "Dr. Calderón, we wish Stefan the best. Really, we do."

Dr. Calderón attempted to step past his adversary, but Richard placed his foot in front of the doctor, forcing him to maneuver around it. "Tell Samantha I'll let her know if there's any change."

Richard slipped out after him, closing the door partway. "Just leave Samantha out of it." He reached over and gave the doctor a light shove.

Miguel turned around. "Don't touch me," he warned.

Richard stepped closer, his expression menacing. "Get out of here!"

Miguel started down the walkway but turned to glance back at Richard again. The look on the doctor's face caught him off guard, and for a fleeting moment, Richard felt afraid.

"You don't intimidate me," Miguel replied at last. He turned to leave, his shoes treading through the water on the sidewalk. The storm was over and evening was falling. The sun shone through the dark clouds on the horizon, illuminating the choppy sea. When he reached his house, the nurse was waiting for him at the door.

"How is he?"

"He's still asleep," she said.

After a brief phone call to Alicia, he seated himself next to Stefan's bed.

"I feel warm."

Miguel knelt closer. "You have a fever."

"Can you open the window?"

"You have pneumonia."

"Please?"

"You'll get chilled."

"I want to hear the ocean."

"You have a temperature of one hundred and three degrees."

"Please?" Stefan gazed at the water in the distance.

"All right, if you insist." Miguel cranked the window open, and the sound of the waves crashing below filled the room. He looked at the ocean, his heart heavy in his chest.

"I've been thinking."

Miguel turned away from the view and seated himself by the bed again. "What have you been thinking about?"

"All the people in my life who liked me."

Dr. Calderón fell quiet. The breakers crashed against the cliff. It was high tide.

"The people who really liked me. . . ."

"What about them?"

"There haven't been many."

Miguel thought of the group next door. "I suppose I could say the same."

"I don't mean 'nice.' "

"I know what you mean, Stefan."

16—El Curandero

Stefan felt cramped from being propped up so high up in the bed. He attempted to shift to a more comfortable position but then remembered, through a haze of misery, that he was gravely ill with pneumonia. He wished the nurse would leave him in peace—she continuously fretted over him in a hopeless way. Listening to the ocean, he noted how each wave pounded on the shore in a timeless rhythm, calming his spirit.

When the nurse departed at last, he opened his eyes and looked out the window at the stars. The day had long since faded away, and he wondered if tonight would be his last on earth. In his feverish state of mind, he tried to imagine a beautiful sunrise and no longer existing to see it. The morning would begin like any other—people would awaken, have their breakfasts, and start their lives anew—but he would be shut up in a drawer at the morgue. His dog would need to go for a run on the beach. Samantha would have to walk Rebel for him in the morning.

His thoughts turned to Samantha, and a great sadness filled him. She hadn't come by to see him since earlier in the afternoon. His body felt hot and yet so cold at the same time. Someone entered the room.

"Dr. Calderón?"

"He's fallen asleep." The nurse stood over him and patted his hand.

"Please don't wake him," Stefan insisted.

"All right," she replied.

The pain in his back felt excruciating—even worse than the crushing sensation throughout his chest. Lying awake for a while, he felt too much discomfort to sleep. It had been like this when he'd first arrived in Acantilado del Mar after ending his relationship with Dr. Gambian. Running out of medication and unable to refill the prescription, he'd popped over-the-counter painkillers to no avail. Night after night had been spent tossing and turning in his motel room bed in an attempt to escape the torture of his body. The agony and exhaustion defeated you in the end, he decided, not the disease.

Stefan felt a warm snuffling against his outstretched palm and became aware of Rebel by his bedside. "Good boy," he assured him, and Rebel wagged his tail against the floor. The dog ambled slowly across the room and collapsed with a grunt. His sad brown eyes still on his owner, Rebel curled up with an air of dejection and sorrow.

Stefan closed his own eyes for a moment, suffering another intense wave of pain. The aching felt so severe; each breath proved a difficult chore. He was suffocating. Stefan passed into unconsciousness again.

He dreamed he stood before the steps of a large medical complex. After checking his watch, he began the long climb leading to the front entrance. He was going to be late for his appointment.

"I'm here to see my doctor," he explained to a woman sitting behind a desk.

"What is the name of your physician?" she asked.

He couldn't recall. His mind drew a complete blank. "I can't remember."

"Is it Dr. Gambian?" she asked, picking up his chart.

"Yes, I think so," Stefan replied.

"He's right down the hall."

Walking along a passageway, he passed room after room. Time was slipping away, and he grew anxious as he checked his watch again. Dr. Gambian would be furious with him. Pausing outside a door for a moment, he decided to open it on the chance that it might be the right one.

"I'm here to see my doctor," Stefan stated to the all people in the room.

"You're late," someone remarked.

"I couldn't find this place."

Just beyond Stefan's line of vision, a man in white appeared. "You can wait in there," he informed him, pointing the way.

Stefan nodded and opened another door, this one leading to an examination room. He hopped up on the exam table in relief and waited. The door opened slowly behind him, and he turned around in expectation. To Stefan's surprise, Dr. Calderón walked in, dressed in his red poncho.

"What seems to be the problem?" he asked Stefan, standing next to him while pushing his black hair from his eyes.

Stefan jumped up again, growing alarmed. His appointment was supposed to be with Dr. Gambian, but he had inadvertently ended up in Dr. Calderón's office instead. Regretful for wasting the wrong doctor's time, he began to apologize.

"I can't seem to draw a deep breath," he pronounced instead, mystified by his own words. "I can't draw a deep breath!"

Dr. Calderón reached for a stethoscope hanging on the wall and, after lifting the patient's shirt, placed it against his back. Stefan sensed the doctor's increasing apprehension over what he discovered with each movement of the diaphragm. Dr. Calderón stepped back abruptly and dropped the stethoscope. It clattered as it hit the floor. He folded his arms around Stefan from behind and pressed his heart against the patient's back. Miguel held on for as long as he could before slowly releasing Stefan and collapsing on the floor, completely drained of all his vitality. Stefan turned and stared in disbelief at the doctor lying at his feet.

Rays of sunlight filtered through the lace curtain, and the sound of children playing in the yard greeted Stefan's ears. He heard Rebel and Toby barking. Sitting up, Stefan eased himself out of bed and trod gingerly over to the window in his bare feet. Roberto threw a stick to Rebel and his dog leaped into the air to capture it. Luis clapped his hands and laughed while Mateo played with his toys in the sandbox several feet away. In the distance, the ocean shone a brilliant blue under the morning sun. Glancing around to the side of the house, he discovered Samantha standing with Dr. Calderón at the foot of the driveway.

"How is he doing?" Samantha asked. She had hurried over upon noticing that Alicia and the boys were back. She dreaded hearing the news that Stefan had passed away in the night.

Dr. Calderón motioned toward the house. "He's much better. Come and see for yourself. When I last checked in on him, he was still asleep."

She almost collapsed with relief. "He's much better? That's

wonderful!"

They walked indoors and turned down the hall for Stefan's room. To his surprise, Dr. Calderón discovered his patient sitting on the edge of the bed, waiting for the two of them. Samantha fought to hold back tears.

Stefan rested his hands on the bed, regarding them quietly. "Hello, Samantha," he said at last.

She rushed to his bedside. "Stefan, we were worried sick about you. You're looking a lot better."

"I'm feeling much better." Rebel trotted into the room, and when Stefan held his hand out to him, the dog pressed his nose against his outstretched palm.

Dr. Calderón folded his arms across his chest. "Alicia is preparing some vegetable broth for you. Do you think you could handle that, Stefan?"

He nodded. "Yes, fine. Thank you."

"I'll be right back." Dr. Calderón disappeared, and Samantha seated herself next to Stefan on the bed. She reached for his hand and held onto it. They sat together in silence, and Rebel rested his head on Stefan's knee.

He turned to her fondly. "Will you take care of Rebel for me for a while?"

"Of course I will."

"Thanks. You're a good friend, Samantha."

"We love you so much, Stefan." She looked away, trying hard not to cry.

He squeezed her hand and patted the top of his dog's head. "I love you, too."

Dr. Calderón reappeared in the doorway. "I have to leave for a while, Stefan. I'll return later this afternoon. Alicia and the nurse will be here to look after you."

"Miguel, hold on. I need to speak to you for a minute." Stefan turned to Samantha. "Can you excuse us?"

"Sure." Samantha stood up.

"But come right back," he requested.

She laughed. "I'll go check on the soup."

"Thanks."

After she departed, Miguel closed the door behind her and settled himself next to Stefan.

Rebel placed his front paws up on Stefan's legs and he gave his dog a long hug. "I can't begin to thank you for everything you've done."

"Your recovery is thanks enough," Miguel replied.

"Yes, well . . . I'd like to go ahead and schedule that surgery."

Dr. Calderón smiled, visibly relieved. "I'm happy to hear that, Stefan. We'll have to wait a few weeks until you've recovered some strength."

"All right."

Reaching for his jacket nearby, Dr. Calderón slipped it on. "Rest up." He smiled again. "*Hasta que nos encontremos de nuevo, Estéfano.*"

The morning of the surgery, Stefan dressed hastily in his motel room while attempting to remain composed. There was no need to worry about breakfast, and after pouring dog food into Rebel's bowl, he broke out in a sweat. His recovery from the bout of pneumonia had been swift and complete. Trying to focus on the recent assurances of Dr. Calderón, he wondered why he had to behave so irrationally. His breathing felt remarkably improved. The surgery would enable him to recover the remainder of his health.

"Eat up," he instructed his dog, rolling down the top of the dog food bag in preparation to drop off Rebel and his accessories at Samantha's house. He paused to study his dog for a moment. Rebel would wonder what had become of him. With any luck, he wouldn't be in the hospital that long.

"Let's see . . ." He scanned the shelf in his cabinet. "We'll bring the doggie biscuits, chew toys, extra collar, and leash." Another wave of anxiety passed over him. Gripping the counter for support, he inhaled deeply in an attempt to steady his nerves. There was no turning back, but the idea of climbing into his car with his dog and speeding away forever held a strange appeal to him in his moment of weakness.

Minutes later, he grabbed his keys and whistled for Rebel to come. "C'mon, mutt. We have to go." Rebel trotted after him down the dingy hall of the motel and out to the car parked in the lot. Outdoors, it proved to be a drizzling, uninspiring day.

"Figures," Stefan lamented. Rebel barked once from the back seat in response. Dark thoughts again began passing through his mind as he turned onto the avenue that led to the oceanfront neighborhood close by. Dr. Calderón seemed certain of his recovery now that he had agreed to the surgery. But the ensuing medical bills would have to be paid, regardless of his current negative income. He contemplated the idea of returning to the city to recapture his former earning potential and status, but doubted his abilities, even if he were in perfect health. He no longer desired the things that had once fueled his motivation to work such impossibly long hours and endure unending stress.

He would have to pay his surgical bills, however. Also, the cancer might recur. Extensive amounts of radiation administered during his treatments with Dr. Gambian might adversely affect his future health, despite Brian's heroic efforts to flush out his body. And who would ever marry an impoverished, possibly sterile, scarred man like himself with an anvil poised over his head? There was also the possibility that once they opened him up, the situation might prove direr than his doctor had anticipated, just like the previous operation.

"Look out, moron!" someone screamed at him, passing on the right.

Picking up his speed, Stefan checked his watch and turned the wipers on. He drove the rest of the way lost in his thoughts. After pulling up in front of Samantha's house, he switched off the ignition and sat in silence for a moment.

"C'mon, Rebel, let's go!" he said at last. Rebel jumped out and Dreamer ran over from around the side of the house. The dogs romped together on the wet lawn and barked excitedly.

Samantha rushed out of the garage. "Stefan, we'd better hurry. Do you realize what time it is?"

"Yeah, I know." He grimaced. The light rain caught in his dark curls glittered like tiny diamonds.

"Here, give me Rebel's things. I'll run them inside and put the dogs in the back. My car's unlocked—go ahead and get in. Don't stand in the rain, Stefan. You'll get sick again!" Grabbing the bag of dog accessories, she vanished; and Stefan turned for her car parked in the driveway. He sat immobile in the passenger's seat, his gaze fixated on the gray, choppy water in the distance.

A minute later, she slipped into the front seat next to him and smiled. "You look like a man going to the gallows."

He sighed and shook his head. "Step on it before I change my mind."

"It'll all be over soon," Dr. Calderón remarked an hour later after Stefan had checked in and been prepped for surgery. He seated himself in a chair next to Stefan's gurney and smiled supportively. Samantha excused herself to go get some coffee.

Stefan exhaled, studying Miguel's face gratefully. Somewhere along his journey back to health, he'd acquired another heartfelt friendship. "I know, but dark thoughts have been going through my mind all morning."

"It's out of our hands now."

"I know. I'm not a trusting person."

"It won't be like the last time, Stefan; I promise."

"I'm behaving irrationally."

"It's going to be all right. We'll all help you out after you're discharged until your strength returns. Especially Samantha. Roberto has even volunteered to prepare meals for you. Alicia's been teaching him how to cook."

"I'm a lucky man," Stefan remarked, and Dr. Calderón laughed.

Two nurses appeared, and Dr. Calderón stood up to leave. "I'll see you later, Stefan."

Stefan looked at his doctor where he now stood leaning in the doorway. "Thanks, Miguel."

Stefan wound his way down the narrow beach trail, reaching out and grasping the railing whenever he felt lightheaded or weak. It was his first venture outdoors alone after Dr. Benson had deemed it prudent for him to resume living alone at his motel, and he wanted to see the ocean again. Rebel loped along ahead, occasionally glancing back at his owner to make sure all was well. Stefan reached a favorite spot up on the cliff above the water and settled on a rock with a sigh of relief. Each new day brought with it a slight increase in strength. His incision felt tender, but he was no longer on the pain medication for the cancer.

"Go ahead, boy." He motioned to Rebel to continue down to where the dog could run unimpeded on the sand. Rebel raced about, sending the sea birds scattering. The sun felt glorious on his skin, and he closed his eyes for a moment, a breeze stirring against his face. A hermit crab scurried across the rock, encountering Stefan's hand in its path. Stefan politely removed the obstacle, and the crab continued on its way, reaching a crevice in the stones where it disappeared.

"I'm going to live," he thought with trepidation, sitting alone in the sun. The beach was deserted today except for one fragile man and his dog. The moment seemed timeless, like that evening on the shoreline before Richard and his fishing buddies had arrived. Stefan gazed up and down the beach and finally at the vast ocean encompassing the horizon while breathing in deeply. "I'm going to live. . . ."

"Are you ready?" Samantha regarded Stefan with undisguised affection as he gathered up a few things for his first official checkup with Dr. Calderón since the operation.

"Yeah, in a sec. Just let me grab my journal." Opening a drawer, he extracted a notepad with doodling all over the cover. "Ready."

Before his bout with pneumonia, he had forgotten the journal on several occasions—annoying the doctor but pleasing the patient. He recalled his former glory days with his files, briefcases, folders—millions of details filed in their appropriate slots. Somehow he'd managed to do it all. Now, he couldn't even remember one item.

Samantha walked alongside him down the motel hallway, recalling the entry she had read over the doctor's shoulder that terrible rainy afternoon. Scrutinizing her friend, she wondered who the author of that baffling admission actually was. Even after all this time, she seemed not to know. He appeared happy-go-lucky this morning as he struggled along holding the notebook, wearing a grin on his face. She wished she could take a peek at the latest entries in the battered notebook. It would have interested her more than anything else in the world right now, but she didn't dare ask him.

Samantha recalled Stefan's humor as being dry and sarcastic during the early days of their friendship; but lately, he seemed uncharacteristically lighthearted and self-effacing. She attempted to ascertain when and for what reasons Richard laughed. He laughed at jokes, usually ones that poked fun at other people. It was the same with her mother. Her father she could not recall laughing at all in recent history.

"You're very pensive this morning. Are you all right?" Stefan studied her from his position next to her in the car, his expression serious and concerned. That was how it was with him. The transformations were instantaneous.

"Oh, sure. I'm fine. Just thinking about the usual stuff." She turned the key in the ignition. What else could she say? Could she admit to him how dear he had become to her or speak about the terrible night when she'd gone for a drive with Richard while Stefan hovered perilously between life and death? Despite Richard's kindness that evening, she'd only been able to think about the man now sitting next to her.

"Oh." He settled back into his seat again, lapsing into a private reverie.

As the car inched along the congested avenue, she glanced his way from time to time as they chatted, studying his face as if for the first time. With his body no longer ravaged by disease, Stefan appeared very attractive. His dark hair looked unruly and his appearance, in general, disheveled. Months earlier, no matter how ill physically, Stefan had been a meticulous dresser. Now that he was healthy, so much stronger, his appearance had gone to rack and ruin. She laughed a little.

"What's up?" he asked.

"You're wearing mismatched socks."

"Oh." He nodded. "I guess I am. I didn't think anyone would notice." It was his turn to smile fondly.

She looked away, delighted. His presence filled her with happiness. Their closeness never diminished; it only increased with each encounter. "Do you write in your journal every day?"

He considered the question for a while before answering. "Well, I'm supposed to. I slacked off for a while there. That's probably why I almost died." He laughed.

"Do you think it helps you?" she couldn't resist quizzing, interested in his reply.

"Yeah, it does. It helps me see who I really am." He leaned back more comfortably in his seat, enjoying the afternoon. "And that's important," he added, his expression once again thoughtful. "It's important to realize how unimportant all the supposedly important things we do really are." He laughed in a comical way, regarding her once again with amusement.

Samantha nodded. He certainly had been successful in the past. "Do you mean like your position at the magazine?"

"To an extent, I suppose, although I'm not sure that simply working for *Paradise* was the real problem. It was more the way I did things as opposed to what I did."

Samantha turned for the medical complex down the block. "Well, I hope you're not too hard on yourself." She cast him a doubtful look. "We all make mistakes. It's only human."

"I know."

They swerved into the lot. She switched off the engine and hurried around to assist him. He maneuvered his body out, his incision obviously still painful. He seemed a little unsteady on his feet.

"Are you okay?"

"Fine." He grinned, inhaling deeply. "I can breathe again." He drew another deep breath. "I can't tell you how good that feels."

Once inside, he checked himself in with the receptionist and Samantha excused herself to run some errands. "I'll be back in a bit, okay?"

"Sure. Thanks for driving me."

"I love helping you, Stefan." She touched his curls. He smiled and turned away.

After her departure, Stefan leafed through several magazines. He disliked waiting rooms and that would probably never change. At last, the nurse called his name and he stood up.

"How are you today, Stefan?" she asked.

"Good."

She led him into the office, and after seating himself, he glanced around in surprise. Dr. Calderón was nowhere to be seen. "He'll be right in," she assured him, closing the door behind her. The clock ticked steadily on the wall while he waited, his gaze drifting around the room. His eyes came to rest at last on the clipper ship, and rising up, he moved closer to examine it. It always drew him in, and today it seemed to hold the promise of better days ahead.

He heard a sound and turned around. Dr. Calderón was now seated at his desk, watching him. Stefan had been so absorbed in his study of the picture that he had not heard him enter the room. His doctor picked up the journal lying on his desk and opened it to the latest entry.

I dreamed I was dead and lying in a closed casket. Yet I was also present, an invisible observer standing on the sidelines. For some strange reason, I wanted to see myself in the casket. After everyone left, I lifted the lid. When I saw myself in the coffin, I felt absolutely shocked. I looked young, incredibly beautiful, and completely at peace. Then I realized that I was under water in the casket. . . .

Dr. Calderón set the journal down, glancing back over at his patient for a moment. They were both silent, the clock ticking on the wall behind them. "You are looking extremely well, Stefan."

"I feel good," he replied.

"I would like you to continue to see me every two weeks for a little while yet. Is that agreeable with you?"

"Yes."

"Are you planning to remain in town?"

"Well, I'm going to look for work. A part-time job to begin with."

"That's a good idea." The nurse appeared and stood next to Dr. Calderón. "Let's step into the next room for an examination," he requested.

Stefan appeared pleased when he emerged back out into the waiting room minutes later. Samantha stood there waiting for him. "Everything all right?" she asked, while assisting him with his jacket.

He shrugged. "Yeah, just fine. Ready to shove off?"

She tried not to laugh. "Sure, Stefan . . . but aren't you forgetting something?"

"What?" He appeared puzzled and looked at her curiously. Finally, he shook his head and shrugged. "I don't think so."

"Your journal!"

He grew embarrassed and smiled self-consciously. "Right!"

With a laugh, he hurried off to retrieve it.

Samantha filled the water dishes hanging on the sides of the cages and then stepped back to assess her charges. There was a young seagull with a broken wing, a sandpiper with a decided limp that seemed to be improving, and a fledgling robin that a friend had found in the gutter.

All three were progressing nicely, and as Dreamer sniffed curiously at the cages, Samantha wondered whether or not to take her dog for a run on the beach. Stefan was well enough now that she no longer needed to check up on him, and Dreamer missed Rebel. Perhaps she would encounter the two of them.

"Hi, Sammie."

Her heart sank when she recognized Richard's voice behind her. He was supposed to be working tonight! Turning around in his direction and filled with dread, she regarded him quietly. "Hello, Richard."

He embraced his fiancée, studying her fondly. "How are all your birds today?"

"Fine." She glanced back at the cages. "I thought you were working late tonight."

"Nope!" He clapped his hands together with enthusiasm. "Got it all done. Knew you had the night off. Want to go bowling?"

Bowling! She just wasn't in the mood. "Not really."

"Have you eaten? We could go out to La Mariposa. The *especial* this week is carne *asada* tacos. Dave says they're unreal."

La Mariposa was her favorite restaurant in Acantilado del Mar, and truthfully, she hadn't eaten; but for some strange reason, she didn't feel like going. "I've already eaten dinner," she lied, immediately feeling guilty and puzzled. Why had she lied?

"Oh, I know! How about a walk on the beach? We could take Dreamer; she looks restless."

She nodded. "All right. Let me run in and change my shoes."

Hurrying inside to her room, she slipped off her shoes and tried to shake the gloom settling in around her. What was the matter with her? Why couldn't she just be happy like she used to be? Instead, she felt an uncanny sensation of doom, as if her life were going to unravel before her eyes. A minute later, she stepped back outside.

"Ready?"

"Uh-huh."

She walked a little to the side of him and avoided holding his hand. He didn't seem to notice and busied himself tossing stones over the cliff down into the water. It bothered her that he took pleasure in this activity; it was possible he might hit something—a bird perhaps, or worse yet, a person. She didn't want to say anything, however, or criticize him. She seemed filled with nothing but denunciations for this man as of late, and it was beginning to trouble her.

"Ha! Got it!" He had been aiming for a particular rock.

They worked their way down the cliff to the sand below. Once down on the beach, Dreamer ran around looking for Rebel, and

Samantha unthinkingly scanned the shoreline for her friend. Her eyes searched for the black windbreaker he always wore, but to her sorrow, he was nowhere to be found. Where might he be tonight, she wondered, and did he think of her as often as she did of him, with so much enthusiasm and affection?

"Go for it, Dreamer!" Richard tossed a piece of driftwood to the dog, and Samantha wanted to protest, to criticize her fiancé for choosing an overly large piece of wood. He threw it too close to Dreamer as well. She held her peace, however, knowing where it might lead. A troubling change had come over her, and the dust was far from settling.

"Dreamer!" She called her dog back and tossed the heavy stick as well. Richard laughed as Dreamer leapt comically into the air after it. She began to wonder if her life with Richard was doomed to become as heavy as the stick that she had tossed against her will, full of secrets and regrets. She hoped above all that he wouldn't bring up the subject of their impending trip to Summerwood next month. It was the last thing she felt like hearing about at the moment.

"So, are you getting excited?"

"What?" She studied him nervously.

"About the trip? It's going to be a blast. I can hardly wait. I still can't believe I got those reservations. Man oh man, did I ever luck out!"

He cared more about his crummy golf game than he did her, she reasoned bitterly, angry at the world and herself. She didn't care for golf, yet her Christmas present had turned out to be a trip that he wanted to take to a golf course. Still, she wanted to see Summerwood and had told Richard as much on several occasions.

Why did she have to have this suffocating, uneasy feeling that she couldn't shake?

"So, are you excited?" he persisted, not one to let anything rest.

"Yes, I'm excited," she lied doggedly once again. She felt like a dead horse being beaten on.

Richard glanced at her doubtfully. "Well, you don't seem very excited."

"I am," she insisted, forcing a smile. "I've just been down in the dumps lately—that's all."

"Yeah, well . . . with that mother of yours, no wonder." He chuckled a little, tossing the stick again.

She remembered when they used to go on and on about her mother, joking about her and criticizing. Their mutual dislike for Maureen's badgering, overbearing demeanor was something they had once found to discuss. But now he was beginning to remind her of her mother, the way he constantly quizzed her as to her whereabouts, whom she talked to, and about what. She resented the way he gloated over her recent estrangement from Miguel, though he tried to conceal his glee. But why should she mind his being glad? Wasn't she now sharing his sentiments?

"Well," she began, attempting to seem diplomatic. "I really should have moved out a long time ago. She's been well for almost two years now."

Richard nodded, wrestling the piece of driftwood away from Dreamer again. "Yeah, but think of all the money you've saved."

It was true; living at home had enabled her to save a lot of money. That was one of Richard's favorite subjects—money. Her money would be his before too long. It made her angry that he thought of it that way—her ability to save money and not of the constant aggravation and interference she'd been forced to endure while living with her parents.

It was also true that Richard's money would be hers as well. Richard made a lot of money; he worked hard and invested his earnings. The problem lay in the indisputable fact that he loved the idea of raking even more money into his pile, whereas she didn't much care.

"There's more to life than money, Richard."

He squinted over at her, trying to decide if she was criticizing him unfairly. "Everyone knows that, Sammie, but money makes the world go round. You want kids, a house, and a decent car. You can't have that without money." He seated himself on a large rock and stared out at the ocean, his hands resting on his knees.

She considered this for a moment, settling herself on a rock next to him. Stefan once thought like that before they'd ever met. He had been just like Richard, probably worse. She thought of him now; how different he seemed from everyone else she knew! The trouble was that she'd become too admiring. Her emotions were outgrowing her means of expressing them.

For a moment, she considered Stefan as a husband. How would he support them? She tried to imagine him the father of their child, burdened down by medical bills and perhaps a reoccurrence of his illness.

"What are you thinking about?" Richard asked, startling Samantha from her private reverie.

"Nothing," she lied.

"Yes, you were," he persisted, gazing intently at her face. "What was it?"

She experienced a surge of exasperation. Now he demanded to

know every thought that passed through her mind, as if she had no right to think privately! And he talked about her mother!

"Nothing," she replied wearily, too tired to think anything false up.

"You know, Sammie, you've been acting really strange lately."

She braced herself. If only he hadn't shown up tonight. She just wasn't in the mood for this. "Richard . . ."

"I mean it! You're moody, withdrawn . . . and you don't ever want to do anything anymore." He glared at her, obviously harboring a great deal of resentment under his easygoing demeanor.

"I don't feel like talking about this." She stood up, but he reached out his arm and pulled her back. She detected anger in his touch, and that alone hurt her far worse than any words might.

"Wait a minute. You're not putting me off. I am really getting sick and tired of it. All you ever talk about anymore is Stefan. That's it. Don't you think I've noticed how you—"

"Richard, stop it. You're being ridiculous. Stefan is my friend—that's all." It infuriated her to stand accused. The man had nearly died just six weeks ago! How could he be jealous of him? It was an absolute outrage.

"Yeah, right . . . a friend. A friend you manage to spend every spare second with, excluding me every time. Poor Stefan. Stefan's going to die. Stefan is so sick. Stefan needs surgery. Look, he doesn't need you constantly—"

She wrenched her arm away and started up the beach, refusing to listen anymore. Angry tears of betrayal filled her eyes. How could he criticize her for wanting to help someone so ill? Did he own her already, her every thought and action? Was she only allowed to have feelings that he approved of and fit into his bowling schedule?

"What do you even know about it? Leave me alone!" Tears splashed down her face. She strode quickly toward home, signaling for Dreamer to come.

"Samantha!" Richard hurried after her, feeling guilty when he discovered her crying. "Samantha, wait up! I'm sorry." He walked alongside her, anxious to get through. "Really, Sammie, I shouldn't have said that about Stefan. I know you were just trying to help him."

She didn't believe he felt sorry for a minute. It was all just an empty show. He hadn't anticipated her having such a negative reaction to his accusations; he had assumed she'd cave in to his complaints like she usually did. Now he was trying to patch up the damage before things got any worse.

"Sammie!" He grew out of breath, attempting to catch up with her. "Please?"

Samantha ignored him, anxious to get away. She was so sick and tired of him and everyone else! The trouble was that she couldn't think and felt caught instead in a swirl of confusion, uneasy hunches, doubts, fears, and anxieties. She needed to catch her breath away from it all and sort it out.

"Sammie, stop!" He grabbed her arm and she turned to face him. "Hew!" He rubbed his eyes, searching for the right words to say. "Look, I'm sorry I said what I did about Stefan. Maybe I am a little jealous. I mean . . ." He pushed his hair back, looking out over the ocean for a minute. "It's been hard. Let's just try and calm down and put a little distance on all this. Tell you what. Call me when you feel better. I don't want to argue, all right?" He took her by the shoulders and held her close.

Her heart felt heavy like a stone. "All right."

"Good." Richard smiled, feeling reassured. He certainly did not want to break off the relationship and he realized he would have to walk on eggshells from now until the wedding. His bride-to-be had always been somewhat moody and unpredictable. Still, this latest obsession with the cancer victim was really upsetting him. The situation had worsened now that the guy was apparently on the mend. With any luck, Stefan would be returning to the city soon to resume his former career, although it was difficult for Richard to imagine the curly haired nutcase being editor in chief of *anything*, much less *Paradise Magazine*.

"I'll talk to you later, all right?" He kissed Samantha goodbye and left her standing on the beach. As he walked away, he prided himself on how sensitively he'd handled the affair. He hadn't lost it! How he'd wanted to! But he would have come across as insensitive, and women didn't like that. Ascending the beach stairwell several minutes later, he checked his watch. If he hurried, he might be home in time to catch the end of his favorite wrestling show.

While standing on the beach and watching her fiancé depart, Samantha wondered at the change that had come over her. A few months ago, she would have felt touched by the tenderness and respect Richard had just shown her. But now she felt as empty as the sand stretching out in front of her. She felt nothing. It was all just a show—he'd wanted to wring her neck. But Richard played to win, and his being nice would eventually get him what he wanted.

Trudging slowly for home, she began to feel sorry for herself. No one really cared about her—not Richard, her mother, or even her girlfriends. Her friends confided in her and she sympathized with all their problems, but in the end, they never really listened to a word she said. Neither did her mother or Richard. Her father was the most painful of all to consider. Her relationship with him felt completely hollow—lifeless.

"Dreamer, come!" She clapped to Dreamer before climbing the stairwell. At the top, Dreamer raced down the trail ahead of her. She observed her dog disappear into Dr. Calderón's garden behind a grove of trees.

"Dreamer, get over here!"

Peering through the Torrey pines, she heard the wind's ghostly murmur through the boughs and spied Miguel in his red poncho hiking down the bluffs to the beach below. For a moment, she considered going after him and apologizing for her behavior on that dreadful night Stefan nearly died but thought the better of it. Truthfully, her neighbor, despite her previous testimonials on his behalf, continued to distress her. She was the one who had taxied Stefan to all of his appointments, helped with his shopping and errands, and cared for Rebel in weeks past; yet Stefan seemed to be turning increasingly to Miguel as a friend and disregarding her. She felt pushed aside and, much to her dismay, increasingly jealous. Starting for home, she decided to seek out her own solitude instead and try to sort out the tangle of conflicting feelings stirring within her soul.

Stefan reclined on his bed in his motel room and studied the balance in his checkbook. His funds were getting low. He'd reached an agreement with social services regarding his medical bills, but he still needed to eat and pay his motel bill. It seemed hard to believe that his money was nearly gone. His large stock portfolio created from saving and investing while at the magazine had been depleted even before his most recent surgery. In short, he was flat broke.

"Rebel, come." He reached for the leash on the table, prepared to spend the day on the beach while thinking his future over. Rebel wagged his tail, anxious to be on their way.

Outside, the white blanket of fog rolled slowly back from the oceanfront, and he breathed the moist, salty air deep into his lungs. It felt so incredible to be able to inhale completely again and walk upright as opposed to being bent over like an old man. Walking the five blocks to the beach, he smiled at everyone he passed, whether they liked it or not.

Up on the cliff ablaze with lavender phlox, he gazed out over the sea beyond. He never tired of the view; every day it appeared altered, completely new. Today the aqua blue water sparkled in the bright sunlight, the white foam from the waves accentuating it brilliantly.

"I feel pretty darn good today," he exclaimed to his dog, laughing a little. He wore his curly hair long and uncombed. They walked along down on the beach, sea birds circling all around and calling out above them. He settled in his favorite place, spreading his beach towel flat and lying back on the warm sand. Thinking for a moment of Dr. Calderón, he found himself looking forward to their follow-up visits together now that he no longer viewed the physician as an adversary. In the interim, he would either need to return to the city for employment or remain in Acantilado del Mar and work. He didn't relish the idea of living in the congested city again, but what could one possibly find for employment in this quaint seaside town? He possessed no marketable job skills beyond his abilities as a journalist.

"Stefan, hello!" Samantha appeared in the distance with Dreamer. She waved in his direction.

He motioned her over. "Samantha, come here!"

Smiling, she complied. The dogs quickly met forces and began a wrestling match close by.

"How are you, Stefan?" Dressed in shorts and a tee shirt, she carried a beach towel rolled under one arm.

"I'm doing great. Why don't you join me?" He pointed next to him.

"All right." She unrolled her towel and laid it out on the warm sand, happiness filling her. She hadn't seen Stefan in over a week and missed him terribly. The purpose of her trek down on the beach had been to potentially meet up with him. She disliked calling him all the time. He rarely called her, and she felt like a pest.

"Do you have the day off?"

She nodded. "Yes, I'm so glad, too. It's such a beautiful day." She noticed his journal lying next to him.

He followed her eyes. "Yep, still keeping the journal."

She frowned, growing curious. "What else does he have you do?"

Stefan lay back on the sand and stared at the sky. "Oh, lots of stuff."

"Does Dr. Sandler still have you on a special diet?"

"Yeah." He nodded. "Only it's not so special anymore. I eat the way I'm supposed to eat and forego all the garbage I used to put in my body."

"I see." It was fun and interesting to be around Stefan, and she treasured their every moment together. She found that with each encounter, they grew just a little bit closer. The phenomenon felt positively magical.

"That's what's so great about the journal, too. The things I used to think were like all the junk I used to eat. It becomes really obvious when you write them down and then read it all later."

"What about the things you write now?" she questioned, wishing she could open his journal and take a peek. "What are they like?"

Stefan turned to study her with amusement. "Actually, nothing so profound." He seemed embarrassed. "Just . . . the changes I've been through. I've changed a lot, I suppose."

It was true; he had changed in the short time they'd known each other. No one else seemed to change. She pondered this thought for a moment, wondering if people were *supposed* to change all the time. She thought of the people she knew and how constant they seemed. Perhaps you changed during the tumultuous times, like during an illness.

"Yes, I think you have," she admitted. "You've changed."

"You didn't know me before either." He smiled and shook his head. "Lucky you."

Obviously, Stefan possessed a great potential for change. She wondered what her possibilities might be. "I like you now, Stefan." Samantha wanted him to know how much she valued their friendship. The thought of Stefan moving away filled her with dread.

"I like you, too." He glanced her way again.

"What are your plans?" She hated to pry but had to know.

He shrugged, pushing the dark curls back from his face. "I guess I'll have to get a haircut."

She giggled, admiring his cascade of curls. They were nearly the same length as her own. "Be serious."

"I am serious." He studied her, still smiling. "I do know one thing: if you and I were ever to get married . . ."

"What?" The statement caught her off guard.

"The children would all have our hair!" He laughed again, lying back in the sand. "But honestly, what am I going to do? I'm going to stay here and finish my treatment with Dr. Calderón, and I'm also going to get a temporary job."

She breathed a surreptitious sigh of relief. He was going to remain in Acantilado del Mar for now. "You're going to get a job? Are you sure you're up to that so soon?"

He sat up. "I have no choice. I'm nearly broke."

"What sort of job are you looking for?"

"I have no idea."

"Well, how about the paper? It's not the greatest publication, but I'm sure they'd jump at the chance to hire someone with your qualifications."

He shook his head. "No, the news has never been a big interest of mine, and besides, I think I'd like to try to do something else. Something new."

"Oh." She fell silent. He didn't want to return to the publication world right away. "Well, you could work for us. We'd pay you."

"You mean at the restaurant?"

"No, silly. I meant our newsletter."

"Sure, Samantha." He appeared amused. "With what? You're barely clearing expenses right now as it is, remember?"

"Yeah." It had been a dumb offer.

"I'd like to try something different," he said, scanning the beach for the dogs. They were running up the cliff after a rabbit. "Rebel, come here!"

Samantha turned to look. "Dreamer!" She glanced back at Stefan. "Whatever you find to do, I'm sure you'll be very good at it."

"Rebel!" he called once again. The dogs were out of sight now.

"I'll go get them," she offered.

"That's okay. Let me do it." He flashed her a beautiful smile and took off for the bluff.

Watching him depart, she grew amazed by how fit he already seemed. While still thin, he no longer appeared ill in any way. Once he disappeared from sight, her gaze fell on the journal, and she felt the temptation to peek inside. It would be a terrible invasion of his privacy. But Samantha couldn't resist, and opening it carefully, she scanned the page.

I passed by two addicts down on the beach last night. As I watched them, I wondered if I wasn't an addict too. I was an addict in my own right, a distraction addict, chasing after my next fix.

He compared himself to an addict? He was too hard on himself! Oddly, her initial glimpse of him ten months earlier had evoked the same thought, but now she considered Stefan to be one of the most beautiful people she had ever known. She continued reading:

To be truly alive requires some vulnerability—a softness, a place to be wounded. So I don't think it's a good idea to build a fortress around myself and become too tough or implacable. People like that lose all their charm. This mysterious softness cannot be faked with kind words or acts; it's either there or it's not. It's a way to survive, this toughness, but in the end you survive only to lose yourself. I don't want to ever lose myself again.

Setting the journal down, she watched Stefan and the dogs approach. She didn't know what to think about the entries in the journal, and she couldn't ask him because she'd invaded his privacy.

"There!" Stefan collapsed on his towel. "Jeez, they must have spring fever or something. They didn't listen to me at all when I called to them."

"Yeah, Dreamer has been a real pill lately. She behaved like this last year in the spring."

"I love spring," he confided, lying down again. "Everything is starting over."

He was beginning anew, she reasoned, and Samantha wondered what he would do with the rest of his life—what his long-term plans were. She didn't want to ask, but the day he left Acantilado del Mar for good would be a terrible one for her.

"How are things going with Dr. Calderón now that the surgery is behind you?" she asked, still wondering about the strange entries in the journal.

"Not too badly," he admitted, the breeze tousling his curls. "Now that we don't argue about cutting me open any longer." He hadn't shaved for a few days. His tennis shoes were worn to shreds and he wasn't wearing any socks.

"Oh, that's good." Observing his appearance more closely, she felt tempted to grow critical. He appeared to be getting lazy. Even in his "sick" days, he had taken more care with his appearance. How much effort did it require to shave in the morning?

"I'm finished with Brian though. He said I didn't have to come back anymore."

"That's good." He sported a terrific suntan. She wondered what he found to do with himself all day long besides sit around on the beach. His only responsibilities were to walk his dog and show up for doctor appointments. The only reason he felt compelled to seek employment was because he had run out of money. "Are you going to work full time?"

He shrugged. "I hope not. I'd rather work part time. I don't really need that much money, just enough to clear expenses."

She wondered why she felt so critical of him all of a sudden. The poor man had nearly died a few short months ago. His blasé attitude bothered her, she decided, not without a twinge of guilt. He seemed so happy without anything. Unless one worked toward a goal in life, there was a danger of ending up a deadbeat, of no earthly use to anyone. "What are your long-term plans?" she could no longer resist asking.

He laughed with delight. "You mean, what do I want to be when I grow up?" He rubbed his nose, feeling childish. He sensed her judgement toward him and found it entertaining.

"Well, Stefan, you have so much talent."

"Do I?" He was still smiling.

"Of course you do, and you know it. Anyone who was editor in chief for *Paradise Magazine* as young as you were . . ." She realized she didn't know his age and decided to ask. "How old are you?"

"Twenty-seven." His expression grew serious. "It wasn't solely talent, Samantha; it was drive and ambition. I don't have that anymore. I suppose I still have motivation but for different things. I hope to pursue other objectives now."

"You'd never work for the magazine again?" She had held this image of him returning to his former employment and regaining the status robbed from him by disease, but this time with more poise and calm. She was ashamed to admit it, but she had even gone so far as to imagine him returning to Acantilado del Mar and asking her to marry him—that was, before she married Richard—a daydream motivated by her deepening affection toward him and her recent disenchantment with her fiancé. But his worn shoes and nonchalant attitude were beginning to alarm her.

"I'm never going back to that life, Samantha."

"You liked helping me and my friends with our publication."

"I liked *helping you*."

"Oh." What could she say? It seemed disappointing, and she felt increasingly uneasy about her own life.

"It's getting really warm out," he remarked, sitting up on his elbows. He felt like peeling off his shirt but only did that while alone on the beach. However, he had to face the fact that his body was scarred, front and back, and that it felt hot today in the sun. Removing his shirt under the present circumstances seemed a perfectly normal thing to do while sunbathing on the sand.

"It is hot today," she agreed, wishing she had worn her suit.

Still feeling uncomfortable, Stefan slipped off his shirt, and the warm sun caressed his skin. It felt wonderful to expose his maimed body to the sunlight.

It shocked her deeply to see his scars. How much he must have suffered! She felt guilty for wanting to throw him back out into the rat race again. Tears filled her eyes; she couldn't help herself.

He glanced over at her in surprise. "Samantha . . ."

"I'm so sorry." She wiped them away. "I just can't stand thinking about how much you've been through."

With a sigh and shake of his head, Stefan settled himself once again on his warm beach towel, basking comfortably in the sun. "It's all good, Samantha."

Samantha grew quiet and reflective. He dozed off beside her and she studied his profile. Despite his scars and lack of interest in his personal appearance, he appeared young and vibrant. Stefan was a very beautiful man again.

"Stay," Stefan commanded Rebel, his voice deep with authority. Lately his dog had been disregarding his orders when his back was turned, as if he suddenly possessed more knowledge and intelligence than his owner and therefore could override his commands. It amused Stefan; it was a sure sign of his health having been restored. Animals knew things, sensed changes. It had saddened Stefan to see his young dog become so docile and ingratiating during the past year. But now Rebel was back to normal with a little dose of spring fever thrown in. Collapsing down on the grass in front of the medical center, Rebel looked purposely away, the whites of his eyes wide with guilt.

"You'd better stay," Stefan warned, clutching his journal. "Or I'll leave you locked up in the motel room next time."

"Hi-ya, doggie!" Two little girls waved to Rebel from the walkway, their mother close behind. Rebel tensed, about to go after them, his face a hopeful mask.

"Rebel!" Stefan eyed him with warning, and the dog sank to the lawn, still refusing to meet his owner's eye. Kneeling down, Stefan held Rebel's head in his hands, forcing the dog to look at him. "You stay."

Rebel pulled his head free, wagging his tail. Somewhat satisfied, Stefan started up the sidewalk for Dr. Calderón's office, feeling relaxed and at peace in the warm spring air. Everything appeared dazzling and fresh this morning; birds trilled in the trees and children laughed.

Once inside, he checked in and seated himself along the wall, selecting a magazine about the coastline. He leafed through it slowly, studying the beautiful photos and scanning the feature article. He heard his name called.

"Hello, Stefan." Dr. Calderón cast a quick smile from across the room where he was busy watering his plants on the shelf above his desk.

"Hi, Doc." He returned the smile and sat on the couch. It seemed like an eternity since his first visit to this office. Dr. Calderón walked over and stood next to him, and Stefan handed him the journal. The doctor seated himself on the sofa and began to read through the latest entries with an intrigued expression.

I dreamed about a little boy and a girl that nobody wanted. It upset me that they were orphans, so even though I was penniless, I took them home. The little girl told me she was a dancer. I brought her to dance classes and went to all of her performances.

Dr. Calderón turned the page.

The boy had never slept in a bed of his own before, so I bought him one. I didn't have much money; I could only provide him with a mattress on the floor. But he was so happy to see it that he ran to it. As he passed by me, he smiled, and to my surprise, I realized he only had one eye—in the center of his forehead.

Dr. Calderón closed the journal and handed it back to Stefan. "You can do it, Stefan. You can pick up your life and start over again."

"I know. I'm scared sometimes, though."

"So am I." Dr. Calderón admitted. "That's okay."

An examination followed, and Dr. Calderón noted an eight-pound weight gain since the surgery, a stellar accomplishment. He reached for his stethoscope hanging on the wall. "Do you plan to stay in town for a while?" He positioned the diaphragm of the stethoscope against Stefan's back while listening carefully.

Stefan thought of his dream about Miguel the night he almost died. "Yes, for now."

"Good." He nodded.

Minutes later, they finished the examination. "Everything is looking as I expected it would, Stefan. I'm exceedingly pleased. Do you have any questions for me at this point?"

Stefan cleared his throat. "Actually, there is one. Do you think I'll be able to have children?" He was thinking about the future now beyond walking his dog on the beach and landing a temporary job.

"I can't really answer that question. But I strongly sense that there are children in your future, Stefan."

Slipping his shirt over his head again, Stefan breathed deeply. His life stretched out ahead of him. He would be celebrating his twenty-eighth birthday soon. "Thank you." He extended his hand.

The doctor accepted it and smiled. "It's been my pleasure to have you for a patient. See you later, Stefan."

Once outside in the bright sun again, Stefan glanced around in annoyance for his dog. Rebel was nowhere in sight. Scanning the courtyard, Stefan attempted to locate him. A group of college students sprawled on the grass, socializing and eating their lunches. Rebel sat in the middle of them, his tongue lolling out and a Frisbee between his legs. Stefan strode in their direction.

"Rebel!"

Rebel cocked his ears and wagged his tail, making no attempt to get up from his position of comfort.

"Is this your dog?" one of the students asked.

"Yes." Stefan clapped his hands and Rebel sauntered over.

"He's a nice dog. Very friendly."

"Thanks." Stefan nodded. "I hope he didn't bother you or anything."

"Oh no, he's great. Doesn't listen, though."

Stefan snapped on the leash. "Yeah, I know. You can say that again."

"It's a beee-utiful morning, isn't it?" Richard smiled around him as he wiped his face with a napkin and took another sip of champagne.

"That it is," Maureen agreed, finishing her Denver omelet and nodding her head in agreement. "It's been such a lovely spring. I can't recall a springtime this beautiful ever in Acantilado del Mar, and we've had some delightful seasons. Can you, dear?" she requested of her husband, who was seated across the table.

"No, I can't. It certainly is unusual. I heard on the radio the other day that the colder winter, late rains, and then the sudden warming trend caused this burst of bloom. Everything seems to be flowering all at once this year."

The terrace garden where they dined was a riotous mass of bloom and color. Samantha poked at her food, thinking, as she usually did, of Stefan. He was not supposed to have survived to see this spring, yet he had, and it had turned out to be the most beautiful ever. She contemplated that irony.

Stefan's former physician, Dr. Gambian, sat dining across the terrace from their table, apparently clued in to Acantilado del Mar's sudden transformation as well. The tourist trade in their little town appeared to be booming. Seated across from the doctor was an enchanting woman who Samantha supposed was his wife, along with another well-dressed couple.

In his late forties and donning an air of great importance, the gentleman reminded Samantha of a doctor. The conversation at their table grew noisy and animated.

"Lively bunch, aren't they?" Richard commented, noting her observation of the foursome.

She nodded, sipping her champagne. "Yes."

"A little tipsy, I'd say," Maureen commented, none too sober herself.

"A hell of a doctor," Richard began and then stopped, suddenly conscious of a truth he disliked. If Dr. Gambian happened to be so exceptional, why was a formerly doomed patient of his—who had left him for a second-rate stand-in—now walking the streets of Acantilado del Mar, apparently a well man? He didn't feel like contemplating that fact; the morning was far too comfortable.

Samantha pondered the contradiction, however, growing thoughtful. The more she watched the doctor, the less she liked him. He dominated the conversation, waving his arms for emphasis and casting the beautiful woman absent looks whenever she tried to get a word in edgewise. He called all the shots. She felt like walking over to his table and informing him of Stefan's recovery. For some reason, the man irritated her, and she wanted to burst his proud bubble. But it was unlikely a busy physician like Dr. Gambian would even remember a former patient, and besides, it was none of her business.

It irritated Richard that his fiancée appeared so focused on the doctor. The man held a connection to her all-time favorite person: Stefan. He wished Stefan would just leave Acantilado del Mar for good. He seemed well enough now, and what possible future could their little town hold for the former highflying journalist?

"Bet he rakes in a lot of dough," Richard commented, attempting to draw her back to their table. He was shelling out a lot of money to treat her and her folks to brunch this morning, and she couldn't even bother engaging in a conversation with him.

"Yes." She appeared to be limiting all her responses to monosyllables. Richard rubbed his clenched jaw.

Samantha continued her inward musings. Stefan was penniless; the doctors and hospitals had taken it all. Now, barely recovered, he needed to go out and slave to stay alive. Meanwhile, Dr. Gambian sat here like a fat cat, hogging the conversation, disrupting everyone else's meal with his loud banter, and acting like a god with his Mercedes Benz parked out front. Her animosity grew.

Richard felt flushed around the collar. He didn't know how much more he could take. "Having a nice brunch?" he offered, feeling like tipping the table over.

She wrenched her thoughts away from Dr. Gambian. "What?"

"I said . . . are you having a nice brunch?"

"Oh. Yes." She smiled insincerely. "Thank you for treating us, Richard." He always had to be thanked ten times for everything he did. He placed so many conditions on his love. It was a necessity to constantly bow and scrape with your gratitude or he wasn't satisfied. She hadn't even wanted to come to brunch in the first place; he had coerced her by inviting her parents first and then getting her to agree.

"You're welcome." His expression remained grim.

Evidently, she hadn't sounded convincing enough and needed to bow and scrape some more. To her surprise, she discovered

226

Stefan standing in the entrance of the terraced dining area. She almost failed to recognize him at first, he looked so changed. He had cut his hair and appeared stylishly attired for the occasion. The host appeared, questioned him, and led Stefan to an empty table. On the way, he spotted them and, smiling reservedly, started over.

"Oh, great," Richard muttered under his breath. Stefan's appearance alarmed him. The curly headed nutcase now appeared startlingly attractive.

Samantha came to life, her expression pleased and animated all at once. "Stefan, hello!"

"Hello, Samantha." He smiled at the rest of the group as well.

"Stefan, you look fabulous." Maureen removed her glasses from her purse and slipped them on. She seemed unable to believe her eyes.

"Stefan, you're well now," Samantha's father marveled, his expression astonished.

"Well, close to it."

Samantha couldn't stop staring. He was cleanly shaven, the curls were gone, and he wore nice-fitting clothes. The transformation proved nothing short of astounding.

Richard recalled his first encounter with Stefan at Maureen's garden party. It just didn't seem possible. "Why are you here?" he asked rudely.

"I'm meeting someone."

"Well, how are doing, Stefan?" Maureen asked. "Have you found a job yet?"

"Yes." Stefan smiled again, and Samantha's heart skipped a beat. The bizarre exchange felt like a mind-boggling dream.

"That's wonderful, Stefan!" she responded with so much enthusiasm that Richard winced. "Where?"

"At the mall."

"The mall?" Maureen blurted. "Doing what?"

"Cleaning up."

"Cleaning up?" Samantha grew astonished. He couldn't mean he was going to be a janitor?

Richard appeared all smiles. He rubbed his eyes, attempting to contain his glee. The guy was going to sweep up at the mall and empty the trash bins. He laughed under his breath. "Congratulations."

"Well, my hat's off to you, Stefan." Samantha's father nodded his support.

"Who are you meeting?" Samantha asked, attempting to recover herself. It made her livid the way Richard kept laughing up his sleeve.

"There he is now," Stefan announced, and the group turned to discover Miguel. "We're celebrating."

Samantha felt her heart pierced. He and Dr. Calderón were celebrating—with her conspicuously absent. Stefan hadn't even called her and told her of his new job. She felt like crying but concealed her emotions. It would have been so wonderful to brunch with Stefan and Dr. Calderón instead of sitting here bored to death with her parents and Richard.

"*Hola a todos.*" Dr. Calderón nodded politely to the group, presenting a striking appearance himself.

"Hello," Maureen replied, her expression grim. She was still nursing a grudge. Richard refused to acknowledge the doctor's presence at all.

"Well, shall we find our table?" he asked Stefan. Stefan was staring across the crowded terrace, his expression sober. Dr. Calderón's eyes followed Stefan's gaze, coming to rest at last on the loudly conversing Dr. Gambian.

Stefan forced himself to look away. "We already have a table. Have a nice afternoon, everyone. Maybe I'll see you later, Samantha."

"All right, Stefan." She watched them depart.

They seated themselves, and Dr. Calderón glanced at Stefan. "Are you okay with this situation, Stefan? We can always go someplace else."

"No, I'm fine. Actually, I was thinking about crawling over there and saying hello to him." He chuckled and studied the menu.

Dr. Calderón laughed. "I personally recommend the asparagus frittata. It's excellent."

"Sounds good." Stefan frowned, listening to Dr. Gambian's voice. "Go ahead and order that for me. If you'll excuse me for a moment, I'll be right back."

Dr. Calderón nodded in acknowledgement as Stefan arose and walked over to the table across the room. Seconds later, he stood next to Dr. Gambian and waited. At last, Dr. Gambian ceased talking and looked up at him. "Yes, can I help you?" he asked.

"I just wanted to stop by and say hello," Stefan replied.

Dr. Gambian appeared uncertain. "I'm sorry, but I'm drawing a blank."

"Stefan Campeau."

Dr. Gambian frowned and shook his head, still mystified.

"I was a patient of yours last year."

Surprise and then shock slowly registered on the physician's face. "Uh . . . hello."

"I wanted to let you know that I'm doing okay now."

Dr. Gambian wiped his face with a napkin to conceal his discomfiture and tore his gaze away. "I see."

Returning to his companion again, Stefan moved his chair closer to the table. "I'm famished. Did you order yet?"

Dr. Calderón nodded. "Yes, I requested the frittata for you."

"Wonderful."

Samantha noted Stefan at Dr. Gambian's table and strained to overhear. It proved impossible; the place was too noisy. After Stefan reseated himself at his own table again, she noticed that Dr. Gambian grew quiet and glanced repeatedly at Dr. Calderón and Stefan. Something appeared to be troubling him. When his party rose to leave, he walked directly over to Stefan and stood next to him. They engaged in conversation for a few moments, after which Dr. Gambian extended his hand to Stefan and then Dr. Calderón.

Richard was watching as well. "A meeting of the minds," he commented sarcastically.

"Doctors . . ." Maureen uttered. "They're all alike. I'm surprised the other one isn't around."

A moment later, Richard spotted a mop of blond hair on the street below and observed Brian locking his bike into the bike rack. "Speak of the devil."

"Why can't you just be happy?" Samantha demanded, tears filling her eyes. "What is the matter with you?" she asked her mother, wiping them away. "Miguel helped you when you needed it. Where is your gratitude?"

"Samantha, calm down. You're making a scene." Maureen glanced around the crowded dining room.

Stefan looked over, noting Samantha seemed upset. He started up, but Dr. Calderón motioned him to stay put. "Please, Stefan, let it go."

"It bothers me to see her like that."

"I know, but our interfering will only make it worse."

Out on the front sidewalk a minute later, Samantha felt so angry and tearful that she had trouble deciding with whom she felt like riding back the least—her parents or Richard. She finally climbed into Richard's truck, hoping he'd sulk all the way back to her house in silence. With her mother, there'd be no such chance.

Once they pulled out into the street, however, he let loose. "That was one hell of a lousy brunch. I'm telling you . . . if you don't pull yourself together, the trip is off."

"I don't want to go on the trip anymore."

"You don't want to go on the trip anymore. Fine, I'll ask Dave instead. He's a hell of a lot more fun than you are lately."

"Good." She lapsed into silence.

"Samantha . . ." He eyed her sullenly. "I think we ought to reconsider getting married." Allowing the gravity of his words to sink in, he hoped to shock her back to reality. If only Stefan were out of the picture for good! There was absolutely no reasoning with her as long as the whimsical man was around. "I can't live like this with all your moods. Your mother is really moody, do you realize that?"

He was comparing her to her mother again. How she hated that! She no longer cared if they were married or not. Anxiety filled her. After Stefan left town, then what? She remembered her mother's dream. In the dream, they had to call off the wedding. It was ludicrous, all of it!

"You know, I think you're spellbound."

"What?"

"Spellbound . . . by the inscrutable healer extraordinaire, Miguel Calderón. He's really got you going. Samantha, your father's a milquetoast. He's completely unavailable. Along comes Miguel with his metaphysical doublespeak and you're hooked. I mean, if you could only see yourself when he's around. You're practically in thrall to him."

"That's not true!"

"Yes, it is! The trouble is you're not some little girl anymore—you're twenty-six years old."

"He hasn't cast a spell on me," Samantha groaned, pressing her face against the passenger's window in despair.

"He has all the answers, and he's going to tell everyone else how to live their lives." Richard shook his head. "He showed up at a council meeting last week demanding we ban weed killer in Acantilado del Mar. He says it causes cancer." Richard laughed.

"He has a right to his opinions. You're a very opinionated person, Richard."

"That's right, but I don't try to ram my opinions down everyone else's throats!"

"He doesn't either."

"The hell he doesn't. He wants to make the entire world over exactly in his image. Underneath all that understanding and perceptibility is just another fascist."

"I'm not going to listen to any more of this." She felt like opening the door and throwing herself down on the pavement.

"Do you want to get out here?" He turned to study her, his expression intense.

"Let me out."

"Fine." He careened to a stop.

She barely had time to dismount before he pulled away. Samantha watched him depart in a cloud of diesel fumes. He could have injured her. What she really needed to do was move far away from Acantilado del Mar. It wouldn't be enough to simply break up with Richard. Their paths were bound to cross constantly, and besides, her mother would badger her for years over the broken engagement. But she couldn't leave. Something was holding her here like an anchor. She didn't want to lose Stefan.

21—*La Despedida*

Samantha seated herself on the bench inside the mall entrance minutes before it closed and glanced around for Stefan. She hadn't seen him in almost two weeks. He and his friend Handy were frequently out of town surfing or backpacking on their time off, and she missed him. Glancing down the nearly deserted beige corridor, Samantha sighed as the elevator music droned on around her. A moment later, she spotted Handy approaching.

"Hi, Handy." She waved.

Handy smiled upon recognizing her and tucked his long blond hair behind his ears. "Hello, Sammie. How are ya?"

"I'm fine. Is Stefan working today by chance?"

"Uh-uh." He shook his head. "He quit."

"He quit?" She felt momentarily stunned. "When?"

Handy squinted, thinking back. "About a week ago."

After recovering from her surprise, she grew uneasy. She knew he wouldn't work cleaning at the mall for long, but he hadn't called to update her regarding his plans. She and Richard were no longer engaged. Richard maintained that she'd eventually see the light and considered it temporary insanity. Her mother harangued her over it constantly, compelling her to rent an apartment downtown. She was all set to move in next week.

"Did he get another job?"

"Yeah, I guess so."

Handy seemed evasive, like he wasn't telling her everything. He also appeared anxious to get back to work, so Samantha stood up, preparing to leave herself. "Okay, thanks Handy. See you later."

"See ya."

On her way home, she decided to swing by the Budget Motel and see if he might be there. She disliked doing it; it bruised her feminine pride to resort to hounding the man, but she couldn't control her affection and curiosity. Standing outside the front door of his room, she knocked lightly. There was no answer.

A housekeeper dragging a vacuum cleaner looked over at her from across the deck. "He's not here anymore."

Samantha frowned. "Really?"

"Yeah. He checked out about week ago."

"Thanks." Returning to her car in the lot, she assessed the situation. He was no longer living in the motel. He must have rented an apartment around town. It seemed a positive step—quitting his janitorial job and moving out of the shoddiest motel in Acantilado del Mar. As she turned the key in the ignition, she resolved to be patient. He'd call and inform her of his new address and phone number when he was ready. She was busy enough herself with her own problems—moving out, her recent job promotion to assistant manager at the restaurant, the bird sanctuary, and the publication. The newsletter had grown into a small magazine, thanks to Stefan's assistance. With his help, they'd drawn out a master plan and devised a way to expand in increments.

When she arrived home, Dreamer greeted her at the door, leaping up on her and barking excitedly. "No, Dreamer, down!"

she scolded, waving the dog away.

"Take her for a run, Samantha. She's been driving me crazy all day."

"All right." It irritated her how her mother handed out an order the moment she stepped into the doorway.

Maureen continued to glare. "Oh, and you had a visitor today." Her tone did not sound pleased.

"Stefan?" she asked, feeling hopeful.

Her mother's expression grew stony. "No, not Stefan. Dr. Calderón stopped by to see you." The ice had still not shifted between her mother and the doctor.

"Oh." She wondered what he could possibly want. "I'll stop by and see him after I walk Dreamer. Did he say what he wanted?"

"No, and I didn't ask." She returned to her magazine, the subject closed.

Once down on the beach, Samantha breathed easy. The lovely spring afternoon felt warm and breezy. Summer was fast approaching, and she wondered what her favorite season might bring. Walking along the scenic shoreline, she felt optimistic and filled with anticipation. The wedding had been officially called off to her immense relief. Richard insisted it was merely postponed. "You're going to miss me when I'm gone," he'd promised her, a sulky arrogance in his eyes. She didn't miss him so far.

"Dreamer, come!" They'd walked a long way, but her dog wanted to remain on the beach. Perhaps she was searching for Rebel. With a sigh, she turned around and began the trek home, Dreamer close by her side. At the top of the stairs, she discovered Dr. Calderón waiting for her at the edge of the bluff.

"Hello, Samantha."

She smiled. "Hello, Miguel. My mother told me you stopped by. I was just on my way to see you."

"Why don't we go over to the garden and talk?" He motioned toward a bench in Alicia's vegetable patch.

She seated herself on the iron seat, and he sat beside her. "Dr. Calderón, do you know where Stefan is?" she asked, certain he would know. "I just found out that he quit his job and isn't living at the motel anymore."

"Samantha, that's what I wanted to speak to you about. Stefan's left town. He's not living in Acantilado del Mar any longer."

A shock wave hit her. "Where did he go?"

"He's moved away, Samantha."

It couldn't be true! He would never leave without saying good-bye to her. "Where did he go?"

"Up the coast someplace. I'm not exactly sure where."

"What?" She couldn't believe her ears.

"A friend offered him a job, and he decided to take it."

"I can't believe it."

"He told me to say goodbye for him."

He'd told Dr. Calderón to say goodbye for him! It was beginning to penetrate.

"I realize how difficult this is." He reached for her hand. She quickly pulled away. "He's going to come back, Samantha. You'll see him again."

"When?" she asked, barely a whisper.

"He's returning next April for a medical check."

He would return in April? That was practically a year away! And he was coming back for a medical examination, not to see her!

Anger filled her. After all she had done for him . . . he couldn't even bother to say goodbye.

"Samantha . . ." His voice sounded oddly composed. ". . . This was a difficult decision for Stefan."

She stood up, tears in her eyes. "Oh, I'm sure it was. Asking you to say goodbye for him. I'm sure it must have been—"

"No." Dr. Calderón stood up abruptly and shook his head. "That's not it."

"No? Then tell me how it was, since you always seem to have all the answers!"

"I advised him not to say goodbye. He'd grown too emotionally involved with you, Samantha."

"*You* didn't want him to say goodbye to me?" The last few times they'd spent time together there had been a subtle shift in their friendship. She would have been able to change his mind about leaving.

"Yes, that's right." Dr. Calderón appeared resolute. "I advised against it."

"You had no right to interfere."

"I felt I had no choice in the matter."

"It's none of your damn business!"

"At this critical juncture, we have to consider what's best for Stefan."

"You think I'm not good enough for him because of Richard . . . you can't stand him!" Rage filled her. "You're just jealous of how close Stefan and I were becoming!" She tried to clamp her emotions down and control her fury, but her grief and attachment to Stefan were too much to handle at that moment.

Dr. Calderón quickly shifted tracks. His expression appeared distressed, but his tone grew even more determined. "You can't marry Stefan, Samantha. He's just barely back on his feet and can't handle many complications right now. Surely you can realize that."

"I would never hurt him!"

"He needs to fully recover his life force."

She turned away, tears streaming down her cheeks. Her heart was breaking. "You had no right," she repeated, refusing to look at him and covering her eyes with her hands. "You're just his doctor."

"I advised him as his doctor and his friend. He needs time now, Samantha. If you really care about Stefan, then let him go."

She stood in silence, gazing out over the immense span of ocean beyond them. Sea birds called out above her in the sky. Her hopes for the future lay in ruins. Stefan had flown away.

Dr. Calderón scanned his appointment calendar upon arriving in his office one thundery spring morning in April. His memory proved correct: Stefan did have his medical check scheduled for eleven o'clock that very morning. The previous summer had passed quickly, followed by a temperate autumn and unusually cold winter, and now they were plunged back into another turbulent spring. The passing year had brought significant changes to the doctor's life. He was anxious to see how his patient was faring out in the world again. His office had been unable to contact Stefan to verify the appointment. Would he remember to come?

"Here are your records for the patients today," his receptionist informed him. He glanced up at her.

"Did he call?"

"No." She shook her head. "We haven't heard from Stefan."

"All right, thanks."

Sorting through the patient files, he selected Stefan's and removed it from among the others, idly flipping through it. The portrait fell out in front of him. Picking it up, he recalled Stefan's expression upon presenting the drawing. After staring at it pensively for several minutes, he slipped it back into the folder again.

Eleven o'clock arrived, his last appointment before lunch. Dr.

Calderón placed his hands behind his head and reclined in his swivel chair, his Earth shoes resting up on the desk. He closed his eyes. The wind blew in frantic gusts, the tree branches tapping against the window behind him. It began to rain and lightning flashed across the sky, followed by a loud crack of thunder.

The door opened and Stefan walked in. He stared at Miguel in silence a long moment before breaking into a smile. "It's so good to see you," he exclaimed.

Dr. Calderón leaned forward in his chair and stood up. His patient appeared to be the picture of health. Stefan looked tanned from the sun and physically fit. He had recouped a healthy weight, but it was the unmistakable aura of equanimity about him that pleased the doctor the most; he knew in that instant that Stefan's recovery was complete. They stood facing each other, both too overcome to speak.

Miguel walked across the room and embraced him. "*Gloria a Dios.*"

Stefan laughed. "Sorry I didn't call to let you know I was coming. I've been out on a ship with some oceanographers."

"Really?" Dr. Calderón and Stefan sat on the sofa together.

"Yes, it's a research vessel. I've been working freelance, and right now, I'm helping with the publication and distribution of one of their studies. I asked to come along and they agreed." He paused to catch his breath, pushing his hair back from his eyes. His dark curls were long again.

"How have you been feeling?"

"Great. I've stuck with Brian's protocol and make sure I get plenty of rest."

Dr. Calderón nodded. "Good."

"And you were right—my former bad habits hold no charm for me now."

The doctor laughed. "I suppose you could say a healthy lifestyle is an acquired taste."

"How have you been?" Stefan asked.

"Not bad. A little tired, but then, we do have a new baby in the house."

"Oh, that's right! How is your baby?"

"She's beautiful. We had a girl."

Stefan studied his friend with admiration. "I'd love to see her."

Miguel nodded. "We'll have to arrange it."

"And how is Samantha doing?"

"I ran into her just the other day. She's doing very well. Her publication is really taking off."

"Good. She didn't marry Richard, did she?"

Dr. Calderón shook his head and smiled. "No, she didn't."

"I'll stop by and see her. Do you have her number?"

"Of course. Are you going to be around for a while? I want to administer a few tests and do some blood work. The results will take a few days. I can give you a call if you can't stay."

"I'll be in Acantilado del Mar for a week."

"Wonderful." It was time for an examination in the next room. They chatted as Dr. Calderón did a complete physical. After the nurse drew blood and provided instructions for the tests, Miguel pronounced their visit at an end.

"Everything looks great."

"I feel great. And grateful," he added.

"I'd ask you out to lunch, but I have other obligations."

"That's all right. It looks like the rain is letting up. I need to take

Rebel for a run. He's been cooped up in the car all day."

"Where are you staying?"

"At my *alma mater*, of course."

"Okay, I'll give you a call."

Stefan turned to leave when a thought occurred to him, and he turned back to his doctor again. "What happened to the café? Did it move to a new location?" He'd driven by on the way to check in at the motel and discovered a clothing store in its place.

Dr. Calderon looked away and frowned. "Unfortunately, Brian had to close it down. But don't worry; he's landed on his feet. Whitney's setting him up in business to manufacture and distribute his products."

Stefan nodded, glancing around the familiar office a final time, his eyes coming to rest at last on the haunting drawing up on the wall. He knew in that moment that he would never stand in this room again. He had survived the storm.

Stefan drove to the motel, enjoying the ocean view as his car swerved along the narrow road bordering the sea. The storm was ending and rays of sunlight broke through the dark clouds. Turning into the motel lot, he parked and slipped out of the car. Rebel stretched and sniffed the air, remembering.

"C'mon, boy. Let's unload our junk and hit the beach." The sun shone brilliantly, lighting the walkway to the motel office with millions of droplets of shimmering crystal as the storm receded into the horizon. The fragrant, salty air filled his lungs, and he spotted the vine he'd once admired. It was much larger now, abloom with cascades of delicate silvery flowers. The antiquated deck creaked as he stepped across it, and upon opening the door to his old room, he glanced around the familiar space. It seemed so long ago, yet everything appeared the same. With a clap, he summoned Rebel, and they jogged the four blocks to the beach.

Along the shoreline, Stefan tossed a stick to his dog and breathed in the sea air. It felt so amazing to walk the picturesque beach again; he knew every curve and rock along the way. The place felt like an old friend who had seen him though the darkest hours of his life.

Dreamer came charging up to Rebel, and Stefan squinted in disbelief. The dogs appeared overjoyed to see each other again and, after a tousle, ran down to the water's edge. Stefan glanced around for Samantha and spotted her rounding the spectacular rock formation just ahead. He waved.

Samantha hurried toward him in disbelief. "Stefan?"

"Samantha!" They hugged each other tightly, a wave rushing up to meet their feet.

"Stefan, I'm so glad you came back!"

He smiled at her, overcome with gladness. Her hair was much longer and fell in a tumble of curls down her back. "You look wonderful."

She laughed. "So do you."

"Dr. Calderón told me you've been working hard on your publication."

"Yes, we all have." She stared at Stefan, still unable to believe her eyes. It was really him, and he looked so well again. "You'll have to come and see our new setup. We've rented a space in town. We don't have to work from Wanda's garage anymore."

"I'd love to see it."

They began walking down the beach together. A fling of sand

pipers scattered in front of them as the waves pounded against the rocks, and it felt like old times again. "How long are you in town, Stefan?"

"For a week. Dr. Calderón's running some tests."

"Just a week?"

He nodded. "I have a permanent address now, though. I don't live that far from here, just up the coast. I've give it to you and also my new number."

"Thanks, Stefan."

"We could see each other."

Samantha smiled. "Really? I'd love that."

The dogs ran past them and up a hill leading to the top of a cliff. "What's on top of the slope?" Stefan asked, preparing to go after them.

"There's a new playground up there—El Parque Infantil."

"C'mon, let's run after them." He took her by the hand.

Samantha looked unsure. "Run?"

"Yeah, c'mon!" They bolted for the trail and raced up the path to the park. When they reached the top, he collapsed on the lawn. "I'm exhausted!"

She sat down next to him. Children played on the swings, and Stefan rested his head in the grass, his hands folded under him while listening. "Have you ever thought about your favorite sounds?" he asked, basking in the sunlight.

"What?" She turned to study him with affection. A year's absence hadn't altered the intimacy between them.

"Your favorite sounds . . . like the sound of children playing. I've always loved that. When I was growing up, we lived near a school. At certain times of the day, the kids would come outside to play. You could hear them in the distance."

Samantha nodded. "I love the sound of birds' wings overhead."

"Me too.

"Church bells."

"Yeah." He smiled. "I love that too."

"Birds singing."

"Crickets?"

"I love crickets." Samantha propped her head up with her hand.

"Rain against the window." Stefan stared up at the sky, listening to the birds in the trees.

"A baby's laughter," Samantha added. "That's a beautiful sound."

Stefan frowned, listening to the children playing nearby. One of the voices sounded familiar. It couldn't be! Sitting up again, he glanced over at the swing set. Sure enough, not twenty feet away, Daniel stood with his brother Robert. Stefan hopped up and walked over.

"Hi, Daniel."

Daniel looked up in surprise. His nose was peeling in chips, just like the last time they'd met. Daniel appeared much taller; Stefan barely recognized him. He continued gazing at Stefan, his own expression unsure.

Robert remembered and nudged his brother. "It's the guy in the hospital at the party. You know . . ."

Daniel grew excited and embarrassed all at once. He ran over to the slide. "Want to see what I can do, Stefan?"

Stefan nodded. "Sure."

Daniel climbed to the top of the slide and then proceeded to run down in his tennis shoes.

"Daniel!" his brother admonished.

Daniel climbed back up the wrong way, glancing back at Stefan to make sure he was watching.

"Daniel!" Robert shook his head.

His younger brother ignored him and, reaching the top, slid down backwards as an afterthought. He raced back and forth, completing one reckless maneuver after another.

"Gee, Daniel. Isn't that a little dangerous?" Stefan asked when the eight-year-old was finished and stood proudly before him.

"Nope." He had a million freckles and a bandana tied around his neck. "I'm going to be in the circus when I grow up."

Robert quickly approached. "That's a stupid job. You don't make any money. Stop showing off before you bust your head open and have to go back to the hospital again."

Daniel grinned, displaying his new front teeth while gazing up at Stefan. "You look a lot better now."

"Thank you."

"My hair's long too." He ran his fingers through his red curls.

"He won't let anyone cut it," Robert said, his own hair a shorter length.

Stefan nodded. "Yeah, I'm having the same problem."

"C'mon, Daniel. We have to go." Robert was heading off.

"Bye, Stefan!" Daniel hurried to catch up.

"See you!" He waved.

"We should go back now, Stefan." Samantha looked at her watch. "I have an appointment later this afternoon. I just stopped by to see my mother and walk Dreamer."

"Okay."

They hiked down to the beach again, walking along the shoreline until they passed the cave. Rebel ran inside to investigate. "Rebel!" Stefan called out. The dog ignored him, and Stefan scrambled up the rocks to the opening, gazing inside where Rebel sniffed at the sand. "C'mon, you lazy mutt!" Rebel raced out and back to Dreamer's side, leaving Stefan alone for a moment. He paused, recalling the darkest day of his life in the middle of the storm.

"Are you ready?" Samantha asked when he returned. She was remembering too.

"Yes." He nodded. "Ready."

Stefan put his arm around her, and they strolled back down the beach together. "I'll walk you up," he told her, ascending the beach stairwell alongside her with ease.

Samantha nodded, holding his hand and thinking about the first time they'd climbed the steps together. The dogs ran ahead, Rebel darting back every so often to be sure Stefan was following. It was a beautiful day, full of promise, and for once, Samantha felt completely happy.

They rounded the curve in the path that led to Samantha's parents' home. Stefan paused a moment in surprise, his eyes sweeping over the familiar house just beyond. A tall fence enclosed the former garden area and many of the trees and shrubs were gone.

"He doesn't live here anymore," Samantha remarked. "The new owners added on and put in a pool right over there," she explained, pointing to the fence while noting his unhappy expression.

"Really?" Stefan turned to study the green lawn stretching out before them. He shook his head. "The neighbors must be pleased," he remarked at last.

She shielded her eyes from the bright sun. "How so?"

He laughed wryly. "No more dandelions."

She grew silent, looking around. The immaculate, professionally landscaped grounds leading up to the home were completely bereft of the pesky round buttery orbs. "Yes," she agreed. "They're all gone."

A week later, Stefan sat at a table in the afternoon shadows of the park, his head propped in his hands. Rebel stood nearby, sniffing at the damp earth. Dr. Calderón was due to join him soon. They had agreed to meet a final time before Stefan's departure from Acantilado del Mar the following day. A man tossed a Frisbee to his dog, and Rebel looked up.

"Stay here," Stefan warned. Glancing across the grass, he noticed Miguel approaching wearing a baby pack.

"Hi, Stefan." Dr. Calderón stood next to him. "Well, here she is." Turning around, he revealed a napping baby nestled against his back.

The infant appeared dollish in perfection. "She looks like an angel," Stefan marveled, leaning closer for a better look.

"They all do. My life is a madhouse," Dr. Calderón admitted.

"What did you name her?" Stefan asked while stroking her tiny hand with his finger.

"We named her Cristina."

Stefan broke into a smile, leaning over to admire the sleeping baby more closely. "Well, let's hope she doesn't flunk the first grade," he remarked, snapping the leash on Rebel again.

Miguel laughed. "Can you make it for dinner tonight? Alicia and the boys would love to see you."

"I'd like that very much. Samantha gave me your new address."

"Great." Miguel repositioned his sweat band and smiled.

"Well?" Stefan prompted.

"Well, what?" The doctor frowned.

"How did the tests turn out?"

"Oh!" He laughed again. "Fine. Everything's good, Stefan."

"Great to know."

Miguel adjusted Cristina on his back and rubbed his hands together briskly, glancing around the park. "Feel like walking
downtown? I'll buy you a cup of coffee. . . ."

www.ingramcontent.com/pod-product-compliance
Lightning Source LLC
Chambersburg PA
CBHW020557180626
46810CB00007B/2544